Of course it w[...]

No mere perfume [...]
one's heart's desire, Casey thought.

Could it?

Gently, carefully, nervously, she turned the bottle upside down, righted it and removed the stopper. The scent of the perfume rose around her like an invisible cloud. Musky, mysterious, spicy, it evoked an image of the smooth, velvety petals of a crimson rose scattered over silky soft white sheets that twined themselves around a pair of lovers, caressing their limbs as their lips met in a deep, searching kiss....

What harm could it possibly do to use a little of the perfume? Giving in to the impulse, Casey gently touched the stopper to her throat and ears and wrists.

Feeling slightly absurd, she replaced the bottle on the shelf.

Suddenly the front door crashed open and a man rushed into the store....

ABOUT THE AUTHOR

"This story came about when I saw a TV ad for perfume and wondered if there really was a perfume that would make a woman irresistible," Margaret Chittenden informed us. *The Scent of Magic* is this talented author's ninth Superromance novel. Margaret has published twenty-two books and more than one hundred short stories and articles. She also writes under the name Rosalind Carson.

Books by Margaret Chittenden

HARLEQUIN SUPERROMANCE

16–THIS DARK ENCHANTMENT
40–SONG OF DESIRE
91–SUCH SWEET MAGIC
123–LOVE ME TOMORROW
175–TO TOUCH THE MOON
214–CLOSE TO HOME
310–THE MOON GATE
366–UNTIL OCTOBER

HARLEQUIN TEMPTATION

40–LOVESPELL
156–THE MARRYING KIND

Don't miss any of our special offers. Write to us at the following address for information on our newest releases.

Harlequin Reader Service
P.O. Box 1397, Buffalo, NY 14240
Canadian address: P.O. Box 603,
Fort Erie, Ont. L2A 5X3

The Scent of Magic

MARGARET CHITTENDEN

Harlequin Books

TORONTO • NEW YORK • LONDON
AMSTERDAM • PARIS • SYDNEY • HAMBURG
STOCKHOLM • ATHENS • TOKYO • MILAN

This book has to be for
Sharon Lynne Lundahl—
my daughter, my friend

Published March 1991

ISBN 0-373-70444-5

THE SCENT OF MAGIC

CHAPTER ONE

THERE WAS something strange about the elderly woman, but Casey couldn't quite decide what it was. It wasn't the old-fashioned nature of her black silk Edwardian dress and jet necklace and earrings; Casey's own outfit was circa 1895. It wasn't her general appearance—she was actually quite an attractive woman—slender and petite, about Casey's size. Her rather frizzy hair was gray-white, her skin somewhat olive in tone, only slightly wrinkled around the eyes and mouth.

Her *eyes*. Yes, the strangeness was in her eyes. Her gaze was too intense, almost mesmerizing, and the eyes themselves were so dark, the irises seemed but a continuation of the pupils.

The woman's booth was squashed in between one selling old military regalia and another that specialized in jukeboxes. Not being interested in either, Casey had almost passed by the small booth. Tired after poking through six hundred of the seven hundred antique stalls in Seattle's Kingdome, she was anxious to get outside before the lovely May Sunday was over.

But then a flash of dazzling white had caught her eye and she had turned in to look at a display of antique linen that included some remarkably beautiful English tea cloths. Turn-of-the-century, probably. Not anything she could use in her shop, but still worth admiring for their own sake.

"Everything on special sale," the old woman said in a heavily accented voice. "I am selling store and house, moving into retirement home. No room for my beautiful things. Big stuff goes to auction. But much smaller stuff here—china, silver, pretty linens."

As she spoke, she studied Casey with great interest and apparent approval, her gaze going from Casey's upswept red hair to her vintage clothing—a lace-trimmed white blouse with leg-of-mutton sleeves, a long black skirt, buttoned boots. "You are antique dealer?" she asked.

Casey nodded. "In a small way. I own a shop, Second Time Around, in Pioneer Square." She didn't really want to get into a conversation; she'd already listened to enough stories from dealers she'd met at previous shows. In general, antique dealers were a friendly and garrulous lot.

The woman's eyes seemed to burn into hers, as though she were trying to see beyond the surface to the woman inside. Always shy with people she didn't know, Casey felt uncomfortable under the intense scrutiny, but somehow was compelled to go on. "I deal mostly in used designer clothing, but I also sell vintage clothing and jewelry. That's why I came to today's show, looking for bargains."

The woman tilted her head to one side without moving her gaze from Casey's face. "So, you wear this clothes for advertisement? For me, I am just very old, and sentimental—this dress very like one my mother wear when I have only ten years."

Casey couldn't quite place the woman's accent. Mid-European, perhaps? Or Slavic?

"You come from here?" the woman asked. "From Seattle?"

"Now I do. I'm originally from a small town in the Midwest."

"Your father, what does he do?"

"He was a minister," Casey said before it occurred to her that she didn't have to answer these inquisitive questions. At least, she didn't have to admit what kind of minister Theodore Templeton had been. "He and my mother died ten years ago in a car accident," she added. It had taken her five years to be able to say that so matter-of-factly. The sense of loss was still there, of course; it always would be. But Casey's grief had been tempered by time into a sort of fondly reminiscent feeling that surfaced whenever she thought of Ellen and Theodore Templeton.

The woman made a clucking sound of sympathy with her tongue. "An orphan. Such tragedy," she said. Tilting her head she gave Casey another appraising once-over. "You are pretty girl," she remarked judiciously. "Green eyes. My favorite kind. My husband had green eyes. Dead short time now. You look like nice old-fashioned working girl. What is your name, my dear?"

"Casey Templeton."

"I am Inga." She gave a small bow, then wrinkled her nose. "This is girl's name, this Casey?"

Casey smiled. "It's actually Cassandra, but that's a mouthful for most people."

Inga's face lit up. "Cassandra. The Trojan princess whose beauty attracted love of Apollo. Was it not unfortunate that her prophetic warnings went unheeded? Do you prophesy, Cassandra?"

Casey wasn't sure the woman was serious. But her direct gaze was making her more and more uncomfortable. "I'm afraid not," she said lightly, dismissively, and turned away to examine a set of old dishes.

"How old are you, Cassandra?"

Well, really... "Twenty-seven," she said shortly.

"You are married?"

"No."

"Why not? You do not like men? You do not want children?"

Casey hesitated. The woman's questions were becoming much too persistent. "I have nothing against men in general," she responded finally. "I would like very much to get married and have children. But nobody's asked me, I'm afraid."

She started moving toward the front of the booth, but the old woman blocked her way, nodding solemnly. "You think I am too much nosy, yes? Please accept apology, Cassandra. I have reason for questions. Do you perhaps have a boyfriend?"

Cassandra smiled ruefully. "Yes, I do."

"He is your lover?"

"No." Now why on earth had she answered *that* question? She knew why. The answer rankled. She had been dating Justin Boyd for six months now. As always, in the beginning, because of her strict religious upbringing and her own instinctive shyness, she had been reluctant to get involved in lovemaking, but she was more than ready now. Apparently Justin wasn't. He respected her, he said often. He had never attempted to go beyond kissing her.

Sometimes Casey wished Justin would just sweep her off her feet. More than once she had fantasized stripping off his button-down-collared shirt, sleeveless pull-over and slacks and making mad passionate love to him, but she was sure he would be shocked if she got so carried away. She shocked herself just thinking about it.

Inga's gaze was fixed sympathetically on her face now, as if she were reading Casey's thoughts. After a moment she muttered a few words in a language Casey didn't recognize, then bent arthritically to pick something out of a box on the floor. "I wish you to look at this," she said abruptly, holding out a beautiful perfume bottle. It was made of opaque amber-colored glass decorated with a gold filigree design edged with blue and red enamel.

"Saracenic glass. Mesopotamia, maybe fourteenth century," she explained as Casey took the lovely thing from her. "Smell inside," she added.

Casey removed the stopper carefully. The was only a little perfume inside the bottle, but it had the most wonderful fragrance Casey had ever encountered. Haunting, ethereal, seductive, it conjured up thoughts of candlelit rooms, bodies entwined in passion, whispering voices vibrant with words of love....

"This is perfect blend of essential oils from natural substances," Inga said. "Sandalwood from India, patchouli, cedar of Lebanon from the forests of Marduk, rose petals from the Balkan countries. Plus other secret ingredients. Very special, yes?"

"It's wonderful," Casey murmured.

"'The smell of thy garments is like the smell of Lebanon,'" Inga suddenly intoned with great drama. "This from Song of Solomon. Many perfumes mentioned in this song. Which you probably know from being daughter of preacher." She lowered her voice. "Our forebears had great faith in power of perfume, Cassandra. Perfume often looked upon as cure for

various ailments. Also associated with religious cere-
monies and magic rituals."

Her voice was hushed now, almost reverent. If this
were a movie, Casey thought, the creepy music would
start up about now. She was conscious of a distinct
sense of unreality. All around her, people were walking
and talking, their voices and footsteps echoing upward
past the bleachers to the far reaches of the huge, domed
roof. Yet it seemed that she and the old woman named
Inga were cut off from them all, alone in a fantasy
world where it seemed quite natural to speak of magic
rituals and the Song of Solomon.

Reluctantly she replaced the stopper and handed the
bottle back to Inga.

"You do not like?" Inga asked.

"I like it very much," Casey said. "I'd love to buy it
to have in my store, but I'm quite sure I couldn't afford it."

"Is not for sale," Inga said. "It is not permitted to
sell. Secret perfume has been in my family many, many
generations. Bottle also. It can only leave family as a
gift. So, is my gift to you."

"But I can't possibly—"

"Romantic story comes with perfume," Inga continued, leaning forward in a conspiratorial way. "You
see perfume commercials on television, yes? All supposed to make person unforgettable, irresistible, like
magic?"

She glanced around furtively, then leaned toward
Casey again. "This perfume *is* magic," she said solemnly. "When young woman of family is age to wed,
she uses little of this perfume and she gets her heart's
desire." She smiled. "Ah, yes, you shake head there.
Crazy old woman, you think. Maybe crazy, yes, but

perfume work for me. Fifty-eight years married, very happy. Sadly, no children. No girl-child to pass on perfume. So I look for girl of good character without lover."

She began wrapping the bottle carefully in several layers of tissue paper. "I give this to you, Cassandra. You accept, please." Placing the package in a sturdy plastic bag, she handed it to Casey with a nod and a smile that had a very satisfied air to it.

"Really, I can't—the bottle alone must be very valuable," Casey protested.

Inga touched her hand to her bosom. "My heart says give to you. My heart never wrong." Her eyes gleamed. "As for value—value is in using." She raised a finger admonishingly. "One caution only. Perfume can be used just once, by each person, in moderation."

Unable to think of anything to say in the face of the woman's solemnity, Casey accepted the gift as gracefully as she could manage. But walking on through the antique show, she felt more and more uneasy about accepting such an extravagant present. Obviously the old woman was mentally disturbed; why else would she so emphatically believe in the perfume's mysterious power?

Finally, after picking up the items she'd paid for at various stalls, Casey retraced her steps, determined to insist Inga take the perfume back. But the long aisles, with their infinite variety of booths, were more crowded now, and Casey hadn't noted the exact location of Inga's collection. She checked the show's directory. No one named Inga. Neither the military stall nor the jukeboxes were listed in any category she could think of. And her feet were beginning to ache in the tightly buttoned boots. Why hadn't she thought to ask Inga's last name?

Finally, after checking with several dealers she knew, asking if they had heard of Inga, and getting negative responses each time, she gave up and went home.

"SHE GAVE IT TO YOU, just like that?" Justin said disbelievingly.

Casey looked up from the cabbage she was shredding for coleslaw and glanced at the bottle, which she had put on the windowsill next to her gateleg dining table. The evening light seemed to be trapped in the dark amber glass, making the bottle glow as if a candle burned inside it. "She was a little strange," she admitted. "Spoke with an accent I couldn't place. And a few words in a harsh-sounding language with lots of consonants and *ch* sounds."

"Affricatives," Justin said. He always knew the right word for everything.

Casey gazed at him admiringly. She liked looking at Justin. He was around five-ten, slender, with blue eyes and blond hair parted just so, always neatly dressed, an escort to be proud of, if not the kind who turned women's heads. Thirty years old, he was a high-school English teacher whose female students adored him. Like Casey, he had come from a poor background. The son of a scrap-metal dealer, he had worked his way through college with the help of any odd job he could find. Someday he hoped to be a principal.

"Is it valuable?" he asked.

Justin was always concerned with the cost of things, and impressed when they cost a lot. "When I'm rich I'm not going to buy anything but the best," he often said. "When I find my rich wife, that is," he usually added with a grin. This was one of his favorite jokes, definitely not appreciated by Casey.

"It's fourteenth-century Mesopotamian, according to Inga," she said shortly. "Saracenic glass."

"Why would she give it to you?"

"I don't know, Justin. Maybe because she liked that my name was Cassandra. She asked a lot of questions. I guess she approved of the answers. Or maybe she just liked the way I was dressed."

He frowned at her. She loved the way his fair eyebrows came together when he frowned, the little twin lines that appeared between them. "You were wearing one of your old outfits, I suppose?" he remarked in an exasperated voice.

"Late nineteenth century. I was at an antique show, Justin."

He didn't comment. He didn't need to. She knew he wasn't too keen on her vintage clothing. He thought it made her look eccentric. Which was why she'd changed into a tan cotton shirtwaist dress before he arrived. She wished he did appreciate her various costumes. She felt so much more comfortable in fashions of long ago. Like a little girl playing dress-up, maybe. Or perhaps she felt more at ease in disguise. When she wore vintage clothing, people looked at the clothes rather than at her. She'd had enough in her childhood of people—kids— looking at her, pointing at her, jeering....

Justin eyed the bottle again. "Better get it insured." He was always practical.

She made a face at him. "Don't you think it's beautiful?"

"I suppose." He smiled. She loved his smile, too. It was an absolutely perfect smile. Modest, unassuming, charming. A nice-guy smile. Unfortunately it was the same smile he gave to everybody. "Not something you can get much use out of," he pointed out.

"Not everything has to be functional."

Again he didn't comment.

She wasn't going to tell him about the perfume inside the bottle, Casey decided.

SHE TOLD HER FRIEND Skip Granger, though, when she had lunch with him the following day. Skip was thirty-nine years old, black, six foot three and built like a linebacker—which he used to be. After retiring from football, he'd opened The Grange, named for his old nickname—an extremely popular bar and restaurant next door to Casey's store. Both establishments were part of a row of great old brick-and-stone buildings that had been built in the middle of the nineteenth century. Like the other buildings, The Grange had been meticulously restored, its only concession to modern times being the huge photograph of Skip in football uniform that hung over the bar.

"Magic perfume," Skip echoed, running a hand over his close-cropped hair and rolling his eyes at the medallioned ceiling. "Women are so damn gullible."

"I didn't say I believed her," Casey chided. "Don't be such a male chauvinist."

He grinned. "It's in the blood, babe. I'm too old to change."

She wrinkled her nose at him. "I take it *you* don't believe in magic."

He snorted. "Let me tell you about magic," he said, leaning forward. "My wife, Brenda—pardon the expression, make that my *ex*-wife, Brenda—used to surround herself with crystals that she ordered specially from somewhere in Arkansas. She's into all that New

Age stuff. These crystals, now, supposedly they had been programmed to make her healthy and wealthy. So what happened when she ran off with my dear old buddy, Luther Everett? I'll tell you what happened. Brenda took sick with mononucleosis and the savings-and-loan company Luther worked for went belly-up, leaving Luther without any visible means of support. Last I heard, they were both on food stamps. Now is that a sad story or not?''

"How do you know they're on food stamps?" Casey asked.

He shrugged a little too elaborately. "Brenda told me. She came in a couple—three—months ago, needing money."

Casey looked at him fondly. "You gave it to her, didn't you?"

"Sure, I did. Numero-uno sucker, that's Skip Granger." He sighed. "Hell, Case, she's family. So's Luther. Where I come from we don't let family starve, we care about them even after they kick us in the teeth."

Casey reached out and patted his big hand where it lay clenched on the polished tabletop. "You need a girlfriend, Skip. Someone to care about *you*." She frowned, mentally running through all the women she knew, wondering if any of them would be suitable.

He looked alarmed. "Don't go making me into one of your pet projects, Case. I need a woman like Seattle needs more rain. I'm happy just as I am."

"Sure you are," Casey murmured, still pondering.

SHE THOUGHT ABOUT Brenda Granger later in the day when she was sitting on the high stool behind the counter of her store, mending a fringe on the edge of a silk shawl. Brenda was an exotic-looking woman with wonderful cheekbones and velvety brown eyes. She had been a fashion model before her marriage, before her addiction to junk-food had shown up on her hips and bosom. Even with the extra weight, she was a stunner, always attracting men's eyes. Skip had adored her. Casey could still remember the way he'd followed her with his gaze whenever she moved through a room, his tough-looking face softening with love. She could also remember thinking she'd like to have a man look at her with that much love someday.

All the same, it wouldn't do to work at getting Skip and Brenda together again. Brenda had hurt Skip badly; he'd been devastated when she let him down. And Casey suspected she couldn't be trusted not to do it again. But somewhere in Seattle there must be a woman who would be right for Skip. How about that woman lobbyist she'd met at Barbara Harriman's Christmas party? Smart-looking lady. Intelligent. Was she single? She'd have to ask Barbara.

Hearing the low-throated blast of a ferry coming into the terminal a few blocks away, she glanced at the watch pinned to the bosom of her antique lace dress, then threaded her needle again. She had an hour yet before she needed to go home to change for her date with Justin. They were going to see a new movie adaptation of D.H. Lawrence's *The Rainbow,* which was one of the offerings of Seattle's International Film Festival this year. Justin had bought two full series tickets. The films were interesting enough, but she did wish the festival would take place some other time of the year. It was such a lovely evening, with just the lightest of warm breezes wafting in the aroma of the blossoming shrubs she'd set in barrels outside her shop.

She'd like to go dancing, she decided as she bit off her thread and set down the shawl. But dancing was out of the question. Justin didn't believe dancing was a productive way to spend time.

So, what else would she like to do? Something outdoors. Seattle was full of possibilities.

They could stroll along the waterfront. Take a ferry ride to Bainbridge Island. One of her dearest dreams was to someday own a house on Bainbridge Island.

They could rent a canoe at one of the lakes. Green Lake maybe. Or Lake Union. Later, when it was dark, she and Justin could find a grassy spot to sit on. Maybe he'd put his arm around her, slide a hand gently down over her shoulder to cover her breast, ease her down beside him and hold her close to his slender body.

Fat chance.

Did she really, really want Justin to do all that? she wondered. She wasn't at all sure. Her brain was too stuffed with mixed messages. She was a young woman, with natural urges. That was one element. Another, unfortunately, was a built-in mental image of her father preaching earnestly to his flock about the sins of the flesh.

Apart from casual acquaintances, there had been three men in her life before Justin. She'd thought herself in love with the first, probably because he *was* the first, and had let him make love to her when he insisted she prove her love. The experience had been pleasant enough, but hadn't lived up to her expectations. The earth had not moved. It hadn't even trembled.

The second man had been too aggressive in his approach and she had turned him down flat, determined not to be a jellyfish this time. She had managed to bruise the poor man's ego irreparably in the process.

The third—ah, the third—had attracted her tremendously. But Winston Perry IV had lacked any real purpose in life. Born to great wealth, he had seen no need to work for a living—not when it was possible to play in all the major capitals of the world. Though recognizing that she had brought her childhood hang-ups into her adult life like so much excess baggage, Casey had found herself totally unable to accept Winston Perry's life-style.

All three men had expected her to leap into bed with them by their second date. But Casey had spent a good part of her childhood reading nineteenth century novels, which were all her father deemed suitable for her. In those love stories, the heroine was chaperoned until the engagement and beyond, and all the hero dared press on her before their marriage was a chaste kiss or two.

Casey's reticence didn't go quite that far. She couldn't imagine anything more horrible than finding out on her wedding night that she wasn't sexually compatible with her groom. But she did want to be courted—wooed—and she wouldn't dream of going to bed with a man until she knew him and cared for him.

The break with Winston had come when he had arranged a trip to Bermuda for both of them. Dazzled by him, and by the prospect of seeing Bermuda, she had gone so far as to get a passport, the first in her life, but then she had discovered that Winston had booked a double room in the hotel without even consulting her. And that had been the end of that.

All three men had been dominating types. Perhaps because of her small size, she invariably attracted the kinds of men who wanted to be boss.

Justin wasn't like that, though. Justin was a nice guy. And he certainly wasn't aggressive sexually. But wasn't there such a thing as a little bit of aggressiveness? Lately she'd found herself gazing adoringly at other women's babies, wishing she could snatch them up and take them home with her. Of course, she'd never do such a thing; but obviously the maternal instinct—the nesting instinct—was working its magic on her.

Magic.

She suddenly realized that she was staring at the bottle of perfume the old woman at the Kingdome had given her. She had brought it from her apartment that morning, placed it on a high shelf where it would be safe and would also catch the evening sunlight. It was glowing again.

Pulling over a step stool, she climbed up and retrieved the bottle. For a while she simply held it, admiring it. Could it possibly be as old as Inga had insisted it was? It certainly looked and felt ancient. The gold filigree on it seemed worn, as though many hands had lovingly caressed the bottle over the years.

While its owners pondered the wisdom of using the contents?

Of course, the perfume wasn't magic. No mere perfume could guarantee someone's heart's desire.

Could it?

The people who worked in the offices above had gone home some time ago and it seemed abnormally quiet in the store. So quiet, Casey could hear her heart beating a staccato rhythm against her ribs. The usual traffic sounds from outside could be heard, of course, but no voices carried in the spring air. No footsteps clattered on the cobbles.

Justin would be with her in less than an hour.

Gently, carefully, nervously, she turned the bottle upside down, righted it and removed the stopper.

The scent of the perfume arose like an invisible cloud, swirling around her, enfolding her, stimulating all her senses. Musky, mysterious, spicy, this time it evoked an image in her mind of the smooth velvety petals of a crimson rose scattered over white sheets. Silky soft sheets that would twine themselves around a pair of lovers, caressing their limbs as their warm, naked bodies pressed ever closer, their lips meeting in a deep, searching kiss of love....

What harm could it possibly do to use a little of the perfume? It smelled so wonderful, so out-of-this-world.

Giving in to the impulse she had been trying to quell since the previous evening, Casey gently touched the stopper of the bottle to her throat and ears and wrists.

''Take that, Justin Boyd,'' she said aloud.

Feeling slightly absurd, she replaced the bottle on the shelf and began briskly putting away her sewing things. Of course, she didn't believe in the perfume's magic power, she assured herself. Inga's story was a romantic one indeed, but hardly credible in this day and age. But at least she smelled terrific. Maybe, at the very least, Justin would notice that.

Five minutes later, she was on her knees busily dusting the shelves in the glass case below the counter where antique jewelry was displayed. As she carefully replaced a jeweled collar on its bed of black velvet, the front door crashed open and a man rushed into the store. He was wearing some kind of uniform—black pants, shiny chartreuse windbreaker, shiny-billed cap.

Alarmed, Casey jumped to her feet. The man halted abruptly on the other side of the counter and began gesticulating, saying something very rapidly in a foreign language. French. He was speaking French. She'd taken a year of French in high school, but had forgotten most of it. Anyway, he was speaking so quickly, she couldn't even make it out. Her alarm increased as she unexpectedly recognized one of the words he used: *voleur*—a thief.

Had he come here to steal from her? Crime had increased recently in this historic quarter, whose lower floors were filled with profitable restaurants, antique stores, art galleries and specialty shops like hers.

"What do you want?" Casey asked. Unfortunately her voice quavered and the question she'd meant to sound demanding ended in a squeak. At the same time, she had backed up until she was pressed against the wall, her hands clasped over her chest. She must look for all the world like a virgin preparing to defend her virtue.

A chagrined expression appeared on the man's face. Snatching off his cap, he shook his head. "Forgive me, *mademoiselle*. I did not intend to frighten you."

He was an extraordinarily good-looking man, she realized, as her fear ebbed. Early thirties. Tall and muscular, with unruly dark curly hair and brown eyes. A tanned, intelligent, aristocratic face that was at odds with his cheap clothing. He didn't look like a thief, though of course there wasn't any special way criminals were supposed to look.

"Forgive me, please, for bursting in like this," he said. "I am...distressed. Someone has stolen my shuttle."

Casey's brain produced a picture of an astronaut. She looked at the man blankly. His uniform didn't fit the image at all.

"My shuttle bus," he explained with a slight air of impatience. "I drive people from hotels to the airport, airport to hotels."

"Oh, I see." Casey's heart rate had slowed. She was able to speak calmly now. "How could anyone steal a shuttle bus? I thought only airplanes got hijacked."

His eyes narrowed as though he wasn't sure if she was making fun of him. "I was eating dinner, around the corner—in the arcade. I left my shuttle bus parked in the street next to your boutique. You did not hear it drive away?"

His English was fluent, but definitely accented, and a little stiff. No contractions. "I hear cars drive away all day," she pointed out. "How did the thief start the bus?"

"I left the keys in the ignition." He looked at her sternly, as though daring her to comment on that.

Casey shook her head. "You want me to call the police?"

He hesitated. "I do not recall my license number." He ran a hand through his dark hair in an agitated way. "You have an automobile I could borrow?"

"I have a beat-up Volkswagen Rabbit, yes. But she won't start for any driver but me. She's even particular about who rides in her. She has to be introduced."

A decidedly impatient expression appeared on his handsome face. Evidently she wasn't cooperating the way she should. "Forgive me again, *mademoiselle*." He made a slight bow, graceful as a prince in a fairy tale. "My name is Michel Gervais Smith," he announced.

Casey frowned. "Smith?"

"Smith." His jawline was firm enough to be called aggressive, Casey noticed.

"I'm Casey Templeton," she said, lifting her own jaw.

He reached across the counter and shook her hand. He had a hard grip, calluses on his fingers. Did fairy-tale princes have calluses? Surely not.

She had been haunted by dark eyes lately, she decided as he gazed at her. His were as intense as Inga's; just as mesmerizing.

"You would drive me to the shuttle-bus depot?" he asked abruptly.

This was obviously a man who was used to getting his own way. "Would I?" she said.

He flushed slightly. "I have tried to find a taxi, but none are available at this time of day," he explained in a more reasonable tone of voice. "If you take me to my depot, I can discover the license number, explain the situation to my boss, get my car, then drive to the police station to make a—how do you say?—statement."

Casey didn't answer him immediately. The man was asking a lot, considering she'd never laid eyes on him before this moment. Did he really think she'd take off with any fairy-tale prince who came along? "You could at least say please," she finally said gently.

He had the grace to look embarrassed. "Once again, I beg your pardon. In my agitation, I have forgotten my manners. Please, *mademoiselle,* will you assist me?"

To go along with this polite request, he produced a whimsical smile that invited her to be amused at his foolish predicament—a smile that curved one corner of his mouth upward, making his tanned face interestingly asymmetrical; an appealing smile that warmed his brown eyes to the color of old brandy. A disarming smile. Practiced, but definitely sexy. As Casey's knees weakened, so did her will. All at once it didn't seem such a lot to ask, after all.

"Okay," she found herself saying, through a sudden shortness of breath.

Their eyes met and held. She couldn't seem to stop staring at him. And he was staring just as openly back at her. It was as if they both recognized at the same moment that they had been coming toward this meeting all their lives; expecting this meeting, waiting for this meeting.

But that was ridiculous, Casey thought. The Frenchman blinked and took a step back, as if his reaction were exactly the same as hers.

Nonsense.

Recollecting her date with Justin, Casey said, "I'll have to stop at my apartment for a moment to leave a note for...someone...."

He nodded gravely. "As you wish, *mademoiselle*." He was still staring at her face.

It wasn't until after she'd left a note for Justin that it occurred to Casey that if Michel Gervais Smith happened to be a burglar or a murderer, she'd just made him aware of her address. Too late to worry about that now, she decided. Besides, the man didn't appear to have any criminal intentions concerning her. He sat on the front edge of the passenger seat, leaning forward as though to urge her on, gripping his shiny-billed cap tightly in both hands. Casey could feel his impatience, but she stuck to the speed limit.

Michel didn't speak; he was obviously too worried. She stole a glance at him from time to time, as traffic permitted. He was definitely worth looking at in spite of the awful chartreuse windbreaker. Intensely handsome. A man women would notice. Strong, but not in a brutish way. His strength was more like that of fine steel. She could imagine him wielding a fencing foil in a costume movie, effortlessly parrying thrusts from an opponent. *En garde!*

Michel's boss *was* brutish—a big beefy red-faced man with little tufts of white hair over his ears and a shiny bald scalp. He looked the type who would have a pretty hot temper, but to Casey's surprise he started laughing when Michel told his story and he didn't seem able to stop. "Double jeopardy," he kept wheezing, slapping the sides of his striped overalls. "Double jeopardy."

When he finally calmed down enough to speak, he informed Michel he'd already called the police and they should arrive any minute.

"You *knew* the bus was stolen?" Michel said in a puzzled voice. "How is that possible?"

That set the man off again. "I didn't know," he answered finally. "I called the police because one of my mechanics saw a young feller get into your Porsche not ten minutes ago and drive it away. Josh said, no way you'd let somebody drive your Porsche without you being in it."

"My Porsche? Somebody stole my Porsche?" If Michel had been distressed before, he was more so now. He seemed absolutely stunned.

"What I said," his boss croaked through more laughter.

"Michel," Casey began, concealing her surprise at learning that Michel drove such an expensive car.

He looked at her as if he'd never seen her before. "Somebody stole my Porsche," he said faintly.

"Were the keys to your Porsche in the shuttle bus?" she asked.

He nodded. *"Oui, certainement."* Apparently realizing he'd slipped into French again, he gave her a repeat performance of his slightly lopsided smile. Once again, it caused havoc in her nervous system. "Yes, of course. They were in the glove compartment."

"With a little tag with your license number on it, I suppose?" his boss asked sarcastically.

"No, no license number. Just the key tag the dealer gave me when I bought..." His voice trailed into silence.

"A disk with Porsche printed on it?" Casey asked.

He sighed, spreading his hands and looking chagrined. *"Oui."*

Casey shook her head. "I guess it wouldn't take a lot of figuring for whoever stole the shuttle bus to work out that the Porsche might be parked at the depot." She touched Michel's arm lightly. "I hear police sirens. Don't worry, the police will get your car back for you, I'm sure."

Michel looked doubtful. With fairly good cause. The police officer who arrived seemed to find his story as hilarious as Michel's boss had done. But he did write down all the details and called them in to his dispatcher. "Probably got that Porsche stripped by now," he said cheerfully, coming back to where Casey and Michel's boss were standing. Michel was standing alone now, off to one side, wrapped in dignified silence, his arms folded across his muscular chest, billed cap tipped down to shadow his eyes.

Gus, the boss's name had turned out to be. He looked like a Gus, Casey thought. She didn't like him at all, she decided. And she wasn't too keen on the policeman, either. Neither of them had offered Michel an ounce of sympathy. Every time either one of them looked at him, they started laughing again.

When the police officer's radio squawked, he strode over to his patrol car and picked up the mike. A moment later he came back and he wasn't smiling anymore. Glowering at Michel, he suddenly yelled at him, "Assume the position!"

When Michel stared at him with frozen disbelief, the officer swung him around, pushed him up against the wall of the building, pulled his arms back and handcuffed him, declaiming his rights all the while.

"But I am an American citizen," Michel protested.

"You could be a Martian, you're still under arrest," the police officer said evenly.

Before Casey could fully comprehend what was happening, he had bundled Michel into the back of his patrol car and was getting behind the steering wheel. "But what did he do?" Casey asked, finally finding her voice. "The bus and the car were stolen from him, not by him. Why are you..."

The rest of her sentence was lost in the sound of the patrol car's engine. A second later the car shot out of the depot's driveway, leaving Casey standing with her mouth still open, her last impression that of a totally stunned Michel looking out at her.

CHAPTER TWO

"WHY ON EARTH WAS Michel arrested?" she asked Gus.

Gus shrugged. "Damned if I know. Weirdest thing." He started wandering back to his office.

"Hey," Casey yelled after him. Normally she wouldn't dream of raising her voice to anyone, but she felt suddenly furious about the treatment accorded Michel. He might be a little on the arrogant side, but he certainly had done nothing to deserve being slammed against a wall.

Gus stopped and turned, his bristly eyebrows raised in an inquiring expression.

"Is Michel some kind of criminal?" Casey asked more quietly.

He shrugged again. "Who knows?"

And who cares? Casey thought as he continued on his way. The whole thing had happened so fast, she couldn't seem to work out exactly what *had* happened. But Michel's dazed face had seemed to entreat her to do *something*.

What could she do?

Nothing. Obviously.

There was no reason on earth for her to feel responsible for Michel Gervais Smith.

Ten minutes later she was at the police station, heading toward a young police officer who looked more approachable than the other men on duty. "You a relative?" he asked, when she explained about Michel.

She shook her head.

"You'll have to ask the chief of detectives," he informed her when she asked why Michel had been arrested.

She looked helplessly around. "Where do I find the chief of detectives?"

He gave her a wry smile. "I'm afraid he's not available right now, ma'am."

It sounded like a runaround to Casey. But she could hardly demand information when she was barely acquainted with Michel.

"May I wait?" she asked finally.

"Certainly, ma'am," he said. Coming around from behind his desk, he showed her to a bench in the lobby. He was very polite, even solicitous. That was because she was still wearing her ivory lace turn-of-the-century dress, she supposed. Perhaps he'd assumed she was Michel's bride, that Michel had been arrested on his way to the altar. Wearing a chartreuse windbreaker?

Probably she should have gone home to change before coming here. But she'd been afraid she'd run into Justin and never find out what had happened to Michel.

Michel was released at eleven-thirty that night. By then, Casey had drawn the attention of everyone who came by and she was feeling extremely self-conscious. But every time she made up her mind to leave, something held her back. Curiosity?

Michel looked astonished to see her when the young police officer pointed her out. "You waited for me!" he exclaimed, taking her hands in his as she stood up. "A thousand thanks, *mademoiselle*."

"I was worried about you," she said nervously.

Charm radiated from him when he smiled. His lean strong fingers gripped hers warmly. Something stirred within her—a butterfly flexing its wings. There was something about that lopsided smile of his, the touch of his callused fingers.... "You can go now?" she asked him, easing her hands free.

He nodded, the smile fading. "It was a misunderstanding only." A frown appeared on his face and settled in around his eyes.

"You don't have to go to court, then?" Casey questioned as she started her car. He had given her his address as they walked to the parking lot.

He shrugged and sighed as he tucked his long legs sideways. "I do not know what will happen to me," he said gloomily.

Something didn't add up here, but evidently he wasn't going to volunteer any information. After having waited four hours for him, however, Casey wasn't going to let it rest. "Why *did* the policeman arrest you?" she asked.

He gave the kind of raised-palm shrug only a Frenchman can manage.

They drove for a while in silence, then he said, "I am sorry, Mademoiselle...Casey, it is difficult for me to be sociable with conversation. I am anxious to be home."

"You didn't have your home address on your key ring, too, did you?" Casey asked.

He shook his head. "I just wish to be home to feel more safe. I did not know in America it is so easy to be arrested."

Casey tried again. "Why did they arrest you?"

Another long sigh. Then he seemed to be thinking hard, perhaps deciding whether or not to answer.

"When I first came to the United States," he said at last, "I received two tickets for speeding. I was accustomed to driving in Paris, you understand, where it is every man for himself. America seemed similar to me. Naturally, I keep up with traffic. But a policeman stopped only me each time. Someone told me a red Porsche is, what do you say, fair game?"

He shrugged. "The policeman each time was quite friendly, understanding. So I thought it was a warning only. I was not so practiced in English at that time, you see. When this policeman, tonight, checked on my car, he was told there is . . . warrant for me."

"You hadn't paid the tickets? How long ago did all this happen?"

"Three years now." He squirmed around a little as if he were uncomfortably squashed in the bucket seat. "I did not pay for them at the right time, no."

"Is there a money problem, Michel?"

A dull flush appeared along his cheekbones. Probably there was a money problem and she had offended him. Men were always so macho about taking care of their own problems. "It is all straightened out now," he muttered.

In that case, why did he say, "I do not know what will happen to me?" Casey wondered. And why was he still frowning in such a worried way? She wasn't at all sure Michel was telling her the truth. As one who had been brought up to prize the truth, she felt disappointed in him. She didn't know for sure, of course, that he had lied, but would a policeman slam someone up against the wall for not paying traffic tickets?

She dropped Michel off outside a very ordinary-looking apartment complex. He'd really had very little

to say and Casey was experiencing a sense of anticlimax.

But he didn't leave right away, after all. He walked
around the car and stopped beside her window, and
when she switched on the overhead light and opened the
window he bent down to look at her solemnly. "I have
been most rude," he said. "Please forgive me. I am
shaken, you understand. I have never been treated like
a criminal before."

"That's okay," Casey replied, a little stiffly.

He held out his right hand and she reached awkwardly across the steering wheel to shake it. He didn't
let her hand go. All at once the expression in his eyes
seemed warmer, as whimsical as his smile. The butterfly that had stirred inside her earlier soared upward on
a breath of air.

"You have been so kind," he told her. "You are a
good person, Mademoiselle Casey. Compassionate."
He hesitated, then went on, his voice acquiring a husky
tone. "Do not think that in my agitation I did not notice how very enchanting you are."

What could she possibly say to that? He was studying her face now as though he wanted to memorize
every detail of it. "A charming combination—red hair
and green eyes," he murmured. "There is much character in your face. You are a beautiful woman. Like a
bird of paradise, the flower of Hawaii. Have you seen
such a flower?"

Casey had never thought of herself as beautiful.
Colorful, yes—how could anyone with red hair and
green eyes be anything else? But a bird of paradise
sounded positively flamboyant, which she certainly was
not.

As he continued to gaze into her eyes, her heart started hammering against her ribs. She was suddenly reminded of movies she had seen of summer landscapes in which a heat haze hovered above the land, turning everything blurry. She felt hot. Her throat was dry. Even in that awful uniform, this was an extremely attractive man. He could be positively dangerous to a woman who didn't have her wits about her.

Without any warning whatsoever, he leaned closer so that his face was only inches away from hers. "Excuse me, please, I cannot resist," he murmured, then he lifted her chin with his fingers and kissed her very delicately on the mouth. It was a fleeting kiss, yet infinitely intimate. There was a rushing feeling inside her body, as though her soul had raced upward to meet his mouth.

"I would like to..." He hesitated. "No, perhaps it is not a wise thing. You would not want to...." He sighed, shaking his head and straightening. "Have I mentioned that you smell wonderful, Mademoiselle Casey?" he said softly, his dark eyes tender now. Then he turned away.

Feeling thoroughly bemused, Casey watched him stride gracefully toward the main entrance of the building. And then his final words echoed in her mind and she remembered, for the first time, the perfume she'd applied to her throat and ears and wrists just minutes before Michel Gervais Smith had come bursting into her store—Inga's magic perfume that was supposed to bring Casey her heart's desire.

Not sure whether she felt horrified or amused or none of the above, she realized that Michel had disappeared into the shadows, as though he had never been. Had she dreamed this evening's unusual events? Had she *invented* this interesting, intriguing, unusual, wickedly attractive man? She glanced at the watch that was pinned to her bosom. Just on midnight. Had Michel Gervais Smith turned into a pumpkin back there?

She was being ridiculous. Of course, she hadn't conjured Michel up out of thin air. Of course, the perfume wasn't magic. If she had wanted to conjure up Cinderella's prince, she thought, as she started the car again, he would not have been dressed in that sleazy chartreuse windbreaker.

How would she have dressed him? she wondered idly as she drove back toward the brilliantly lighted towers of the city. He wasn't stuffy enough for a suit, but she could imagine him in a blazer—bottle green maybe, with beige slacks and a white shirt. Polished shoes. Dark tie with a little emblem repeated on it. Fleur-de-lis? That would be fitting.

Later, getting ready for bed, she caught herself chuckling. It had been quite an adventure, after all. A lot more interesting than a trip to the movies. In spite of the evening's worrying aspects, she had enjoyed herself. *You are a beautiful woman.* There was no more attractive accent than that of a Frenchman. *How enchanting you are.*

Yes, an exciting little interlude. But only an interlude. Of course.

IN THE MORNING she called Justin to apologize for canceling their date. "It was a terrific film," he said, with a trace of umbrage in his voice. "Glenda Jackson was wonderful as Gudrun's mother."

"I'm sorry I missed her," Casey murmured.

There was an expectant silence.

"I was doing a favor for someone," Casey said. "I'm sorry it was such short notice. It sort of came up unexpectedly."

"Oh?"

"A man had his shuttle bus stolen."

"His shuttle bus." Justin's voice was flat. She was going to have to tell him all of it. Well, maybe not everything. Certainly she wasn't going to mention the perfume, or the compliments, or the kiss. Quickly, she explained the circumstances.

There was another silence. "I couldn't just let him rot in jail," she said with an attempt at humor.

"He was hardly your responsibility," Justin pointed out. "The whole story sounds suspicious to me. Maybe we should check it out with the police. What was his name?"

"I didn't get it." Casey was appalled at herself. The lie had just popped out. She could hear his father scolding her, *Never consort with people who aren't totally truthful. Their dishonesty rubs off.*

Justin made an exasperated sound. "He might have been a rapist or a mugger, or a serial murderer. Didn't you even think of that?"

"Briefly, yes. But he looked . . . decent."

"The grisliest murders are committed by men who look just like the guy next door."

Michel looked nothing like the guy next door, she thought contrarily. Justin looked like the guy next door. Michel looked like a prince in exile, a darkly glamorous movie star traveling incognito, the ultimate hero of a romance novel brought to life by a magic spell. Luckily, she had the sense to keep her thoughts to herself.

Justin sighed. "Do you remember what happened in February when we had that cold snap?"

"February?" Casey echoed innocently, though she knew perfectly well what was coming.

"You found that . . . street person lying in your shop doorway and nothing would do but you should take him a blanket."

"It was freezing. He could have died."

"And where was the blanket next time you saw him?"

"Gone," Casey admitted.

"No doubt swapped for a bottle of cheap wine."

"Probably," Casey agreed meekly.

"You've got to stop being so trusting, Casey," he went on. "You need to develop more sense of self-protection."

"I'd rather trust people," she said firmly. "I've got enough common sense to know when someone's a crook. My father taught me it's better to trust everyone and get let down sometimes than to go through life distrusting my fellow man."

"Your father would have approved of you sitting around in a police station in the middle of the night, I suppose?"

Not much argument to offer there. And not much sense arguing with Justin when he had right on his side. "I'm sorry, Justin," she said contritely.

He sighed, and she was afraid he was going to chastise her some more, but instead he merely warned, "Do be more careful, Casey," then went on to arrange their date for the evening. "Eric Rhomer's *Four Adventures of Reinette and Mirabelle,* tonight," he informed her.

"Lovely," she said warmly, almost meaning it.

ON THE WAY to and from work over the next few days, Casey saw several airport shuttle buses. Each time, she craned her neck to see the driver. None of them looked remotely like Michel Gervais Smith. Had he disappeared as magically as he had appeared?

Every once in a while she felt tempted to stop by Michel's apartment complex on the chance of catching him at home and finding out if his bus and car had been recovered. She just wanted to be sure the man was real, she rationalized.

On Friday it occurred to Casey that she couldn't try the perfume out on Justin now. Inga had said she could only use it once. So she'd blown her chance to galvanize Justin into some kind of action. Probably just as well. To tell the truth, she was really quite content with the way things were between them. It was such a civilized friendship. Enjoyable. Rewarding.

Boring, a little voice murmured in her mind.

She sighed. If only the weather wasn't quite so balmy this last week in May, and flowers weren't bursting into bloom everywhere she looked, and the air didn't smell quite as sweet, and she didn't see so many women walking around with tiny babies nestled in carriers against their breasts, she could go back to feeling settled with Justin. She wouldn't have this strange yearning feeling all the time.

Had she really used all she could of the perfume? she wondered, glancing up at it as she tidied her store that night.

Exasperated with herself for even being tempted to try the perfume again, she plucked the bottle from the shelf, took it home with her and closed it firmly away in the medicine cabinet over her bathroom sink.

THE FOLLOWING MONDAY did not start out well. A gray, drizzly day, it began at eight in the morning with a telephone call from her landlord—something Casey always dreaded. Vern Gilbert was always trying to catch his tenants out in an infraction of one of his many rules. Casey had tried to be charitable. After all, the man had gone to a lot of trouble and expense to faithfully restore the old mansion in which her apartment was located. Naturally, he didn't want anyone messing it up. But was it really necessary to be quite so rigid?

"I told you when you signed the rental agreement that the rules must be strictly adhered to," he said without preamble when she picked up the telephone.

Casey searched her conscience, but could find no blemish.

"I've been adhering like mad," she replied, hoping to lighten him up.

"You left a note on your door last week."

The note for Justin. Had Mr. Gilbert read it? *Sorry I can't make it tonight. Will explain tomorrow.* What could he possibly object to in that? Wasn't she supposed to have a social life?

"You fastened it with adhesive tape. It states clearly in the rules that you must not use nails in the paneling or any other fastener that could possibly mar the finish of the wood."

Guilty as charged. She put as much girlish ingenuousness as she could manage into her voice. "Gosh, Mr. Gilbert, I'm so sorry. It was an emergency and I didn't even think."

He grunted. "I was going to let you get away with it this once, but I can't let you off on this new infraction. The rules are quite clear on this point. All apartments are studio apartments, designed for one-person occupancy—no pets."

Casey frowned. "I'm not sure what you mean."

"I'm referring to your cat," he said.

"I don't own a cat."

"I've seen it myself, Miss Templeton. On your windowsill, west side of the building."

Casey bit her lip so she wouldn't laugh out loud. Tabby. The man was talking about Tabby, a gift she'd bought herself when she arrived in Seattle. Something to hug. "That cat is stuffed, Mr. Gilbert," she stated as solemnly as she could manage. "It's a toy."

Silence. Then he said indignantly. "It looks real."

"Doesn't it?" she responded pleasantly, then decided to try to turn his probable embarrassment into achievement. "As long as I'm talking to you, Mr. Gilbert, what about the doorknob that's loose? The one on the bathroom door. I dropped you a note a month ago, remember? You particularly asked me not to try to fix anything myself, so..."

"All in good time, Miss Templeton," he said. Then he hung up. Casey laughed, but underneath she felt uneasy. She definitely did not want to know that Vern Gilbert was keeping a watch on her windows or hanging around her doorway. At the same time, she hated the idea of looking for another apartment. This one suited her so well, and it was affordable if not cheap.

The bad start gave way to a second upset. When she arrived at her shop she found evidence that a mouse was inhabiting her storeroom. It took her an hour to track down the mousetraps she'd used the previous year. Then she had to run next door in the rain to beg a little cheese from Skip's chef, and when she came back she found that the mailman had delivered her mail while she was gone, without picking up the stack of advertising fliers she'd had ready for him.

What next? she wondered.

Michel was next. And suddenly the day did not seem so frustrating, after all.

He came into her shop in the middle of the afternoon carrying a flat box filled with velvety purple pansies. Casey was helping a customer decide between two antique necklaces. She glanced up and felt heat rush to her face. A second later she felt cold, as though she were frozen in place, but she quickly melted again in response to Michel's whimsical, lopsided smile. Smiling nervously in return, she hoped the customer wouldn't notice that the chain she was holding had developed a tremor. He was real, then. She had not imagined him. Boy, was he real.

He was not wearing his billed cap and abominable chartreuse jacket today. His shirt sleeves were rolled up, showing some very respectable muscles. She was astonished at the impact his tall muscular presence made on all her senses.

Her customer, a middle-aged matron, was obviously just as affected. She became positively giddy after one solemn glance from Michel's dark eyes. Casey thought the woman would never decide whether to make a purchase or not.

"Which do you think?" the matron asked Michel, holding one necklace after the other round her neck, batting her eyelashes like crazy.

"They are equally lovely," Michel said politely, somehow giving the impression that they were equally lovely on *her*.

The customer finally left with both necklaces and many a backward glance before she fumbled her way out the door.

"I hope you do not mind that I visit you again," Michel said.

"No, of course not," Casey replied. Her voice had developed a gravelly undertone due to the extreme dryness of her mouth.

He handed her the box of pansies. "I regret the flowers are not properly arranged. I picked them for you myself."

She glanced at him sharply.

"With permission," he added gravely. There was a glint in his dark eyes that told her he knew she'd wondered.

To cover her embarrassment, she turned away to hunt for a dish. "They're beautiful. Thank you," she said. "I've always loved pansies."

He nodded as though he'd known that.

She had found a suitable bowl and had no choice but to look at him again. Then it was difficult to look away. "I've been wondering how...things were going for you," she said awkwardly. "Did the police find your Porsche?"

"Not yet. But they discovered the shuttle bus the next day, at the side of a residential street in West Seattle."

"Any clues to the thieves?"

He shook his head and made a dismissive gesture with one hand as if he didn't want to talk about that. "I have wanted to come to see you before, but I was... embarrassed that I was arrested." His compelling dark eyes held hers. "But at last I had to come. I could not forget such a charming young woman, you see. That is why I bring you pansies. In my country we use the same word, *pensée,* for thought as for pansy." He shrugged gracefully. "It was like the advertisements you see on television for the perfume," he added. "I am drawn back to you."

Casey flushed guiltily, her mind flashing a picture of the golden bottle safely closed away in her medicine cabinet. Without comment, she went into the small bathroom at the back of the store and filled the bowl she'd found with water, taking a long swig from the faucet herself while she was at it.

"I am sure you think I am very stupid for being arrested, is it not so?" Michel asked when she returned.

"Not so at all," Casey replied, then realized she'd spoken too warmly. "I mean, it wasn't as if you'd done something terrible. It was all a misunderstanding, you said?"

"Just so."

"Are you managing all right without your Porsche?"

"It is a nuisance, but I have rented a car temporarily. But not so good, I am afraid. If my automobile is not found soon, I must buy a new one."

"Another Porsche?"

"I like the Porsche, yes."

He must get generous tips, Casey thought as she gently arranged the pansies, her fingers lingering on the soft petals. Or else he had very good insurance. "Well, at least you are out of trouble with the law over those speeding tickets," she told him.

For just a second, he looked...bewildered. "The tickets," he murmured. "The tickets, yes."

Casey experienced a moment of doubt, but before she could explore it, that whimsical smile of his came into play again. Putting his hands on the counter that separated them, he leaned toward her. "I have another larger favor to ask of you, *mademoiselle,*" he said softly.

It seemed very stuffy in the store all of a sudden. The scent of the pansies he'd brought seemed overpowering, far stronger than any pansies had ever smelled before. She needed to open a window, let in some air so she could catch her breath. "The police station again?" she asked.

"*Mais non*. I wish to arrange to take you to dinner this evening. To show my gratitude."

"Oh, well, that isn't necessary."

"But it would be my pleasure. I am so very grateful, you understand." His smile became more intimate. "I am acquainted with an excellent French restaurant, in the Pike Place Market. Chez Étienne."

"I know the one you mean." She hesitated. She could hardly ask him if he could afford a place like that. "I'm afraid I have an engagement tonight."

"Tomorrow, then? I could come for you in my rented car, if you do not mind this."

She couldn't possibly go out with him, of course. "I'm sorry," she said. "That sounds too much like a date."

"There is some reason you cannot date?"

"I'm afraid so."

The whimsical smile was very much in evidence again, playing around his mouth, making her own mouth quirk at the corners in automatic response. "Perhaps we can effect a compromise," he suggested. "Let us suppose that I find myself at Chez Étienne tomorrow evening at eight o'clock. Let us suppose that by coincidence you also happen to be present. We could perhaps contrive to sit together?"

He was so very charming, so blatantly roguish, it would really be very churlish to refuse. Anyway, it was natural that he'd feel grateful. She *had* gone out of her way to help him. And she was really very curious about

Michel Gervais Smith. Face it, she scolded herself, there was a lot more than curiosity operating here.

Justin had a staff meeting the following evening, she suddenly remembered.

"Could we make it eight-fifteen?" she asked, capitulating. "I'll have to change my clothes first."

He glanced at the vintage blouse and long skirt she was wearing—the same outfit she'd worn when she'd met Inga at the Kingdome. "Must you?"

"I'd look a little conspicuous like this, don't you think?"

He raised an elegant dark eyebrow. "*Charming* is the word I would have selected." He hesitated, and for a heart-stopping moment she thought he was going to lean over the counter and kiss her again. Instead, he inclined his head. "Thank you, Casey. I will look forward," he said softly. Then he smiled and turned away without even attempting to kiss her, leaving her wondering if that was really relief she was feeling, or disappointment.

CHAPTER THREE

THE MOVIE THAT NIGHT was one of the best thrillers
Casey had ever seen. It wasn't classic enough to suit
Justin, however. He thought it was too contrived.
"Why would the woman go swimming alone late at
night when she knew the killer was nearby?" he wanted
to know as they sat over coffee in Casey's studio apartment.

"She was hoping he'd make a move. So she could
prove he was the guilty one. The detective was watching out for her, remember."

"Well, I thought it was unbelievable. Women don't
usually court danger."

Sometimes Justin could be as chauvinistic as Skip,
even though he prided himself on being a feminist. But
she let the remark pass. Actually, the comment had hit
home in a different way. Wasn't *she* courting danger,
agreeing to see Michel again?

"I'm going out to dinner tomorrow night," she confessed as she got up to bring the coffeepot to her small
dining table.

Justin smiled. "Good. I'm sorry about the meeting.
Which restaurant are you going to?"

"Chez Étienne."

He whistled softly. "Who are you having dinner with,
Barbara Harriman? It has to be someone with money.
Chez Étienne's one of the first places I plan to eat when

I find my rich wife." He chuckled when Casey made a face at him. "Shall I lend you the season tickets? Barbara likes movies. She and Marilyn used to go all the time when they were in school together."

Marilyn was Justin's sister, Barbara Harriman one of Casey's most frequent customers. In fact, it was Barbara who had introduced Casey to Justin, at one of the fabulous Halloween parties she and her husband hosted every year.

"I'm not going out with Barbara," Casey said awkwardly. "Actually, it's not a woman friend."

"Oh?" The little frown that she usually loved had appeared between Justin's fair eyebrows.

Casey took a deep breath. "It's the man I told you about the other night—the man whose vehicles were stolen."

The frown deepened. "You're having dinner with a man who was carted off to jail? Why?"

She deliberately misunderstood the question. "He's grateful for my help, I guess."

She thought Justin was going to protest, but after a moment of silence, he evidently remembered how enlightened he was. "You're a grown woman, Casey," he said, a little too evenly. "You must make such decisions for yourself, of course. But as your friend, I'd advise you to be careful of getting involved with someone you know nothing about. Especially someone you met under such unusual circumstances."

If he only knew *how* unusual. Thank goodness she hadn't said anything about the perfume when she showed him the bottle.

Did Justin really see himself as just her friend? she wondered. Contrarily, she wished he had become angry.

I can't bear the thought of you seeing another man! he could have yelled.

She'd have wanted to yell back at him if he had, she conceded. All the same, a little passion once in a while wouldn't offend her. It might even be welcome.

THE RESTAURANT MICHEL had mentioned was one Casey had seen only from the outside. She had wanted to eat there, but it was much too expensive for her tight budget, or Justin's. She wondered again about Michel's tips and hoped he wasn't beggaring himself in order to impress her.

Michel was there ahead of her, standing in the lobby, talking in French to a short, bearded man. His back was toward Casey as she entered, which was just as well— she was afraid for a moment she was going to faint dead away from shock.

She couldn't believe it.... He was wearing the bottle-green blazer and beige slacks she had imagined for him. His shoes had been buffed to a high gloss, his dark hair neatly brushed. And when he turned, there was the white shirt and the dark tie, complete with fleur-de-lis pattern.

"Casey." His voice seemed to caress her name. He had taken her right hand. She wouldn't have been surprised if he'd kissed it, but he kissed her cheek instead.

Somehow Casey managed to find her voice. "You look very...elegant," she said.

He laughed. "You expected to find me wearing that so awful jacket? I must confess to you, Casey, the uniform I must wear offends my soul. This is better, no?"

"Much better," she agreed faintly. The jacket was beautifully tailored, smooth over his shoulders, fitting him as if it had been made for him, which it obviously had been.

It was a coincidence, that's all, she told herself. Or else she'd experienced some kind of telepathic insight into the kind of clothing hanging in his closet. Or maybe she had become prophetic as Inga had suggested, like her namesake Cassandra. Did that make Michel Apollo? Perfect casting. She could just see him standing naked on a marble base, a laurel wreath around his head. Was she losing her mind?

His hand was still holding hers. "We are both new people, yes? You are a twentieth-century lady today."

She nodded mutely.

"I approve of the change in you also," he said. "Though I admit to admiring your—what do you call it?"

"Vintage clothing."

"Just so. But you are as alluring in this dress."

Alluring. No one had ever called her alluring. And the dress was just a plain apple-green cotton, slender, buttoned all the way down the front, with a tie belt of the same material.

She became aware that the short man Michel had been talking to was looking at her curiously. Michel must have remembered his presence at the same moment. He turned and said something very rapidly in French, then introduced the man. "Casey Templeton, Étienne Vincent. Étienne is the owner of this fine establishment," he added.

"So you are Michel's guardian angel," Étienne said, shaking her hand. He laughed, his dark eyes twinkling. "I am supposed to tell you, *mademoiselle,* that I have only one table available, so you must unfortunately share one with this gentleman here." As he led the way into the dining room, he smiled back at her over his shoulder. "Michel has told me about his adventure. It was kind of you to take him under your wing. I must tell you, I have also played the role of guardian angel to Michel." He made an airily dismissive gesture. "My assistance dealt only with a couple of traffic tickets, however."

Michel looked embarrassed as Casey darted a sharp glance his way. "I have something to explain to you, Casey," he murmured.

She nodded, feeling suddenly cold. "I think you have," she agreed.

The decor of the restaurant was very elegant, with snowy damask linen and gold-rimmed white china, flowers and crystal lanterns on every table, brocade-covered settees instead of chairs. Michel and Casey were shown to a corner table and seated side by side on the single oval-backed sofa. After a long discussion of the menu, a snap of Étienne's fingers brought the wine steward, who greeted Michel by name, as did the waiter. Michel was evidently well-known here.

"I found this restaurant by chance when I first came to Seattle," Michel explained when they were totally alone. "It became my home away from home for a while. I have not come for some time, because I decided I must—" he searched for a word, finally came up with "—integrate...into American society. But I thought you would enjoy this place and it would be good to see Étienne again."

"It's lovely," Casey said. Before she could say more, the wine was brought and had to be sampled and decided upon. Casey had always felt impatient with the few wine snobs she'd run into, but then again, Michel was a Frenchman and the quality of a wine was of utmost importance to the French. Actually, she suspected Michel was mainly interested in delaying the questions that had to be answered. And in any case, a wicked little voice murmured in her mind, it was nice to have an opportunity just to look at this gorgeous man, to study the planes and angles of his face, the sensual curve of his mouth, the dark depths of his brown eyes, and thick dark hair that seemed to invite her fingers.

Evidently the entire staff of Chez Étienne knew Michel. And every one of them had to come to their table to pass the time of day. Casey and Michel had finished their hors d'oeuvres and were waiting for the paupiettes of flounder to be served before they had a chance to speak privately again.

"I've an idea you haven't been entirely truthful with me, Michel," Casey said as soon as their most recent visitor was satisfied that their comfort was assured.

Those dark eyes of Michel's could look soulful, she discovered. He nodded. "You refer to what Étienne said about the traffic tickets."

"Exactly."

His mouth quirked in apology. "I did not tell you all the facts before, because I did not wish you to think ill of me, you see."

"So you lied." She kept her voice stern, but it took an effort. It was almost impossible to feel angry when he was looking at her with such an earnest, open expression and incidentally holding her right hand between both of his, absentmindedly stroking the back of it with his left thumb.

"I lied," he agreed. "I referred to an earlier occasion rather than the one in which you were involved. There *were* speeding tickets, three years ago, when I first came to Seattle. And Étienne, as he said, helped me explain to the police that I had not understood. It is something common, the police told me at that time. Many people do not pay tickets, even parking tickets. But the other night is more serious...." He took a deep breath. "It is so terribly embarrassing. But you must believe me, Casey, it is truly a misunderstanding, a mistake."

"Try me," she suggested.

"There was apparently a young couple involved in a... What is the expression you use in this country? A con game. That is it. What does it mean, exactly?"

"It means to swindle a victim after first gaining his or her confidence," Casey said, looking him straight in the eye.

He met her gaze directly, with every appearance of complete honesty. "Yes, that is it. Well, this is what happened. The couple approached elderly people in Seattle and Tacoma, the police told me, selling them a miracle treatment for...." Again he searched for a word. "For carpenter ants." He frowned at Casey. "You know about carpenter ants?"

"Enough to realize they are a constant problem in the Pacific Northwest, yes. They get into houses and chew up the wood."

He nodded. "It seems the miracle cure turned out to be salt water only, but the young man and woman have cheated many people of many dollars. They charge five hundred dollars for each useless treatment."

The paupiettes arrived. There was some ceremony to the serving, but finally the food was in place.

"The police thought you were the young man?" Casey asked as she cut through the tender roll of stuffed fish with her fork.

Michel used his knife and fork in the European way, making it look like the only possible way to eat. He had wonderful manners for a shuttle-bus driver, Casey thought, and was immediately shocked at herself. Since when had she become such a snob?

"He drove a Porsche the same color as mine," Michel said after a moment. "Red, you see. Very noticeable. Does that not seem stupid?"

"Did anyone get the license number?"

"Apparently not."

"Then perhaps it wasn't as stupid as it seems. If people remember only the red Porsche and not the license number."

He rested his knife and fork on his plate and looked at her admiringly. "But that is very clever of you, Casey. I must mention this to the police."

"You have to see them again?"

"It is possible."

"Just because you drive a red Porsche?"

He sighed. "The man spoke with a foreign accent also. And had dark hair and eyes." He hesitated. "And was tall."

"I'm amazed the police didn't stash you away for life."

"I convinced them it was a case of mistaken identity."

"And was it?"

They had both stopped eating. The flickering candle in the lantern cast shadows over his face, making his eyes look darker than ever and even more intense. "Casey," he said chidingly. "Do I look like a man who would cheat others?"

"In your chartreuse windbreaker, you do."

He laughed. "Ah, you are so quick, Mademoiselle Casey. In my country we prize a rapid wit above all things. It is even more important than beauty."

"You're changing the subject," she replied sternly to cover up the emotional fireworks his admiring gaze had caused.

"I beg your pardon," he said at once, picking up his knife and fork again. He seemed to be selecting his next words with care. "I must point out to you, as I pointed out to the police," he continued, "that it would be very stupid of me to report my Porsche stolen if I had used it previously for...nefarious dealings."

"Almost as stupid as a con artist driving a car as memorable as a red Porsche," Casey said drily. "In any case, you didn't report the Porsche stolen. Gus did."

"But I would have done so, of course. You do not believe in my innocence?" Once again he was gazing at her very intently, but now there was an injured note in his voice.

Would he have told her about the con game if he *had* been involved in it? she wondered. Perhaps. He had told her a lie before.

Show me a liar and I will show thee a thief, her father said in her memory.

It wasn't really an out-and-out lie, Casey argued with him. The traffic-ticket incident really happened.

Three years ago.

You've never heard of lying by omission? her father questioned.

"You have doubts about my character?" Michel asked.

"Uncertainties, perhaps."

"Shall I call Étienne over to vouch for me?"

"That won't be necessary." Who was she to talk about truthfulness, anyway? She certainly hadn't told Michel there was a good chance she'd attracted him with magic perfume. Wasn't that lying by omission, too?

Did she really believe the perfume had brought him to her? Yes, she did. How else to explain that explosion of feeling that had arced between them almost right away? The stillness. The sense that they had been meant to come together.

"You like the paupiettes?" he asked, obviously wanting to change the subject before she could come up with any more questions.

She picked up her fork. "They're delicious. The crab sauce is wonderful." Her father's voice had faded out, but in the back of her mind she could hear Justin snorting about people who were too trusting. She shut her ears to the sound of his voice. What did it matter anyway? She was probably never going to see Michel again after tonight.

Now, why did that thought make her feel so depressed?

"You told the policeman you were an American citizen," she said to prevent herself from exploring the reason for her sudden depression. "Was that true?"

For a minute, she thought he wasn't going to answer. There was something definitely cautious about his expression, and a deliberate hesitation in his manner. But then he said, "Oh, yes. My father was an American. From Los Angeles. I was born in this country."

"That's where you got the name Smith, then. I wondered."

"Not a romantic name, I'm afraid. But my father was a romantic man, my mother says."

"Was?"

He nodded. "Conrad Smith was stationed in England with the United States Air Force from 1953 to 1956. In 1955 he took a small vacation in Paris, where he met my mother, Jeanne. They were both twenty-one. He carried her off to England and then to California. I was born one year later, their only child." He paused, a bereft expression showing in his eyes. "My father was killed in a crash on takeoff in Florida when I was four years old."

"It's tough losing a father," Casey murmured.

His dark eyes studied her face. "You also?"

"Both parents. In a car accident. A drunk driver sideswiped them. I was luckier than you. I had them for seventeen years. You never really knew your father."

"From stories only. And one or two vague memories."

"Your mother took you back to France?"

Why did she keep getting the idea he was selecting his words carefully, editing them in advance? Because he was speaking very slowly, pausing between every phrase. "My mother Jeanne is of a big French family, very close. She was never happy in America, so homesick, so she and I returned to live with her family."

There was a silence. Evidently he didn't want to talk any more about his past. At least he *had* a past, Casey thought. She was relieved to hear that. She hadn't invented him. Unless her brain had also invented a cover story to explain his existence.

About to ask him why he had come back to the United States, she realized he was looking at her in a very thoughtful way. "I am wondering if you ever let your hair down," he said when she glanced questioningly at him.

"Symbolically or literally?" she asked.

He looked blank for a second, then laughed explosively. "Either one."

"I wear it down sometimes," she replied. "You don't like it this way?"

"Very much. When I walk beside you the view of the little knot on top is most charming. But I was imagining how it would feel to touch your hair. Such a vibrant color. Such shining. It would feel like silk, I think."

She could not in a million years imagine Justin saying something like that. Probably she should be offended. After all, she hardly knew the man. But she wasn't offended. She was...excited. She wanted to touch him. She wanted him to touch her. Quite suddenly, she was remembering the images the perfume had evoked; the tangled sheets, limbs brushing against limbs, lips meeting.... Somewhere low in her body, heat formed and spiraled upward.

His fingers tenderly brushed a tendril of hair away from her forehead. For a moment, Casey thought she was never going to be able to breathe again. But then a waiter appeared at Michel's elbow. "May I show you the dessert tray?" he asked.

"Not for me," Casey answered quickly, always calorie conscious.

"Some fruit, perhaps?"

"Well, fruit. I guess that would be okay."

The waiter said something in French to Michel and Michel chuckled appreciatively, and the next thing Casey knew she was looking at a dish of plump strawberries that had been individually dipped in chocolate.

"How could you do this to me?" she groaned.

Michel smiled. "Let me tempt you," he said softly, then picked up one of the strawberries and held it to her mouth until she bit into it. His gaze on her lips, he held the rest of the berry until she took it into her mouth. She couldn't remember anyone ever putting food into her mouth before. It was a very intimate thing to do. Especially as Michel ended the whole procedure with a kiss. Again it was a delicate kiss, too fleeting to properly object to. Not that she felt like objecting; actually, she felt more like melting against him and begging him to prolong the kiss. She must have drunk too much wine, she decided, ignoring the fact that her glass was still two-thirds full.

Michel's dark eyes held an expression that told her the kiss had not been as casual as it had seemed. No doubt about it: Michel found her as attractive, as desirable, as she found him. All at once she began to worry about what might happen when this meal was over. Would he want to come home with her? So far, she hadn't managed to refuse him anything.

"Why did you come back to the United States?" she asked, when it seemed he would be perfectly happy to continue looking at her without talking.

He shrugged and tried a strawberry himself. Casey hurriedly took another before he could try feeding her again. He smiled at her, his gaze meeting and holding hers for a long, still moment. Then that cautious expression descended over his features again. "When I became thirty," he said slowly, "I awakened to the fact that I was not spending my life in the way I wished. So I came to my father's country. I had always been curious about it."

"You came alone? Your mother's family still lives in France?"

"Yes." He hesitated, then shrugged.

Evidently he didn't want to talk about his family. Okay, she wouldn't push him. A big family, he'd said. Perhaps not too well-off? If the only work Michel could find in this country was as a driver, it would seem safe to assume that, like her, he hadn't been able to afford the privilege of a higher education.

"I wanted a chance to do my own thing, *tout seul,*" he concluded.

"Driving a shuttle bus is your own thing?" Casey exclaimed.

He laughed. "You do not think anyone would have ambitions to drive a shuttle bus? By why not, Casey? There is much freedom. I meet many interesting people. I make excellent tips. You would be amazed at what some people will pay for me to lift a bag from the van to the sidewalk. *Incroyable!* I would never be so generous." For a moment he looked as if he were going to say something more, but he changed his mind.

"We **have** talked enough about me, I think," he said, with another of his charming smiles. "Let us have some liqueur and coffee and talk about you. I wish to hear your whole life story."

Very nifty footwork, Casey thought. But he did seem interested in hearing how she had grown up in the Midwest with parents who could easily have qualified for sainthood. "They were truly good people," she told him. "There was never any money, but they scraped up enough to send me to a private school. They were determined I should have a good education."

She hesitated. He was such a sympathetic listener, she was almost tempted to tell him how tough getting that good education had been. But she restrained herself. Few people had heard that story. Why should she tell it to a virtual stranger?

"Mom was a warm, loving, bustling sort of person," she continued. "Always busy tending the sick and the elderly, tending my father, tending church affairs."

Always busy, Ellen Templeton. Too busy to notice how unhappy her daughter was.

"And your father? A minister, you said?"

She nodded. "A sweet man," she told him, smiling reminiscently. "Absentminded, good-hearted. Everyone in the congregation adored him. But he had his tough moments when it came to religion. Do you know what a puritan is?"

"A person who is very strict in morals?"

"That and someone who looks upon some kinds of fun and pleasure as sinful. My father was a wonderful man, but he wasn't easy to live with or up to." She shook her head. "He was always quoting aphorisms from the Bible, Shakespeare, Publilius Syrus—anywhere that would do the most good. I still remember most of them. I can even hear his voice saying them."

No need to go into the painful parts of her background she decided. No need for Michel to know why she had left her hometown.

He was smiling at her. "I will try out my powers of extrasensory perception, I think." Picking up her left hand, he turned it over and studied it solemnly. "This hand is for the past, you understand. I think that you were a very good little girl. No trouble to anyone. Alone a great deal. Always very shy."

She felt a little uneasy. He was uncomfortably close to the truth. He was still holding her hand. She extricated it carefully and picked up her coffee cup.

"When my parents were killed, I was a senior in high school," she continued. "I came to Seattle, finished school, worked at several jobs, then started Second

Time Around on money borrowed from the bank.'' She told him a little about the methods she had used to get the shop going. He really was a good listener—very attentive, with pertinent questions that led her to open up more than she might have. ''It's not exactly the source of great wealth,'' she concluded. ''But I manage. And it's very satisfying to me. I've always wanted to be around beautiful clothes.''

''You are very resourceful, Mademoiselle Casey,'' he said admiringly, his dark eyes fixed on her face.

And you are so very charming, she thought as she melted one more time. ''You have not married?'' he asked.

She shook her head and seized the opportunity to ask, ''How about you?''

He shrugged. ''I have come close twice, but escaped each time.''

''Escaped?'' Remembering the way Inga had questioned her, she asked rather accusingly, ''You don't like women?''

He looked astonished. ''How can you say such a thing, Casey? I adore women.'' The charmingly lop-sided smile flashed once more. ''Perhaps that is my problem. It is difficult to settle for one woman when there are so many, *n'est-ce pas?* What about you, Casey? Have you come close also?''

She shook her head. ''I do have a boyfriend, though,'' she said. ''He's an English teacher.''

''Ah, that is why you did not wish to consider this outing as a date,'' Michel replied softly. Then he looked at her directly, his dark eyes liquid in the candlelight. ''I cannot bear to think of you with another man,'' he said with great drama.

The exact words she had wished Justin would say to her.

Every time she imagined something, it happened. Michel made it happen. Or she made it happen. What forces had she set in motion when she used that crazy perfume? She opened her mouth to say something, closed it, opened it again.

"You are offended," Michel told her. "Forgive me, Casey. My grandmother tells me often I am too... arrogant in my approach to women. I have shown my admiration for you too soon. When you know me better we will speak of such things again."

When you know me better.

But this was supposed to be a one-time-only meeting, a thank-you meeting—not the first of a series. She couldn't possibly see him again.

Nonsense. She had to see him again.

Michel was studying her face intently, probably reading her mind, she decided, almost hysterically. What should she imagine now, taking him home to her apartment, inviting him into her bed? Had she made up her sofa bed this morning? She wasn't sure. Better make it his apartment.

"I would like to suggest you come to my apartment," Michel said, jolting her almost out of her seat. "However, I would prefer that you come in daylight rather than at night."

One thing she could say for Michel—he wasn't at all predictable. Most men with amour on their minds would want to meet under cover of darkness. Perhaps he did turn into a pumpkin at midnight. Or a vampire. He was handsome enough to be a movie-type vampire. Without the vampire teeth. He had perfect teeth, beautifully even, white against the tan of his face. All the same, she could picture him in the requisite evening clothes with a cape lined in red satin. No. Better not picture him in anything more outlandish than jeans and a knit shirt. He'd look good in jeans and a knit shirt. White jeans. A dark polo shirt. With short sleeves to show his muscles.

"Why in daylight?" she asked huskily.

"I have something to show you."

"What?"

He smiled mysteriously. "Everything."

The thought of Michel showing "everything" to her was not one she could allow herself to pursue. *If you think a sinful thing, you might as well do it,* her father said in her head. *A sin in the mind is as bad as a sin in the flesh.*

"You aren't going to tell me what you have in mind?"

He shook his head. He was still smiling his crooked smile, his dark eyes glinting in the candlelight. "Shall we say Saturday? About ten in the morning?"

Saturday seemed a long way off. What would he be doing in the meantime? Ripping off senior citizens who had carpenter ants in their basements?

"I am especially busy during this week," he explained, reading her mind again.

"I suppose I could get my friend Fumiko to help out at Second Time Around," she said, thinking aloud. "She's always happy to oblige. She and her husband Goro have five children. They need the money, so I give her as much work as I can."

He raised his eyebrows. "I am not the only person who has you for a guardian angel?"

She smiled absently. Justin was going to be busy on the weekend, she had just remembered. Some kind of open house for parents. Immediately she felt awash with guilt.

"Saturday it is," she agreed. After all, she had told Justin about Michel—she had no reason to feel guilty.

Yes, she had.

CHAPTER FOUR

"So what are you worried about, girl?" Skip asked.
"You want to see this Prince Charming again? Do it.
I've no objection. Even if he did take you to somebody
else's restaurant."

Casey had regaled him with some of the details of her
meetings with Michel Gervais Smith while they jogged
along the waterfront. They jogged together two morn-
ings a week. Tuesdays and Thursdays. At least Casey
jogged. After his injury-dogged years of football, Skip
refused to subject his knees to any more stress than was
necessary, so he merely walked rapidly alongside Casey, his long legs keeping up easily.

Casey hadn't told Skip that Michel had turned up
right after she'd used the magic perfume. He'd made his
feelings about magic perfectly clear.

But now that he'd asked what was troubling her, she
did tell him about the supposed mix-up between Michel and the con artist who sold miracle cures for carpenter ants.

Skip chuckled, then strode along beside her in silence for a while, obviously mulling the story over. The
two of them must make an odd-looking couple, Casey
thought—she in her size-eight lime-green shorts and T-
shirt, his muscular bulk wrapped in his extra-large gray
sweats. What would anyone think, seeing them trot-
ting along together? That he was in training for a

heavyweight title and she was his somewhat puny coach? The question was moot. Later in the day the area would be crowded with sightseers, but at this hour of rosy dawn over Puget Sound, none of the import or specialty stores or restaurants on the piers were open, so there were no tourists around to stare at them. Nor were there any other joggers in view—most of the regulars were office workers or store employees and would turn out later on their lunch break.

"The thing is," Casey said, "he wasn't exactly truthful the first time around."

Skip snorted. "You and your search for absolute truth." There was enough affection in his voice to take any possible sting out of the words. "Few of us tell all of the truth all of the time to all of the people, Case. We fudge here and there, out of self-protection, or to spare people's feelings, or to make people like us more."

"But how can I tell he's not still lying?"

He sighed. "You can't. So if you feel strongly about it, then maybe you shouldn't see him again."

"But I like him," she argued. "He's a bit on the arrogant side, but terribly attractive."

"Con men usually are. Tool of the trade." He glanced at her sideways. "Think, girl. This dude supposedly had a female partner. Suppose Michel *is* the con man—police are going to think you're his accomplice."

Casey laughed. "You've been watching too much TV." She frowned. "He wants me to go to his apartment for some particular reason, but he wouldn't tell me what. I wish I knew what he had in mind."

"Show you his etchings, maybe?"

"Well, I'm pretty sure he does have something like that in mind, but there's something else, too, I think. He was just kind of mysterious about it."

Again Skip didn't reply for a minute or two, striding briskly along, his face upturned to the breeze off the sound. Apparently he was watching the antics of some sea gulls that were wheeling and dipping overhead. The morning looked as if it had a fair chance of becoming beautiful—the rugged Olympic mountain range was etched hazily in the west against a gradually lightening sky. "Us guys like to indulge in a little male mystique sometimes," Skip offered at last.

Casey laughed and aimed a mock punch at Skip's broad shoulder. Then she frowned again. "I got the impression Michel wasn't quite what he seemed to be. Several times it seemed to me that he was censoring himself, keeping all sorts of stuff back deliberately."

"Did you bare *your* soul?"

"Well, not completely. It's a little soon for that. Oh, I see what you mean."

"I rest my case," Skip said. "Guess you just have to weigh the downside against the upside."

Casey immediately thought of the flowers she'd received yesterday morning after her dinner date with Michel. Definitely upside. A young black man on a bicycle had brought them. Irises of the most incredible shade of powder blue. Unwrapped. Handpicked again? The buds had been tightly furled, and had opened slowly, beautifully, after she'd placed the flowers in water.

Here again was a mystery. The young man—Sidney Arundel—didn't work for a florist's shop, he'd told her when she questioned him; he was just doing a favor for Michel. "We live in the same apartment complex," he'd volunteered. Then he'd hesitated as if he were going to say something more. But instead he'd just accepted the tip she offered and gone on his way. Yes, definitely mysterious. Also intriguing.

"Then there's this business of him leaving his family, going it alone," Casey said, speaking more to herself than to Skip.

"I can relate to that. Can't you? You and I are both loners. Your folks hadn't died, you think you'd have lived at home forever? People don't usually, you know."

"Well, I wouldn't have stayed on in my hometown," Casey allowed. "But I had good reason not to."

"Maybe he does, too."

"Whose side are you on?" Casey demanded.

"The side of truth, justice and the American way," Skip intoned solemnly.

Casey punched him lightly again, then sighed. "So what is he? Just a hardworking man trying to make ends meet? A hardworking man who drives a Porsche, and dresses in tailor-made clothing when he's off duty." She frowned. "There's something about him, Skip—an aura—like deposed royalty or something. Makes me nervous."

"So maybe he is a con man."

Michel came alive in her mind, his whimsical smile in place. *You have much character in your face. You are a beautiful woman.* Could she trust him? She still didn't know for sure. "Life sure is difficult sometimes," she said hesitantly.

"You overdoing the jogging?" Skip asked. "You're supposed to be able to carry on a conversation while you're jogging."

Obviously he'd caught the shortness of breath that had assailed her along with the image of Michel. "I'm fine," she answered firmly, picking up her pace a little, pumping her arms. "Well, anyway, I had fun, whether I see Michel again or not." Her voice sounded far more wistful than she had intended.

"That's what you need, fun," Skip told her. "You're too serious all the time."

"Life is serious," Casey said.

Skip snorted. "That's not you talking. That's your father. Trouble with you, Case, your daddy's walking around in your head all the time, telling you if it's fun it can't be good for you."

"How did you know that?" she asked, amazed.

"Lucky guess." He laughed. "You mean he really does talk to you?"

"All the time. 'Pride goeth before destruction, and a haughty spirit before a fall.' 'Blessed are they which are persecuted for righteousness's sake, for theirs is the kingdom of heaven.' I used to try to remember that one when the kids gave me a hard time at school, but it never did seem too comforting."

Skip winced. "You deserve a break, Casey Templeton. Maybe this guy Michel is the guy to liven you up, whether he's a con man or not."

"Listen to who's talking," she teased. "How much livening up are you getting?"

"I have fun just hanging out in The Grange."

"You really don't need a woman in your life?"

"No way. Women mean trouble for yours truly. Sleepless nights. Acid indigestion. I drank half a gallon of milk a day when Brenda lived with me."

"You never get lonely?"

He didn't answer for a full minute. Casey glanced up at his face and missed a step, almost falling over her own feet. He was looking straight ahead and there was such *longing* in his expression. No more teasing, she vowed. But she'd definitely check with Barbara about that woman lobbyist, first chance she had.

Even as she thought this, Skip's face cleared and assumed its usual tough expression. "Don't know the meaning of the word *lonely*," he said firmly, then gave her a sidelong grin. "We were talking about you, as I recall. I'm supposed to help you make this big decision, right? Do you, or do you not, go out with the shuttle-bus driver slash possible con man? My vote is take a chance, for once. Go for it. Just don't buy anything from him without checking with the Better Business Bureau."

"But I'm dating Justin," Casey protested worriedly.

"So you are," Skip said flatly. He never had liked Justin.

WHY WAS THAT? he wondered as he hiked up the hill to his own apartment after leaving Casey. He sure as hell admired Casey—there was a lot of spunk wrapped up in that little bundle of energy. The way she'd got that store of hers going on sheer nerve had impressed him. After losing home and family, she'd traveled thousands of miles across the country, put herself through the rest of high school, then worked for a while at three or four part-time jobs—clerking in a dress shop, freelance typing, waitressing in his restaurant.

Then she'd worked the fashion scene for a few years, learning the ropes—selling, tailoring to fit, modeling at shows for the petite department of a department store. Five years ago, she'd decided she was ready to go into business for herself. She'd typed up a loan proposal herself—including every light bulb and clothes hanger and box of potpourri she would buy—and bearded one of Seattle's major bank managers in his den and dazzled him into lending someone with zero net worth enough capital to launch Second Time Around. The poor man, one of the shrewdest in the business, hadn't known what hit him. He hadn't even asked for a co-signer.

In the meantime Casey had managed to talk some of the wealthiest women in town, including Justin Boyd's sister, who had married one of the city's foremost attorneys, into not only selling their barely used designer clothing on consignment in her store, but buying from her, too.

So, okay, he admired Case for her guts and her stamina. But did he really have anything against Justin Boyd?

No.

Except instinct. And instinct told him Justin wasn't right for Casey. He was a bit of a know-it-all, for one thing. He took himself too seriously, for another. Which Casey was also inclined to do—as a result of her religious upbringing, no doubt. But Casey had a sharp wit and a sense of fun under her seriousness. And around Justin, both would get dulled in time. It had been obvious to him, the few times Casey and Justin had eaten in his restaurant, that Casey was attempting to obscure her naturally outgoing personality, to behave in the shy, ladylike manner her dead father and mother had required of her. What good was a friend if you couldn't be yourself around him?

None of his business, he told himself, shaking his head as he strode up the steps of his condo building. He responded with a grin to the doorman's raised eyebrows. "Having an argument with myself," he told the man.

"Hope you win," Felby said cheerfully, then called after Skip as he went by. "I let your wife into your apartment, Mr. Granger. Hope that was okay. She said you were expecting her."

Skip sighed, but managed a smile when Felby looked worried. "Okay this time, but in the future, ask her to wait until I get home."

"Yes, sir," Felby said in a subdued voice. "I'm sorry, Mr. Granger. She was very insistent. You know?"

Skip nodded. "I do indeed, Felby, my man."

"What is it this time?" he asked the minute he entered his living room, taking the offensive before Brenda could get the upper hand.

"Now what kind of greeting is that, honey?" his ex-wife purred. She was reclining on his eight-foot white sofa, looking exquisite in a blue silk blouse and white slacks. She'd shed twenty pounds since her last visit. And had her hair straightened into a silky-looking bob. On his money.

"I thought maybe you'd like to take me to breakfast," she said, looking at him from under her lashes in the way that used to make him putty in her hands, and still had the power to elevate his blood pressure.

"I've given up eating breakfast," he informed her.

"Since when?"

"Right this minute. Unaccountably lost my appetite. So, what can I do for you? I have to take a shower and get to work."

"You want me to take a shower with you?" she suggested.

"Wouldn't that mess up your makeup? Wasn't that usually the reason you didn't want me to make love to you?"

"That was the old me," Brenda said.

"And this is the new you?"

"Absolutely." She sat up straight and looked at him directly. "I want to come back to you, Skip."

There was a time he'd dreamed of her saying those words. "What ever happened to my old buddy Luther?" he asked.

She pouted, then stood up, swayed over to him as provocatively as only she knew how, and put her arms around his neck. With an effort he held his fists clenched at his sides. She smelled as wonderful as ever. Obsession. A great perfume. Also expensive. She was going all out for some reason.

"Luther Everett is history," she said.

"Sure enough? What did he do, walk out on you?"

She backed up a step, removing her arms from around him, to his relief. He had almost been tempted to pull her close and let bygones be bygones. And that would have landed him in a whole mess of trouble.

"I'm leaving Luther," she announced indignantly. "He would never leave me."

"Too much the gentleman, that Luther," Skip said. "With only one historical exception, for which I'm not sure he should be blamed. Does he know you're leaving him?"

"Not yet."

"Didn't want to burn any bridges, huh?" A pang from his incipient ulcer made him wince and he retreated into his kitchen, took a milk carton from the refrigerator and poured a tall glass.

Brenda followed him. "You are being very hostile, Skip," she said as he drank the milk down.

"I learned how from a good teacher." If she only knew how much he longed to take her in his arms. The look of her, the smell of her. He hadn't touched a woman since she left him a year ago; hadn't wanted to. Now he wanted to.

"I miss you, Skip," she said huskily. "I made a mistake. Surely you aren't going to hold it against me forever? We could start fresh, start over."

Could it possibly be true? His reason, his famed instinct, told him she was running scared and needed him to bail her out again. But his emotions were something else. Give her a chance, they were urging him. Give her one more chance.

With maybe a small test first.

"You out of money already?" he asked.

She smiled ruefully. "When am I not?"

True. "That what this is all about—you needing money?"

There was a sudden glint in her eye. "You told me last time not to come asking for more money."

Something hardened inside him. "Changed my mind," he said evenly. "Feelin' generous as all get out. How much you need?"

"Used up all my credit cards," she admitted sadly. "Too many new clothes. You know how I like new clothes. And the spa..." One graceful hand with long lacquered fingernails indicated her slenderized figure.

"You get off food stamps, you really get off," he commented. "A thousand do you?" he asked grimly.

She tilted her head, considering. "Two?"

He pulled his checkbook from the kitchen drawer where he kept his household bills and wrote out a check.

"I guess we aren't going to have a reunion after all, huh?" he asked.

"Probably wouldn't work," she said. At least she had the grace to sound a little regretful.

"You going back to Luther?"

"Wouldn't be surprised."

He swallowed. "Well, that's good news. Wouldn't want you treating my best friend the way you treated me."

"Skip," she began chidingly. She looked at him for a moment and again something regretful showed up, in her eyes this time. "You're a good man, Skip. Too good for me."

Such honesty was rare. If only her inside matched the beauty of her outside, Brenda would be quite a woman, Skip thought as he watched her sashay along the hall to the elevator. He found he was holding his breath, couldn't seem to let it out until she'd disappeared behind the sliding doors without looking back.

Why was it, he asked himself, that he could know how bad that woman was for him, yet if she had just turned down that check, had just meant what she said about coming back to him, he would probably have been in bed with her right this minute.

Because if she *had* turned down the check, she wouldn't have been so bad for him, he acknowledged.

But Brenda always would take the money over the man. Now, he admonished himself as he closed his apartment door and leaned against it for a moment, if he could just remember that, next time she came calling.

The apartment seemed emptier than usual after having had Brenda in it. He could still smell her perfume in the air. *Don't you ever get lonely?* Casey had asked him.

Lot of insight in that young woman. *You really don't need a woman in your life?*

Sure I get lonely, Casey, my friend, he answered her truthfully now. *And yes, I need a woman. I just can't seem to find one who truly needs me.*

AFTER HER SHOWER, Casey decided to walk up to the downtown area to do a little shopping before opening her store. Not that she really needed a new outfit. After all, she had all that designer clothing in her own store to choose from. Except that most of it was fairly formal—dresses and skirts and blouses, suits and tailored jackets. Nothing casual enough to wear on Saturday if she did happen to decide to visit Michel's apartment.

After purchasing a nifty yellow jumpsuit and matching tennis shoes, she emerged from the department store, so busy castigating herself for needless extravagance that she almost bumped into an elderly lady who had stopped on the sidewalk in front of her. Apologizing, she saw the reason for the woman's abrupt halt. The woman was staring with marked disapproval at a pregnant black teenager who was sitting on the sidewalk against the wall of the store. The girl was a younger version of Whoopi Goldberg—wide mouth, multiple dangling braids and all. In front of her was a coffee can with several bills and coins in it and a sign that read: I Need Money. Please Help Me And My Baby.

The old woman immediately started haranguing the girl, telling her she should be ashamed to beg in public. "I am," the girl said with a remarkably sweet smile. "I just don't have a whole lot of choice, ma'am."

"There are welfare agencies designed to take care of problems like yours," the woman insisted.

The girl shrugged, then glanced at Casey and smiled again. "Hi," she said brightly.

"The police are going to move you on soon as they see you," the woman warned.

The girl sighed. "Probably."

Apparently the well-dressed elderly lady was going to keep on offering her unwanted comments for some time—her feet were firmly planted, her stance aggressive. Edging around her, Casey placed a five-dollar bill in the coffee can. "Good luck," she said.

"Thanks," the girl replied.

Compared to that poor girl, she was very fortunate, Casey thought as she walked back to her store. Seeing someone like that made her realize she should count her blessings, just as her mother and father had always told her. She might have had a tough childhood, but at least she was economically solvent now, if only marginally. At least she could afford to buy a bright yellow jumpsuit to go visiting a handsome young Frenchman.

Was she going to visit him?

Had there ever been any doubt?

CHAPTER FIVE

AFTER SHE'D PARKED, Casey sat looking up at Michel's apartment complex for a while. The wooden building was far from luxurious, even though it was in a good part of town. It was obviously well cared for, but very ordinary—no outstanding architectural details to it at all; it was just a series of staggered boxes, six up, twelve or so along. Painted beige and brown. Strictly utilitarian.

"Good morning, Casey," Michel said from behind her as she fed coins into the parking meter. He did have a way of popping up from nowhere.

Schooling her expression into one of friendly greeting, even though her blood was abruptly circulating at a dangerously rapid rate through her body, Casey turned around. She had carefully refrained from guessing what Michel might be wearing, afraid her guess would turn into fact once more. As he took her hand between both of his, she noted with a feeling akin to despair that he was wearing a dark polo shirt and white jeans—just the clothing she'd decided was less dangerous to imagine than a vampire suit.

Michel gazed down at her, thinking that he would plan to spend the entire day looking at her: her sweet, delicate face; that mass of red hair piled on top of her head; her small, beautifully formed figure in the bright yellow jumpsuit; the shy smile that glowed in her bewitching green eyes; the thick, curling sweep of her mascara-darkened lashes. Looking at her, he wanted to grab hold of her and throw her over his shoulder and rush off with her to his lair. He had wanted to do that since that first strange moment when they had stared at each other so silently.

Why had men had to get so damn civilized over the centuries, he wondered. Early cave dweller had the right idea. He realized he hadn't moved since he took hold of her hand. She must think he'd gone into a trance. He could not remember ever having been drawn so irresistibly toward a woman before, as though he had no will of his own. It was a wonderfully erotic feeling, but unnerving at the same time. "You look like the essence of sunlight," he managed to say finally. Then he leaned to kiss her mouth, restraining himself with difficulty from making the kiss more than an affectionate greeting.

She glanced down as she always did when he complimented her, then up again, her shy smile tugging at the corners of her mouth.

"I guess my new jumpsuit was worth ninety-five dollars, after all," she replied.

One of the things he liked about her, *adored* about her, was the sudden flash of humor that would break through her shy manner so unexpectedly.

He drew her across the sidewalk, his hand tucked intimately under her elbow, excited now by what he was about to show her. "Come," he said. "There is something I wish you to see."

He took her with him through the opening in the middle of the building. *"Voilà—"* he gestured "—what do you think?"

Most people did not suspect that the apartment complex surrounded a central courtyard. There was a full-size swimming pool, with several young people and children playing in it, but instead of the usual wide concrete surround and plastic chairs dotted here and there, the area had been landscaped into an inviting garden.

"How beautiful!" Casey exclaimed. She glanced up at him, mischief showing in her eyes. "Is this where my flowers came from?"

He nodded. "The pansies from over there, the irises there, beyond the birch trees."

"The owner didn't mind you helping yourself?"

"Not at all."

She did not yet understand. She was too busy gazing around her. He followed her gaze, trying to see the garden as she would see it.

Beyond the pool, swaths of rich green ground cover led to multilevel beds that contained rhododendrons, azaleas, small trees and a dazzling variety of flowers. And still there was ample room for comfortable conversational groupings of benches, several of them occupied, a barbecue area with round picnic tables and gay umbrellas, a quiet corner with a scattering of Adirondack chairs, where young Sidney Arundel was sitting in the shade with a book. Casey waved at him and he waved back.

"He is a very nice young man, Sidney," Michel said. "He has helped me with many things, including the delivery of your flowers. He is most ambitious, attending university to become an accountant. I am thinking I will offer him a full-time job when he graduates."

"Driving a shuttle bus?" Casey asked with a puzzled frown.

She still didn't suspect. He smiled at her. "Do you like my garden?" he asked.

"It's fabulous," she answered, then quite obviously realized exactly what he had said. "*Your* garden?"

"People rarely used the pool except for brief spurts of exercise, you see," Michel said as she gazed up at him. "It was so stark, so exposed. Nowhere shady to sit. But since I persuaded the owner to let me redesign the area, everyone enjoys it more. It is more livable, I think."

"You designed all this?"

"Mais bien sûr." He laughed at the astonishment on her face. So lovely a face. It showed every emotion she was feeling. He wondered if she knew that. Few people's expressions were quite so open. It made her strangely vulnerable. Endearingly so. "I did most of the work, at first," he explained. "But then other tenants became interested and soon we had work parties evenings and weekends. As I said, Sidney was a great help to me. Now everyone enjoys, as you see. And we have used low-maintenance plants for the most part. Easy care."

Casey murmured something too low for him to understand.

"The best part is that now everyone is more friendly together. The garden is convenient, as you see, and safe for children—I use no pesticides, but rely on good soil composition and disease-resistant plants. It is also comfortable, so everyone has come to know his neighbor. We have even a romance or two." He accompanied this last statement with a deliberately mischievous glance that brought a flush to her cheekbones. Then he took her hand and walked with her through the garden, enjoying her amazement at the beauty he had created. The other tenants greeted him with their usual friendliness and looked curiously at Casey. There would be gossip around the pool after they moved on—he had not brought a woman here before.

"Where did you learn to design gardens?" Casey asked as Michel escorted her up the steps to the balcony that ran along the front of his building. He didn't answer immediately, as he was worried about her reaction to his apartment. It was so very plain, as boxy inside as it looked outside; clean and tidy, but definitely stark. But he need not have worried. After one quick glance, Casey seemed, if anything, reassured.

"Gardening is my business," he said then. "Perhaps you will understand more clearly if I tell you I have recently received my degree in landscape architecture and design. I have also passed the national examination for my license. And this week I have been offered a partnership in an established company—Harlan and Fawcett. They are remodeling an office for me. I expect to specialize in corporate business. More and more companies are realizing that pleasant surroundings with access to the outdoors make for happy employees. And happy employees are good for business."

He smiled at her. "I am very pleased about this, Casey. It is our company policy to do the contracting and occasional maintenance, as well as the initial design, so I will be able to supervise every stage of the work. I will not be shut up in an office all the time. I will be doing the work I love best. Can any man be more fortunate?" he asked as he waved her toward a dark blue sofa and went into the kitchen nook to make coffee. She seemed slightly dazed. Which, he supposed, was understandable.

She shook her head, not wanting to sit down yet, wanting to be alone for a minute so that she could try to assimilate his new image into her mind. "May I use your bathroom?" she asked.

"Certainly." He gestured at a closed door. "Use the one off my bedroom, if you do not mind. The other little one is full of boxes of seedlings."

His bedroom was as characterless as the living room, except for several thriving houseplants set on a long table in front of the window. His bed was a big one, queen size at least, the white sheets turned back at one corner over a navy blue and beige comforter.

White sheets. They reminded her of those she had imagined when she smelled the perfume. White sheets covering a pair of entwined lovers, whose voices murmured as their lips caressed.

She felt a wave of heat go over her as the lovers she'd imagined changed into a clear image of herself and Michel.

What was she thinking of? Not quite two weeks ago she had fantasized stripping Justin's clothes off and making wild, passionate love to him. Now she was contemplating doing the same thing with Michel.

And quite obviously Michel was contemplating the same thing. Those sheets were turned back as though this were a hotel and the maid had just prepared the bed for the young couple to sleep in.

Casey felt uneasy and disappointed in Michel. She hadn't expected him to be quite so obvious. But then she hadn't expected him to change into a landscape architect, either. She had a strong feeling that she shouldn't have come here. But she could hardly walk out on him now. Or could she?

After washing her hands she went back into the living room. Michel was still working in the kitchen nook. "Are you going to give up the shuttle bus?" she called to him as she seated herself on the very edge of the sofa.

He laughed. "I will keep driving for a few weeks more until I have clients of my own. You are surprised that I make gardens? It is hard to imagine for a shuttle-bus driver, perhaps?"

He returned to the tiny living room, wanting to sit with her while the coffee finished percolating. She was gazing thoughtfully at the drafting tables that stood in front of the long windows. He wondered what she was thinking. He wished she would smile. "I think, myself, I was born with a love of beauty," he told her as he sat down and gazed appreciatively at her lovely face. "Which you, Casey, should already know."

Her gaze came up to meet his, then shifted away as she smiled self-consciously. It was obvious that compliments had not been a feature of her life. Perhaps her parents had believed they would turn her head. And the English teacher? Did he not think they were necessary?

"You designed gardens in France?" she asked awkwardly.

She was evidently still tense. Now she was untying the knot in her belt, retying it tightly, her gaze concentrated on it as though it were extremely important that she get the ends matched perfectly.

He hesitated. "For part of the time."

She was obviously curious about his past life. Which was only natural. But he wasn't quite ready to tell her all of it. Not yet. Not until he could be sure of her reaction. A new relationship was a fragile, growing thing. It had to be treated with great care.

"Are you sure you're not a con man?" she asked suddenly.

Another unexpected flash of humor. Laughing, he put his arms around her and hugged her, which created some interesting sensations in parts of his body that seemed unusually sensitive around this woman. As usual, she smelled wonderful—more fragrant than the most fragrant blossom in his garden. "You are so charming, Casey," he said admiringly, kissing her lightly. "I enjoy so much how you make me laugh."

Setting her away from him, he stood and went to bring the coffeepot and a pair of mugs. To his surprise, when he returned, she was on her feet. "I'd better go now, Michel," she said as stiffly as a little girl forced to remember her manners. "Thank you for showing me your garden." Picking up her purse and placing its strap carefully over her shoulder, she headed briskly for the door.

Michel was in shock. It took him a moment to recover. By then she was opening the door. "But Casey," he exclaimed. "I thought you were joking about my being a con man. Surely you were joking? I planned to spend the whole day with you. I thought we would have lunch and talk and—"

She shook her head without turning around. "I have to go," she repeated. And closed the door behind her.

Michel stared at it for a full minute, totally unable to understand what had just happened. What had he said to change her in less than fifteen minutes from a warm, friendly young woman to the iceberg that had just walked out on him?

Dismay finally gave way to action. Hastily setting down the coffee things, he strode to the door, yanked it open and emerged onto the balcony. She was already on the pathway into the garden—a bright splash of yellow, topped by even brighter red, moving rapidly away. "Casey!" he yelled down to her, getting everyone's attention except hers. She just kept on walking.

He ran down the steps and loped after her, aware that every eye was on him. "Casey!" he called again.

She shook her head and kept on going. "What did I do?" he demanded. "What did I say?"

She didn't answer until he caught up with her at the end of the swimming pool. Then she said, very stiffly, "I'm sorry, Michel. It's not your fault. It's mine. I have this hang-up about honesty."

He took hold of her shoulders. "You cannot leave this way."

"I'm doing it," she pointed out. She glanced around. "Let me go, Michel. Everybody's looking at us."

"Let them look," Michel said, not trying to hide his exasperation. "It is a public service to provide people with free entertainment. Don't worry about them. Tell me why you are so angry with me."

"I'm not angry. Just...disappointed, and confused."

"Why should you be disappointed? I thought you would be pleased. Are you saying you liked me better as a shuttle-bus driver?" He didn't realize he'd raised his voice again until she flinched. He apologized at once. "Forgive me, Casey. I am being arrogant again?"

She nodded. "Your grandmother was right," she said tersely.

"Then I must use a humbler approach." Dropping to one knee, he took her hand in his and looked up at her with a deliberately pleading expression. "Please tell me what I have done to make you so angry."

Embarrassment flared color into her cheeks as someone nearby laughed and a male voice called, "Way to go, Michel!"

"Please get up," she begged.

"Not until you agree to come back to my apartment and explain yourself."

She sighed. "All right."

He stood up and put an arm around her shoulders and started easing her toward the pathway. There was a scattering of applause from the people gathered around the pool, but he refused to acknowledge their presence. For one thing, he was afraid that if he let go of Casey she would bolt again. There was such stiffness in her shoulders!

She refused to be persuaded back to the sofa. "What did I do?" he demanded.

"First of all, you misrepresented yourself," she said hotly. "You let me think you were a shuttle-bus driver, then you changed into someone else altogether. You let me think you were supporting yourself with that job. I was pleased that you were an ordinary working person like me. I had you firmly fixed in my mind in this certain slot. It did not occur to me to think you could be something else. And now I find out that was all an illusion. That's not the person you are. If I could be so mistaken in you, then perhaps I am mistaken in believing you are not a con man."

"I *am* a working person like you," he insisted. "And I have not changed into someone else. I am Michel Gervais Smith, just as I introduced myself to you."

"But you aren't a shuttle-bus driver. Not in here, are you?" She had rapped him sharply on the chest.

He shook his head. "Not in my soul, no. In my soul I am a gardener."

"A gardener who is about to go into business for himself and do very well for himself with his corporate business and his new office and his new partners. Isn't that so?"

"It is to be hoped."

"And is that or is that not deception?" she demanded. "To let me feel sorry for this poor man who is being railroaded by the police, this poor shuttle-bus driver?"

Her eyes were bright with anger, her cheeks flushed. She had never looked lovelier.

"I didn't tell you about my new business because I wanted to surprise you," he told her.

"Well, you succeeded." She turned away as if to leave again and Michel grabbed her arm. "Let me go," she said angrily.

He held on to her. "No." He was quite sure that if she walked out a second time he would never see her again, and he wasn't about to let that happen.

"Mon Dieu, Casey!" he exclaimed. "I'm not going to let you go until you—"

"Until I what?" She yanked her arm free. He had to let her go or risk hurting her. "Until I go to bed with you? As you obviously intend, with your covers so invitingly turned down."

For a minute he had no idea what she was talking about, but then he remembered the turned-down bed and realized how it must have looked to her, especially when he'd insisted she use the bathroom that would necessitate her going through his bedroom. "That was last night," he said firmly. "I was getting ready to go to bed and an idea struck me for a garden I'm working on, and I came back out and worked on it for an hour or more, then decided to watch television for a little while and fell asleep on the sofa. I never did get the bed put back together again." He smiled wryly. "Not that I have not thought about making love to you, Casey. But I would hope to be more straightforward about it—not so sly."

"Oh."

All the wind had gone out of her sails. He put his hands gently on her shoulders. "Now, would you please let me explain why I deceived you?"

"Okay," she said.

Her eyes were as green as the depths of the ocean; less stormy now, but not yet tranquil. They were looking at him questioningly, steadily, waiting. He could not imagine what he had been about to say. Looking at her, smelling the fragrance of her, he could not even remember what they had been quarreling about.

His hands tightened on her shoulders. "Casey," he said thickly, and saw an immediate response come into her face. Pulling her down to the sofa he kissed her, his mouth gently brushing hers in a tentative way as his arms went around her and eased her close.

He heard her give a little sigh, then her body relaxed against his and her mouth moved under his and he tasted the full sweetness of her for the first time. He felt as if he had come home.

Her hands moved slowly upward over his polo shirt, and his body tightened in response to the gentle exploration of her fingers.

"Not fair," he murmured against her lips. She was so well protected in her jumpsuit. All he could do was hold her tighter, letting his mouth do all the lovemaking, now pressing gently, now brushing against hers, the tip of his tongue seeking the corners of her mouth where it curved so sweetly.

A torrent of desire raged through him as he felt her body move slightly against his. In immediate response, his mouth became more demanding. Her intensity matched his all the way. Time hung suspended while they kissed. And before the kiss was over, Michel knew that he was lost.

They stopped at precisely the same moment and drew back so that they could look at each other.

Casey gave a delightful gurgle of laughter. "That was some explanation," she said.

"It was, yes," Michel agreed seriously. "It was an explanation of what is between us. It has been there from the beginning, has it not, Casey?"

She nodded, then laid a hand on each side of his face. "I'm sorry, Michel," she said. "I acted like a child. It was as if you had suddenly turned into someone I didn't know at all. And if that could happen, how could I ever be sure exactly who you were?"

She frowned. "I would like to try to explain why I felt so threatened." She let out a long breath. "I guess it comes of growing up with my slightly unusual parents. They never bent the truth, never deceived anyone, never told even a small white lie. My friend Skip teases me about truth, justice and the American way. I'm an anachronism, he says. But I can't seem to get away from the fact that truth is very important to me."

She was trying to keep her voice light, but he could see that this was very serious to her.

"Couple that with their discipline policy," she added. "I wasn't allowed to be upset or angry in front of them. If I showed signs of any excess of emotion, I was sent to my room. We were a happy family and nothing could be allowed to spoil that image."

She shook her head. "I sound bitter, and I didn't mean to. Most of the time we *were* a happy family, but I've never learned how to handle anger. An immediate flight-response takes over."

"So when I caught up with you, you were 'going to your room'?"

She laughed. "I guess so."

He touched her cheek lightly, then drew his thumb over her lips, delighting in the tremor that went through her, feeling one of his own.

"I'm sorry I misled you, Casey," he said softly. "I really did want just to surprise you. And I really was— still am—supporting myself mostly with the shuttle-bus job."

He picked up the coffeepot and poured coffee for both of them. "I had to support myself while I was studying for my degree," he explained. "I was able to find some fieldwork with Harlan and Fawcett to help me qualify for licensing, but I did not earn enough to take care of all my expenses. So I drove the shuttle bus at night."

He sighed. "I did not wish to tell you I was a gardener, because I was afraid you would imagine me as someone pulling weeds and spreading fertilizer. I preferred to show you. It did not occur to me that you would look upon this as deceitfulness."

She took a sip of coffee, not looking at him.

"It all sounds so logical when you explain it," she said with a faint, slightly crooked smile. "But when you told me the scope of what you are attempting, I was overwhelmed. I felt . . . inadequate compared to you." Clasping her hands tightly together, she gave a self-deprecating smile. "I 'go to my room' when I feel inadequate, too," she added in a shaky-sounding voice.

He took her hands into his, kissing each one separately. "Casey, *chérie,* there will never be a need for you to feel inadequate. You are a lovely, intelligent, warm woman and I am very strongly attracted to you." He grinned at her. "Obviously. Anyway, this country is a democracy. We are all equal, *n'est-ce pas?*"

"It doesn't always work that way," she said with a sigh. Then she smiled. It wasn't quite her usual smile, but it was close. "Tell me why you became a gardener," she suggested.

"I have always loved working in a garden," he told her. "To bring bare ground alive with color and texture—ah, that is such pleasure. Like painting a picture, you understand, only this picture has many more dimensions and touches all of the senses. Even when I was sixteen I would go out and work in the garden without anyone telling me to do so. In fact—" He broke off. He must be careful, or he'd be giving too much away. He was more than ever convinced that this was not a good time to tell all.

"I have always felt a garden should reflect one's relationship with nature," he continued. "It should be wild, exuberant, exciting, beautiful. People need beauty in their lives."

He laughed. Casey had glanced around the small, barely furnished living room. The implication of her glance was clear. "You wonder how I can say that in such surroundings?" he asked, then shrugged. "This is temporary only. Again for economy. Soon I will move to something more...suitable."

Another frown. Why? Surely she must agree that this utilitarian apartment was not the most exciting place to be?

"I take it Harlan and Fawcett is in Seattle?" Casey asked.

He smiled and nodded, his spirits rising. Did that question mean she would not like to think of him moving away?

"Why Seattle?" she asked. "I mean, you never did tell me why you chose this particular city. You said your father came from California."

"But he was stationed briefly at McChord. And my mother told me of Washington State when I was of an impressionable age. She spoke of huge forests and a temperate climate and good soil. She spoke of salmon to be had for the taking from the ocean, trout from the lakes and rivers. And then I read an article about Seattle's Freeway Park, which seized my imagination. Any city that could build a flowering park complete with a waterfall to straddle an interstate freeway seemed a fine place for me to be. I love trees and water, and in Seattle one is never far from either. I have found this to be a very livable city. With my gardens, I wish to make it more so. Do you like gardens, Casey?"

"Oh yes. I've never had one, though."

"Never?"

"When I was growing up we lived in a house by a little stream on the outskirts of town." She broke off, conscious that it wasn't quite truthful to paint such a pastoral picture. The house had been small and ugly, surrounded by rough grass—the stream a mere trickle of muddy water. Was there really any need to tell all that to Michel? Ah, now *she* was rationalizing. How difficult it was to know where to draw the line. But the last thing she wanted from Michel was pity.

"My father was always too busy saving mankind to bother with flowers," she said evenly. "My mother never had the time for it, either." She sighed. "I sold our house after my parents died, and came to Seattle. Since then, I've lived in apartments that didn't have Michel Gervais Smith around to create beautiful gardens."

"I admire you very much, Casey," he told her solemnly. "It cannot have been easy to cross the country alone at the age of seventeen." He hesitated. "Why Seattle?" he asked, as she had asked him.

Fair enough. "I just pointed myself west and kept going until I was as far away from home as I could get and still live in the same country," she confessed.

"You wished to escape from too many memories?"

She nodded agreement, realizing that he was thinking of happy memories. There was no need to tell him it was the unhappy ones that had driven her away. "I knew nothing about Seattle, but when I saw it, I loved it."

She looked at him directly. "I'm sorry I was so silly, earlier," she said softly.

"My fault. I should have had the sense to realize you'd formed certain impressions of me based on what you knew." He touched her hair lightly. "Sometimes there are good reasons for not telling all the truth all the time, Casey."

There was a frown shadowing his eyes. Was there still something he hadn't told her? Could he still be holding something back? Surely not.

His hand was still touching her hair. He was going to kiss her again. She could see the intention dawning in his eyes. And she was going to let him kiss her again. In fact, if he didn't do it soon, she was going to reach for him and . . .

His lips met hers, his right arm slipping naturally around her shoulders, his left hand lightly cupping her face. His mouth was warm, firm without being too demanding, his breath mingling sweetly with hers. Her arms went around him, pulling him closer, her fingers climbing to his shoulders, his neck, his hair, urging him closer.

Jezebel, her father said in her mind, as he had once said about one of their neighbors he had deemed unchaste. *Harlot, strumpet, seducer.*

Shut up, Daddy, she said back to him. *I'm a grown woman, and times and circumstances change. I have needs, desires—all of which are perfectly normal.*

For a moment, as though he had heard the conversation going on inside her mind, Michel lifted his head and looked at her, his dark eyes glowing with mischief, his mouth tender, and then he reached to take the pins from her hair, letting it fall down around her shoulders. "Literally and symbolically," he murmured.

They laughed softly together. And then he was kissing her again, more deeply, his lips almost harsh on hers. She could feel his heart beating as strongly as hers and no less erratically. *"Ma chérie,"* he murmured against her lips, so that they opened to his.

She had known, she thought, that first time when he kissed her, she had known that he was a man who could arouse her totally. He smelled clean, earthy, and his taste on her tongue was exhilarating, causing an electric tremor to surge down her spine to her loins with a potency that made her shudder.

His hands were touching her, exploring gently at her throat and her breast, his body tensing as hers relaxed beneath his fingers. Her own hands moved over him, delighting in the softness of his knit shirt, the smooth, hard flesh of his forearms.

His lips had found the tender area at the base of her throat where the collar of her jumpsuit was open. "You smell so wonderful, Casey," he murmured against her skin.

She stiffened immediately, remembering the perfume. But she hadn't used the perfume again. Actually, she had been so unnerved by the apparent effect of Inga's magic scent that she had been afraid to use any perfume at all. And she was quite sure that her soap, pure and fresh as it was, didn't smell like roses. Yet, all of a sudden, she could smell what Michel was apparently smelling—the soft yet heady aroma of roses with dark red petals. Was that why Inga had told her to use the perfume no more than once? Did its effect never end?

Perhaps aware of her sudden nervousness, Michel raised his head and removed his hand from her breast. "I am sorry. I go too fast for you?"

She shook her head, then nodded, then grinned in confusion. "I'm just not...I'm still not sure...why you are attracted to me," she stammered, which was surely the stupidest thing she'd ever said.

Instead of answering, Michel stood and held out his hands to hers, easing her up off the couch when she gave them to him. Turning her around, keeping his arms loosely around her, he faced her toward a rectangular mirror that hung on the wall behind them.

Her hair was tangled around her shoulders, vividly red against the yellow cotton of her jumpsuit. Her eyes were at their greenest, looking strangely exotic, her cheeks flushed with the residue of passion. She could hardly recognize herself.

"I didn't . . . I wasn't looking for compliments," she told him.

"You will never need to look for them," he answered.

How did he always know the perfect thing to say?

"It is not only the way you look that attracts me," he said softly. "I admire also your sense of humor and the courage you displayed when you came to my assistance so promptly. And I think there is very strong chemistry between us."

"Chemistry?" she repeated nervously.

"That certain je ne sais quoi that brings people together, powerful as a chemical attraction. I literally cannot resist you. Is that not an amazing thing?"

"Amazing," she echoed, her blood running cold. It *was* the perfume that had attracted him to her. An accident. If he hadn't come into her shop, the perfume would have worked on Justin instead.

An image of Justin appeared in her mind, accompanied by a twist of guilt.

"I want to make love to you, Casey," Michel murmured.

She turned to face him, feeling nervous again. "Just like that, straight out?"

"Why not?" He smiled and touched her cheek. "It eliminates much confusion from a relationship." He put his fingers over her lips. "I apologize. I make the—what is it?—wisecracks, when I am nervous. And I am very nervous with you, Casey. I am afraid to say or do the wrong thing that will turn you against me. I feel today that you do not altogether approve of me, now that you know more about me. And I am remembering that you told me you had a boyfriend. You are reluctant to go too far with me because of him, perhaps?"

She flinched. He had read her mind again. "I'm not—I mean, we don't have—it's not as if we're engaged or anything, but I think there's a sort of understanding between us."

"I see," he said gravely, as though she had spoken with great clarity. He touched her hair again, stroking a strand down its length, lifting it to his lips. "So, does this hesitancy mean you do not wish to see me again?" he asked.

"No," she replied flatly.

He laughed and hugged her. "*Voilà!* You see how much easier it is when you say something straight out, Casey. No room for misunderstanding. So. We wish to be together, you and I. Yes?"

"Yes."

"Then let us try this again." He cupped her face in his hands. "I want to make love to you, Casey."

She looked up directly into his eyes. His face was very serious. What would he say if she told him straight out she was afraid his attraction to her *was* caused by chemistry—*real* chemistry? What would he say if she told him she'd thought for a while she'd conjured him up to fill needs she hadn't even known she had? That for many and diverse reasons, she still didn't feel confident that he was attracted to her for her own sake? Why couldn't she have met him without having used that damn perfume?

"Casey?" he prompted gently.

She sighed. He wasn't asking her to marry him, after all. He was asking for something temporary—a love affair, a relationship. All the same, it seemed too soon, too quick.

"I want to make love to you, Michel," she said slowly.

"But not yet?"

She was grateful for his understanding. "Not yet."

"But someday you will come to me and tell me you are ready to make love?"

"Yes." So much for the woman who wasn't sure she wanted anyone to make love to her. Quite suddenly it was clear to her that her problem had not been that she didn't want to make love—it had been that she didn't want to make love to Justin. And probably she had put out signals that told him so.

"So we must decide what to do about this boyfriend, then," Michel said. "I understand that you wish to be honorable. You wish to speak to him about me?"

"Yes."

"*Bon.*" He stepped back from her, ran a hand through his dark curls and smiled his whimsically crooked smile. "And after you have spoken with him, we will do things together so that we become acquainted."

"Yes." She hesitated, feeling a return of her usual shyness. She might admire honesty, but Michel had made her speak of things that seemed less than discreet. "What sort of things do you like to do, Michel?"

When he answered, she thought that she had known all along what he would say. His response was not all unexpected—it was all part of the general enchantment that had surrounded him from the moment she met him.

"I think I will try my extrasensory perception again and tell you what I think *you* would like to do," he said gravely. "Then we shall see whether I am a competent judge of character. Is this a good idea?"

She nodded.

"You understand, of course, that these are all things I would enjoy doing also, so perhaps I am prejudiced on my own behalf." He smiled, taking her hands in both of his. "So then—I can see you dancing, Casey. I think you like to dance as much as I do. You have a graceful body and you will like to move it in rhythm with mine."

Was he really talking about dancing, she wondered, feeling heat suffuse her as his words created an erotic image of their bodies pressed closely together, moving, loving.

"Yes," he said softly. "I will want to take you dancing. To hold a beautiful woman in one's arms and move to music, there can be nothing more enjoyable."

If he kept talking like that she was going to fall in love with him. So said *her* extrasensory perception.

His hands dropped hers and reached to cup her face, his gaze studying her as though he were looking inside her, reading her thoughts, her dreams, her desires. His expression was unusually solemn. "I think you will like to be outside whenever possible," he continued firmly. "Do you like to ride in a canoe?"

She shivered.

"It is possible to rent a canoe, you know," he said, with an air of great discovery. "I know of one such place at the University of Washington's water activities center, behind Husky Stadium. We can explore the arboretum—such trees, Casey—and the Japanese garden!" He hesitated, obviously thinking. "You will like to walk along the waterfront also," he went on after a moment. "To admire the sound and the Olympic Mountains and to see all the many people jogging. And around Green Lake—it is interesting at Green Lake, *n'est-ce pas?* So many people doing so many different things. Fishing and boating and swimming and scuba diving and playing tennis.''

He lifted her hair in both hands, smiling into her eyes. ''And I think I would like to find a place where I could sit with you on soft grass beneath a darkening sky. Do these things seem interesting to you?''

So easily and casually he had listed almost all of the things she'd wanted Justin to suggest instead of going to the movies on a warm spring evening. Too many things for the list to be coincidental. There was definitely something unnatural going on here.

For a moment Inga seemed to be in the small room with her, smiling conspiratorially, talking about family secrets and magic perfume.

Michel hadn't suggested a ferry ride, she realized thankfully. He had left out the ferry ride. And she had imagined all those other activities *before* she used the perfume.

But *after* she met Inga...

''Casey?'' he prompted.

''Definitely interesting,'' she managed through a throat gone tight with panic.

''*Bien*. Then, for now we shall go buy a picnic lunch at a delicatessen I know and take it on the ferry. We can ride to Bainbridge Island and back with all the other people. I enjoy Bainbridge so much. It has the rural character, yet it is only thirty-five minutes on the ferry to downtown Seattle.''

The ferry. Bainbridge Island. How did he know? How?

''So then, with all the people on the ferry, we shall not be tempted to become too friendly until you have spoken to this boyfriend of yours,'' he continued.

''His name is Justin,'' she murmured.

He nodded as though he now understood everything she hadn't said about Justin. As perhaps he did, she thought, as she walked with him again through the beautiful garden he had created. He seemed able to read her mind, her moods, her needs, without any difficulty at all.

Whatever was between them was like nothing Casey had ever experienced. Michel himself had said he literally could not resist her. Just as she could not resist him. Something new was definitely at work here. Something magical. Something scary.

CHAPTER SIX

CASEY KEPT GLANCING at Justin as they drove home, discussing the movie they had seen. At least Justin was discussing it, dissecting it. "Of course, it *was* Si Maximilian's first attempt as a director," he said with deadly fairness.

He was a very critical person, Justin, Casey realized suddenly. Why hadn't she seen that before? Really, he rarely had something good to say about anything. And his mouth, when he talked, looked . . . pinched.

"Justin," she said abruptly, interrupting him when he started talking about the film they were to see the following day. "I won't be going with you tomorrow."

He glanced sharply at her, then away. "Really, Casey, you did commit yourself to the whole month before I bought the tickets."

"I wanted to pay for my own ticket, if you remember," she pointed out. "I'll be glad to buy it back from you."

"That's not what I meant at all," he said. "It just seems a shame to keep missing performances."

Casey took a long, slow breath. Not much point in reminding him he'd missed some himself. "I'm afraid I'm going to miss the rest of them."

His fair brows drew together. "You're finding the festival boring?"

"Well..." She hesitated, then said hastily, "That's not the reason, it's just that, well, I have something to tell you, Justin."

"I have something to tell you, too," he replied unexpectedly. "It think it's time we discussed our relationship. I've been meaning to speak to you about—"

"Not now, Justin," Casey interrupted, suddenly alarmed. "What I have to say will directly affect our relationship."

"In what way?" he asked, looking puzzled.

Say it straight out, Casey, Michel murmured in her mind. "I'm seeing someone else. Another man," she said firmly.

"I see." Justin's voice was flat. Silence stretched between them, almost vibrating in the air.

"Aren't you going to ask any questions?" Casey asked.

His mouth tightened perceptibly. "You've been behaving very oddly ever since you met that...that Frenchman," he said. "I imagine he's the one you're talking about."

"Yes."

He made a sound of disgust. "Really, Casey, I've always given you credit for a lot of common sense. It's one of the things that first interested me in you. But you are behaving like a child—dazzled by false glamour. Just because he's a Frenchman. For heaven's sake, he's just a shuttle-bus driver."

She hadn't suspected Justin was a snob. "Driving is honest work," she said contrarily, not about to tell him that Michel had other interests, or to remind Justin that he was the son of a scrap-metal dealer himself. She had no desire to get into an argument with Justin about Michel; that wouldn't be fair to either man. "I'm sorry, Justin," she said carefully.

"There is nothing to be sorry about," he answered stiffly. "I've never suggested you shouldn't have other friends. I see no reason to quarrel over this."

"I think Michel is going to be more than a friend," Casey added gently.

"I see. Very well. That does alter the picture, doesn't it?" He glanced at her sideways. "I think you are making a big mistake, Casey. But in a way, this is a relief to me. I have meant to tell you for some time that I should probably not see you so often. I'm thirty years old. It's time I was looking for a wife."

Stunned, Casey stared at him. "I didn't know the two things were mutually exclusive," she said.

He frowned. Sometimes he was a little slow on the uptake. After a moment or two his brow cleared. "Oh, I see what you mean. Why couldn't I have asked *you* to marry me?"

"The thought occurred to me," Casey remarked drily.

"But my dear Casey," he stated in the pedantic tone he adopted from time to time, "there wasn't much sense even thinking about marriage between us. Our prospects aren't all that bright, are they? Friends, yes. No reason we can't be friends. But it behooves us both to look for a partner who can help us realize our goals. I've told you all along that I meant to find a rich wife."

"I thought you were joking," she said faintly.

"Why would you think that? Marilyn and I decided when we were quite small that we would have to marry someone with money. She managed to do so, as you know. So there's no reason I can't do the same."

Out of interest, Casey decided to try a little test. "What if I were to tell you my father wasn't really a poverty-stricken minister, after all? What if I told you I'd just discovered I was adopted and my real parents were very wealthy?"

"You're joking," Justin said. But there was uncertainty in his voice and he was looking at her with a glint of interest in his blue eyes.

"I'm joking," she agreed.

The glint of interest died. He nodded twice, shifted his hands on the steering wheel, then went back to talking about the movie.

Casey was conscious of a sense of anticlimax. And of resentment. What if she had fallen in love with Justin? How had she failed to realize that he was serious about his quest for a rich wife?

Thank God he hadn't arrived right after she had used the magic perfume, she thought as his voice droned on. She'd have been stuck with him. She might even have married him if the perfume had overridden his objections to her lack of a significant dowry. She'd have had to spend the rest of her life listening to him, analyzing whatever movie they had seen, or concert they had listened to, or play they had attended. He should have become a newspaper critic. He could always, infallibly, find the weak points of any artistic work.

She was tired of listening to criticism, she decided. And she wasn't all that crazy about movies, anyway. Or concerts. Or plays. Winston had adored obscure plays whose point she had invariably missed. Another boyfriend had loved classical music—especially Wagner and Bach. Not that she had anything against Wagner and Bach, once in a while. But there were other things to do—fun things that required exercise or fresh air, or both.

She'd entertained similar thoughts before, but she'd always ended up feeling guilty about them—as though she ought to like the things other people liked. Why had she felt that way? Why shouldn't she like other activities? Why shouldn't she yearn to rock around the clock, or to go to a Mariners game once in a while, to sit in the bleachers and shout?

She had tailored her activities to suit Justin's wishes, she admitted to herself, just as she had tailored them to fit other men's preferences. She had never really allowed herself to be herself. With Michel, she could be anyone she wanted to be. With Michel she could have much character in her face. She could be a beautiful woman. She could let her hair down—literally and symbolically.

The memory of Michel going down on one knee before her in the middle of his garden brought her close to giggling aloud. *It is a public service to provide people with free entertainment.* What a wise man he was. Remembering those words, how could she possibly feel embarrassed by her own behavior ever again?

So what if magic was involved? So what if eventually the magic ended?

Justin was still happily rattling on about the movie. What had she expected? That he would try to argue her out of breaking up with him? Yes, that was exactly what she had expected. She had thought she would be breaking his heart. What an incurable romantic she was.

But in all fairness, given her enchantment with Michel, would it have done Justin any good to argue? Probably not. All the same, she would have felt much more satisfied if Justin had passionately declaimed, "I can't possibly live without you."

Passion. That's what Justin was lacking. That's what she had been yearning for when she used the magic perfume.

"Don't worry," Justin said kindly when he dropped her off. "I'll probably be able to find someone to use your series ticket."

Shaking her head as she climbed the stairs to her studio apartment, Casey wondered if Justin would even miss her. But she didn't wonder long. As she pulled out her sofa bed and made it up for the night, she became conscious all at once that a heavy burden had dropped from her shoulders.

She was free.

Free to love Michel.

Love?

A figure of speech only.

IT WAS AN ENCHANTED MONTH. It seemed to Casey that Michel was determined to spend as much time as possible fulfilling all her secret longings, encouraging her to do all the things she'd wanted to do for so long. On several of the long warm summer evenings, he took time off from the shuttle bus and they rented a canoe. By some unspoken mutual consent, they didn't talk as they paddled through the water lilies and cattails alongside the university's serenely quiet arboretum, both of them content to listen to the soft splash of their paddles dipping and lifting in the still water, scattering cascades of glittering drops into the air, scaring up mallards and mud hens from among the wild yellow irises.

On weekends, they walked together, hand in hand, exploring the city and its numerous parks. They rode ferryboats to Bremerton and Bainbridge Island. They even drove up to Anacortes and took a ferry to the San Juans. They hiked amid the alpine flowers on Mount Rainier, and attended a couple of Mariners games, arguing the merits of the various players, cheering lustily when they weren't yelling remarks at the umpire. Michel announced with great satisfaction that he might just be beginning to learn what "le baseball" was all about.

On one rainy evening, they went dancing in a popular nightclub, their steps matching wonderfully to dreamily slow music. Casey had worried that she was too short to make a comfortable partner for Michel, but she wore her highest heels and they seemed to fit very well together. "Dancing is a wonderful invention," Michel murmured into her hair. "How else can a man make love to a woman in public, without causing any comment at all?"

He did make love to her in a way, one hand pressing her close to his hard body, his left hand holding her right hand folded in against his shoulder so that he could lift it and drop a kiss on her knuckles from time to time. She was aware of his breath catching in her hair, his fingers changing pressure subtly against her back, his hips brushing hers. From time to time, he held her away from him and looked at her solemnly. And she knew, as clearly as if he had spoken aloud, that he was thinking of how it would be when they did make love.

Almost every day, he sent her flowers. Daisies, violets, roses. The roses came after their trip to the San Juans. Around one of the island doorways a luscious pink-and-white rose had climbed a trellis in untamed profusion and Casey had thought that nothing could be lovelier. She had not commented on the sight to Michel, but the roses he sent were almost duplicates. He must have seen her admiring the trellis, she thought. Perhaps he had read her mind again. Or else it was all part of Inga's magic.

Sitting at her dining table inhaling the fragrance of the old-fashioned roses, she shivered.

A test, she thought. What were the most unusual flowers she could think of? Wallflowers. An old man who had frequented her father's mission regularly had once planted wallflowers in the strip of land next to the mission's side door. Surely no one grew wallflowers anymore.

The next morning, Sidney Arundel arrived on his bicycle carrying a huge bouquet of yellow, orange, brown and red wallflowers.

It became a game, with a kind of nervous fascination driving her on. Gladioli, she thought, and within twenty-four hours was hunting for a vase tall enough to hold them. Hyacinths. Bluebells. Pansies again.

It had to be telepathy, she told herself. The extrasensory perception Michel had joked about.

And there was Inga, smiling in her memory, nodding her head and smiling with satisfaction. Always smiling.

On July 4th, they celebrated Independence Day together, watching an air show complete with sky divers. Later, fireworks blazed across the night sky.

"Is it not odd," Michel commented, "that so many countries find some excuse to blast off fireworks at some time in the year—England with her Guy Fawkes, France's Bastille Day?"

Michel knew a great deal about a great many things, Casey had discovered. She had heard, vaguely, of Guy Fawkes, had known that Bastille Day was the anniversary of the storming of a prison called the Bastille, but didn't know until Michel told her that it had triggered the French Revolution in July, 1789.

She and Michel held hands throughout the fireworks display. She could feel her own pulse beating against his wrist. Her whole body felt in tune with his, connected to his. Soon, she thought. It must be soon. Hazily she visualized Michel making love to her in surroundings that seemed vaguely romantic. A soft, soft bed. There was a fire burning in a fireplace. Good Lord, did she have to wait until winter?

Four nights later, they were lying on their backs on the soft green grass near Green Lake, arms linked, holding hands as they looked up at the night sky through the leaves of a huge maple tree. Earlier they had swum together, playful as a pair of porpoises. Then they had eaten the picnic meal Casey had prepared—a simple but delicious feast of cold, tender chicken and fruit and cheese, with some of Casey's home-baked bran muffins. For the past hour and a half they had been content to lie together, watching the sun go down through trailing clouds of salmon-pink and black, studying and naming the constellations as they appeared, admiring the silver moon that had floated up to the now-clear sky.

Michel was very conscious of Casey's firm young body so close to his. He wanted to touch her. It was difficult for him to allow any time to go by without touching her. He was always finding occasion to tuck an errant strand of hair behind her ear, or to put a hand on her back or shoulder, or touch her cheek.

He was obsessed by her, he thought, then changed his mind—obsession sounded too heavy for the delight-fully light-filled feelings he had when she was near. No, he was not obsessed; he was enchanted. And he thought he would go crazy if she did not tell him soon that she was ready to make love.

"You have not yet told me how your friend Justin reacted when you told him about me," he said, feeling he had also waited patiently long enough for her to tell him that.

During the past month they had managed not to discuss anything that might lead to arguments. It had been a time for pleasure only, a time for getting to know each other. A time out of mind.

Casey sat up, but didn't answer at once. He hadn't expected her to. She usually thought things over before coming up with a response. Her grave deliberation was one of the things that delighted him about her. There were many things that delighted him about Casey Templeton. She took such pleasure in such simple things. She smiled often. She was always good-natured, a friend to the world, patient, kind, undemanding, honest. She was unique in his experience.

"He took it very well," she said flatly.

"American men!" Michel exclaimed, not even trying to keep the sarcasm from his voice.

Casey had been sitting forward, her arms clasped around her knees, her face turned up to the moon. The light breeze was tossing her hair around her shoulders—she'd been leaving her hair down more often lately. Now she turned her head and grinned at him. "You're an American man."

"But I have the French background, do not forget. My heart is American but my soul is French." He frowned. "He must not have loved you, Casey."

"Actually, he was getting ready to dump me," she said.

"That is difficult for me to believe," he protested.

"Believe it. He said he needed a rich wife. My prospects weren't good enough for the long haul."

"And you? Did you love him?"

"I admired Justin," she replied slowly, considering in her grave way. "I found him very attractive. And I was...fond of him."

"That is a weak word—*fond,*" he pointed out.

"I guess it is."

"I would never let a woman go so easily," he declared.

"What would you do?" she asked with a teasing smile.

He sat up, put an arm around her shoulders and pulled her down to the grass beside him, then leaned over her to kiss her lightly.

"First, I would tell her that I could not possibly live without her," he declared.

Her body stiffened. "You do not approve of this statement?" he asked.

"It's not that I don't approve, though I hope you're exaggerating. It just shakes me when you read my mind."

She had mentioned mind reading before in connection with the flowers he sent her. She had tested the theory, she insisted.

"You were thinking I could not live without you?" he teased.

"Of course not. But I did think, a while back, when I was breaking off with Justin, that it would be neat if he—" She broke off. "Never mind, it's too complicated. Tell me what else you would do to hold on to a woman."

"I would smother her face with kisses," he said, suiting his actions to his words. How wonderful she smelled, always; like a red rose unfurling its petals in the morning dew.

She tasted wonderful, too; sweet and spicy all at the same time. For a while he forgot the conversation they were having, concentrating instead on kissing her deeply, touching her, murmuring softly to her in French. Try as he would, he could not murmur endearments in English. "My darling," for example. Impossible to say on a sigh. How much easier to murmur *"Ma chérie."*

"I would remind her of all the enjoyment we find in each other's company," he said against her mouth after a time. He kissed her again, his lips lingering against her sweet mouth—another rose. Then he lifted his head and gave her his wickedest smile. "And then," he added, deliberately making his voice vibrantly sensual, "I would take her to bed."

Her smile gleamed in the near dark. "Whether she wanted to go or not?" she queried.

"But by now, of course, she would want to," he replied. Without his planning it, his voice had become completely serious. "Would she not?" he questioned.

She met his gaze directly. "Yes, she would," she whispered.

He lay down beside her again, folding her closely in his arms. *"Bien,"* he murmured.

For the moment, he was content to just hold her, delighting in her closeness. It was beginning to get cold and the grass felt damp to him, but he didn't want to move—not yet. Whenever he was with Casey, he wanted time to stand still. There was never enough time. They both had busy schedules. His had been especially trying as he was working on readying his office, talking to prospective clients, bidding on various jobs, while at the same time completing jobs he had begun for his partners. Perhaps that was why the time when they managed to be together seemed so precious.

Her body felt warm and pliant. Her arms were around him also, her hands gently stroking the back of his neck, arousing him to a state that would shortly reach a point of no return. He could feel her breasts against his chest, and her heart beating in erratic unison with his. He bent his head in search of the sweet vulnerable hollow at the base of her throat, touched it lightly with just the tip of his tongue and felt her shudder.

And then he was kissing her deeply again, his mouth more demanding than he had previously allowed it to be, his whole body thrilling to the fact that she was returning his kiss just as passionately, just as demandingly. I must touch her, he thought. I want to put my lips to the place where her blouse is unbuttoned at her throat. I must touch her breasts and her flat abdomen and her sweet, rounded buttocks and all of her secret places.

But not now; not here in this public place where city traffic was not that far away and where other people still strolled by the water's edge and he could hear their laughter. He had waited more than a month, he could wait a while longer.

"Casey," he murmured, forcing himself to slacken his hold on her.

"Mmm," she answered, refusing to let his mouth leave hers.

"I want to talk to you," he said, and felt her smile.

Then she sighed. "Okay, talk away."

"I want to take you away for a weekend," he told her. "Next weekend, if possible. Your friend Fumiko could take care of the shop on Saturday, perhaps?"

"Probably."

"Bien." He kissed her lightly. "It may be my last free weekend for some time. I have been approached by two very large corporations to offer plans for gardens for their new buildings—one in Bellevue, one in Seattle—that one on the rooftop of the new Cartright Tower—a challenge, *n'est-ce pas?*"

"Congratulations!" Casey exclaimed.

"Later, perhaps. Nothing is certain until they view my plans."

"But you are on your way at last." She laughed softly. "I suppose you will finally be giving up your shuttle-bus route."

"I have already turned in my jacket and cap to Gus. Without regret."

Strangely she felt rather sad. Why? she wondered. Had she really grown that attached to Michel's chartreuse windbreaker?

No—it was the recurring fear that Michel was about to move out of her sphere. With his talent, he was probably going to become a very rich man—maybe even as rich as Winston Perry IV had been.

But why should his income make any difference?

It shouldn't. But it did.

"So," Michel continued, apparently unaware of her thoughts for once. "Our lovemaking for the first time must be a ceremony, a celebration. I cannot take you to my apartment, the walls are like the tissue paper. And your apartment—"

"I know," she said. "My squeaky old sofa bed—not conducive to seduction."

"Ah, then you *are* going to seduce me?"

"I am indeed."

Go away, Daddy, she told the voice that had started muttering in her mind.

"The ocean, perhaps?" Michel suggested.

Her ferocity had silenced her father's voice. She was able to laugh. "You want to make love to me in the ocean? Wouldn't that be uncomfortable? Think of the riptide." She kissed him lightly. "I'm sorry, Michel, I'm obviously temporarily unhinged at the thought of making love to you. Where on the ocean?"

"I will make the arrangements. I want to take you somewhere very special. Somewhere you have never been before. Have you visited a place called Pacific View Lodge?"

She shook her head.

"*Alors,* it is settled. And you must not worry about the contraception. I will take care of all such details. Frenchmen have a practical side as well as a romantic one." He patted her rear. "Now we must get off this grass before we develop rheumatism."

"I take it this isn't your romantic side?" Casey teased as he hauled her to her feet.

CHAPTER SEVEN

THE KNOCK ON HIS DOOR was peremptory. "Mr. Smith," a male voice called out.

Michel looked down at the bag he was packing for his weekend with Casey. He had overslept this morning after having worked on drawings half the night. That rooftop garden was creating even more challenge than he had expected. Now he barely had time to get his socks and shoes on and get over to Casey's boutique.

The man at the door was evidently impatient. He was knocking again. One of his fellow tenants? Whoever it was would have to be dealt with in a hurry. Michel didn't want to be late on this important day.

The sight of two uniformed police officers outside his door made his stomach coil into a hard knot. "Something is wrong?" he asked.

The younger man smiled reassuringly. "Not a thing, Mr. Smith." There was that heavy emphasis on his name again. The policemen on that last embarrassing occasion had thought his name amusing. Sidney had explained to him that Americans sometimes used the name Smith when they wished to remain incognito, especially in sexual situations.

"We'd like you to come down to the station," the older man said.

"But I have a— I am late already for an appointment."

"I'm sorry about that." He didn't look at all sorry, just blandly unconcerned.

"I am under arrest?" Michel asked.

"No, sir. No way. We'd just appreciate it if you would cooperate with us."

"I may make a telephone call?"

"Sure. From the station."

He looked down at his feet. "My shoes and socks?"

"We'll just come on in while you do something about that," the younger man said jovially.

He wandered into Michel's bedroom while Michel was lacing up his sneakers. "You planning on going somewhere, Mr. Smith?" he asked.

Michel stood. "A weekend at the beach," he said.

"Uh-huh."

In the patrol car, the older man—Sergeant Bennett—told him he was to take part in a lineup. "You know what that is?"

"I have seen such things in movies, of course. Victims of a crime are asked to pick out the criminal from a line of people who look something alike."

Bennett nodded. "You got it. Got some people want to take a look at you."

Michel was beginning to feel angry. "They will not know me. I have done nothing wrong."

The younger man, driving the car, laughed. "Mr. Smith, you'd be amazed how many people tell us that."

MICHEL WAS LATE. Casey had finished going over instructions for Fumiko fifteen minutes earlier. Her packed bag was at her feet, her hair clipped back tidily in a barrette, and she was dressed in a pink sweatshirt, shorts and sneakers.

She went to stand in the shop doorway and looked out at Pioneer Square. A few tourists. A couple of street people camping out on one of the benches. A man sweeping his shop doorstep. Lots of pigeons. No Michel.

"You will be gone for the whole weekend with your handsome Frenchman?" Fumiko queried. She had dressed herself in one of Casey's vintage blouse-and-skirt outfits and was admiring herself in the cheval mirror. "You're staying overnight? Together? It's that serious?"

"I think so," Casey answered.

Fumiko raised an eyebrow, her mischievous face alight with interest. "What do you mean, you *think* so? Has your Michel not yet declared himself?"

"Well, he said he couldn't resist me. And he said some other things in French." She had gone over and over in her mind the time when they were lying on the grass, trying to translate exactly what he had murmured to her. But most of the French she had learned in school had been lost to her.

"You don't know what they mean?"

Casey sighed. "I'm afraid not. They sounded good, though."

Fumi's face lit up again. "*Je t'aime* means I love you."

"I remember that one. Don't remember hearing Michel say it, though." She smiled at Fumiko. "I didn't know you spoke French."

Fumiko grinned. "I know the important words in several languages. I have worked as a part-time maid for many different families, remember, many of them from other countries. If Michel ever says *Je t'aime,* then look out. Next thing you know you'll be like me and Goro, up to your ears in babies."

Fumiko Watanabe looked more like a teenager than the mother of five children. But Casey knew for a fact all those children existed. Since the company Goro worked for had contracted to clean the businesses in Pioneer Square, she had met all of them. And a lively bunch they were. According to Fumi, Japanese people spoiled their children until they were of school age, then lowered the boom on them. Only one of Fumi's sons was in school. Casey hadn't noticed any huge difference in his social behavior so far; perhaps the discipline didn't begin until second grade.

"I wouldn't mind," Casey replied, wandering back into the store. "At least, I wouldn't mind two children. I can't quite see myself with five."

"Nor could I," Fumi said cheerfully. "But there they are, so I must have had them."

"Who's taking care of them today?"

Fumi looked surprised. "Goro, of course. We are American Japanese, don't forget. Very liberated. Goro has promised to take them to Woodland Park Zoo. They are in seventh heaven. So am I. Today I'm pretending I'm a single woman."

Casey suppressed a mild shudder at the thought of those children invading the zoo. She had accompanied the whole clan to Seattle Center once, and had vivid memories of the children climbing on and slithering through and jumping off everything that appeared in their paths. The eldest, Kenji, had gone wading in the international fountain.

"Goro is a good husband," she commented.

Fumiko nodded, looking slightly wistful. "Good, yes. Very practical and kind. But not romantic like your

Michel. Whenever Michel comes in here, he kisses my hand. And I like it.'' She touched the bright gold petals of the marigolds Casey had arranged in a vase on the counter—Michel's latest offering. ''So many flowers,'' she murmured. ''Goro has never sent me flowers.''

''Never?''

Fumiko shook her head. ''When the children were born, he brought me practical gifts. For my birthday and Christmas and New Year he buys me another pot or a food processor or a new sewing machine—all very nice presents, but definitely not romantic.'' She grinned. ''I have told him about all your flowers. He shakes his head so.'' She demonstrated, rolling her dark eyes. ''Such foolishness, he is thinking.''

Casey gave her a sympathetic smile, then glanced at the clock. Michel was forty-five minutes late. Should she call him? No. She'd wait. He was usually punctual; he wouldn't be late without reason.

She became aware that Fumi was regarding her solemnly, evidently aware of her nervousness. To distract her she repeated her instructions. ''You will be sure any consignments have been washed and ironed or dry-cleaned?''

''Of course.''

''And you won't accept anything that isn't in fashion?''

''Except for vintage clothing, no.''

''Right. And a lady might be bringing in a couple of poodle skirts—they're not really vintage, but I've had some requests—people go to sock hops, so there's a demand. If you sell anything, be sure to keep all the tickets together so I know who to split the money with.''

''You've told me all this before, Casey,'' Fumiko said gently.

The phone rang. Casey grabbed it on the first ring. "I have been unavoidably detained," Michel told her. His voice sounded strained.

"That's okay," Casey said. "I've been explaining things to Fumiko."

"To a fare-thee-well," Fumi murmured.

Casey ignored her, waiting for Michel to explain. "I do not know exactly how long I will be," he continued. "Another hour, perhaps."

"That's okay," Casey said again, then added, "Is anything wrong?"

"Not at this moment, no. I will be there as soon as I can."

Casey put down the receiver. "He hung up," she said flatly.

"Trouble?" Fumiko asked.

Casey was still staring at the telephone as though that could give her an answer. "I don't know. He just said he'd been unavoidably detained. No trouble at this moment, he said. No proper explanation. I could hear a lot of voices in the background."

"A business meeting, maybe."

"He didn't have a business meeting scheduled. He's hoping to get a contract to put in a roof garden at the new Cartwright Tower. He met yesterday with Roger Prestergard—the developer—and then they walked the site with Cartwright and the project engineer. Michel told me on the phone last night that the meeting went well. Prestergard called him an imaginative genius. Cartwright was delighted with his ideas." She frowned, looking at Fumi. "He *has* been having problems with Harlan and Fawcett's landlord. The landlord was supposed to put some partition walls in Michel's new office and he's dragging his feet. I suppose something could have come up on that."

"You are worried?"

"I guess I am. Michel sounded . . . strange."

"He has given you cause to worry, Casey? That's hard to believe. He's such a . . . nice man." She rolled her eyes. "And so very charming. And tall. I think I shall ask Goro to become taller. Don't you agree that if he can't manage to be romantic, it is the least he can do?"

Casey grinned, recognizing that Fumiko was trying to cheer her up. But the truth was, she did worry—mostly that the spell, or whatever it was that had brought Michel to her in the first place, might wear off; that the "chemistry" he'd mentioned might fade away. Was this the day on which it was scheduled to happen? Was Michel having second thoughts about the weekend? Was that why he was late?

"Are you mad at Michel, Casey?" Fumi asked.

"I guess I am. Dammit, yes. He could at least have explained what was holding him up. This was supposed to be an important day, a special day—" She broke off, looking down at herself. "I can't hang around here looking like this. I think I'll take off for a while, Fumiko. Do you mind?"

"What I'm here for," Fumi said.

"If Michel calls again, tell him I'll be back within an hour."

"Okay."

She felt better when she was outside, doing something, if only walking. She'd walk along 1st Avenue to Pike Place Market then hike down the hill and take the waterfront streetcar back, she decided. If Michel hadn't arrived by then, she'd . . . what? She'd wait; that's what she'd do.

She took her time in the market, admiring the freshness of the fruits and vegetables, the humor and vigor of the men tossing fish back and forth as customers made requests, the ingenuity of the crafts people who made everything from silver jewelry and leather belts to herbal wreaths and dried flowers. She was paying for a small wreath—a gift for Fumi—when she recognized the young pregnant woman beside her who was fingering a bunch of dried lavender. "Hi," she said.

Putting the lavender bundle down with obvious reluctance, the young black woman smiled as sweetly as before, but without any light of recognition. "How's it going?" Casey asked.

The girl frowned, then tossed her dangling braids so that the gold beads that held each one together jingled. "I remember you. You gave me five dollars. Who could forget that red hair?"

"You're getting closer," Casey remarked, with a nod at the girl's swollen belly. "Are you managing okay? I haven't seen you downtown lately."

"Changed my location," the girl replied. "Keep moving around, the law doesn't get so antsy. But at least now I've got a roof over my head. Friend of mine and her boyfriend been letting me sleep in their room the last few weeks. It's some crowded, but it's better than the streets."

"It must be awkward, though," Casey said sympathetically.

The girl's smile looked strained this time. "Only when they fight. Or when they make up." She shrugged.

"My name's Casey Templeton," Casey told her.

"Sarah Bailey. You work around here?"

Casey nodded. "I have a secondhand clothes store in Pioneer Square, Second Time Around."

"I've seen it," the girl exclaimed. "Got an old-fashioned wedding dress in the window. Prettiest dress I ever did see."

Casey nodded. "That's the place." She hesitated, wondering how to frame an offer without seeming patronizing. "If you have problems you can't handle, come and see me, okay?"

Sarah looked at her directly. "You mean that?"

Casey nodded again.

Sarah's smile shone out. She must be beautiful when her eyes didn't have dark circles under them, Casey thought. "Are you seeing a doctor?" she asked.

"Sure," Sarah said. "I want a healthy baby. And I'm trying to eat right. Vegetables, even." She showed Casey the contents of the brown paper bag she was clutching. Two carrots, a potato, a small cabbage. "Trouble is..."

"What?" Casey asked when she hesitated.

"Costs an awful lot to have a baby."

Casey nodded. Then, as she received her change for the wreath she'd bought, she passed it on to Sarah.

"Hey, I didn't mean— Listen, you're a friend now. I'm not going to hit on you for money." Very firmly, she pressed the few dollars back into Casey's hand. "I'm going to be just fine," she insisted.

"Remember what I said," Casey told her.

"I will." Sarah moved away, walking so awkwardly, Casey's heart ached for her.

MICHEL HAD NOT YET arrived when she returned to her shop. It was another hour before he showed up. He even looked elegant in a white sweatshirt and khaki shorts, Casey thought, almost forgetting that she was supposed to be angry with him for keeping her waiting.

From the corner of her eye, she noted that Fumiko's expressive face was registering total approval of Michel's strong-looking legs.

Michel did not seem himself, she thought. He had greeted Fumiko as always, with a kiss for her hand, setting her giggling, and he had kissed Casey discreetly but affectionately on her mouth, again as usual. But his face seemed pale under his suntan, his expression grim—a certain tightness around his eyes. Casey didn't have the heart to ask him to explain his lateness.

He drove out of the city and was well along I-5, heading toward Tacoma, before he said anything beyond comments on the traffic and the weather. Then he took a deep breath and made an obvious effort to relax. "It has not been a good beginning to our weekend, Casey," he said apologetically.

"I noticed that," she responded carefully.

"I had to take part in a lineup at the police station."

Casey's stomach did a backward somersault. She had very carefully put out of her mind the thought of Michel's arrest and the con game that had triggered it.

"It took a long time because one of the...victims...was late arriving, because of heavy traffic," he said slowly, not looking at her.

She waited.

"He picked out someone else. A clerk who worked at the police station."

"You said there was more than one victim there?"

"The rest couldn't make up their minds about anybody."

She stole a glance at his set face. "That's good, isn't it?"

"I suppose it is, yes. But I would have preferred that they all say very loudly— 'But no, this could not possibly be the man.'"

"The police haven't accused you directly, have they?"

"No. But I was asked about a visit to Portland, Oregon I made in February. It seems several people were also defrauded there. And the police placed me there during that time by a credit-card purchase of gas."

"You *were* there?" A strange iciness was trickling into her stomach, making her whole body feel stiff and cold.

"Oh, yes. I went to see a particular garden I had heard about. The owner of the house was away in Europe, but he had invited me to stroll through his garden. So I did. It was very beautiful, on a hill overlooking the city." He shook his head. "The police were not impressed that I went to look at a garden, but they are willing to check with the owner that I was invited for that purpose."

Casey could think of nothing to say, and Michel was silent for a long time. After they turned off I-5 and left the traffic behind, he made an obvious effort to cheer up. "So, we will put this annoying business out of our minds, shall we, and enjoy ourselves?"

"Of course," she assured him.

Almost immediately, her father's voice sounded off in her mind. *Be sure your sins will find you out.*

But he hasn't sinned, Daddy, she responded silently. *Where there's smoke there's fire.*

That wasn't her father. That was her own mind speaking, questioning.

"This isn't going to work," she blurted out.

Michel glanced at her face, then slowed the car. There was a rest area ahead, and without consulting her he pulled into it and parked.

Leaning forward with his arms resting on the steering wheel, he said, "There is no need to say anything, Casey. I understand. It is just that I am disappointed— no, I am distraught that you have lost faith in me. I must sit here a moment before driving back to Seattle, all right?"

He *looked* distraught, and tired to the bone. There was something defeated about the angle of his head, a lack of luster to his dark curly hair.

"I'm sorry, Michel," she said.

"It is not your fault," he told her. "It is all mine. If I had not misled you in the beginning, you would not have cause to doubt me now. I was mortified, you understand, Casey, when that policeman pushed me against the wall and arrested me in front of you. But at that time I was more embarrassed than worried. I cared more about how stupid I must look. And so I lied to you. Which was even more stupid. Today, I began to worry for my reputation. Now that I am becoming established with Harlan and Fawcett, I cannot afford any breath of suspicion to fall on me."

"I think it's time you found a lawyer," Casey said.

He nodded glumly, pushing a hand through his hair. "I have thought this also. I do not wish to use the company law firm, but I know a good man who is a friend of Étienne's. But still I feel so helpless. There seems nothing I can do to clear myself. I have tried." He shook his head. "I had the idea this week that I could check around the state of Washington. I could perhaps find out if this young couple had been heard of in places other than those I knew about. If I could prove I had not been in those places, then I would be in the clear, perhaps. I made telephone calls to all Better Business Bureaus in Washington State. There are five of them. But apart from those in Tacoma and Seattle, no one knew anything.''

"It was a good idea, all the same," Casey replied softly.

"But I was so stupid, I did not think of checking other states. Now I find out about Portland."

"The couple were there in February, you said."

He nodded.

"And Tacoma?"

"In March."

"Seattle?"

He frowned, looking at her. "The middle of April and during May."

"They moved north, then. Up the I-5 corridor."

"I suppose so."

"Then it would seem reasonable to suppose they might show up farther north yet."

"Possibly." His whole face brightened. "Thank you, Casey. You have made me feel much better. If reports come to the police from cities in the north, I will be cleared. I have never traveled north of Seattle."

"Can you prove that?"

He was crestfallen again. "Probably not. How does one prove such a thing?"

"Well, at least no one can prove you *were* there."

"That is true."

"Will the police want to see you again?"

"I do not know. Sergeant Bennett said he would see me later, but in this country that does not necessarily mean anything, *n'est-ce pas?*"

He was still gloomy. "When I was in that lineup, Casey, standing there with those other men with a light on my face, turning sideways when I was told to, speaking when I was told to, I wondered, what will happen if someone makes a mistake? If someone says, there, that is the man? How can I prove it is not?"

"In this country you are considered innocent until proven guilty, Michel," she said.

He darted a glance at her that held an edge of cynicism. "And it always proceeds that way?" he asked.

There was such pain in his eyes. She had been so busy worrying about Inga's magic perfume and the reasons for Michel's attraction to her, she hadn't stopped to think of what Michel's arrest and the suspicion hanging over him was doing to his dignity. Looking at him, she thought of all she knew of him—his patience, his tenderness, his thoughtfulness, the beautiful garden he had created for his neighbors, his love of beauty, his sense of fun. And suddenly, every doubt vanished. She *knew*, totally and unalterably, that this man would never deliberately cheat anyone.

"It proceeds for me," she said firmly.

The shadows lifted from his face as they had lifted from her thoughts. As quickly, as easily as that, the air became charged once more with all the tender feelings that had increased between them over the last weeks. Silently he held out his arms to her. Awkwardly, they leaned to each other over the console as best they could and kissed each other with great delicacy and tenderness. "Thank you, Casey," he murmured against her hair.

Looking at him as he straightened and started the car, she felt that they had both passed a test in the progress of their relationship. They had crossed an abyss together and had emerged stronger for it. "Onward to the ocean?" she queried with lightness in her voice and in her heart.

He laughed. "Onward," he agreed, and the way he said it was almost a commitment.

WHILE THEY WALKED on the beach and ate dinner in the gourmet restaurant, someone had brought firewood to their cabin.

As Michel greeted the sight with pleasure, Casey wondered again about this new interpretation of her thoughts. It was too damn uncanny that she had imagined a fire when she thought of making love to Michel. All the same, now that the heat of the day had dissipated, the warmth of the fire felt wonderful.

They showered together, soaping each other without embarrassment, though this was the first time they had seen each other naked. As they showered, they deliberately suppressed their rising excitement, wanting to stretch out these last peaceful moments of the day that had started so badly and ended so well.

Wrapped in the terry robes the hotel had furnished, they sat at a small table in the bay window drinking the *café mocha* Michel had ordered. "It is ten o'clock," Michel said softly after a while.

"Mmm-hmm," Casey murmured. She had decided not to worry about the fire or the bed, which was as soft as she'd imagined—she'd checked. There didn't seem to be anything she could do about these strange coincidences, so there wasn't much point in worrying about them. Besides, she had better things to think about. For one, she was enchanted by the vista outside the cabin window. Pacific View Lodge had lived up to its name. The view of the ocean from the cliff top was incredible.

Darkness had just fallen and floodlights had been switched on. Far below their cabin, the frothy edges of the gentle waves glittered like ruffled snow.

"We have only seven hours until dawn," Michel pointed out.

"You think we should get some sleep?" Casey asked mischievously.

She expected a humorous response from Michel, but it did not come. When she turned to look at him, she caught her breath at the expression on his face. His eyes were darker than ever, though she would not have thought possible. His beautiful mouth, usually curved in the promise of a smile, was stern.

"I am waiting for you to ask me to make love to you," he said. "You promised you would tell me when you were ready."

"I'm ready," she answered promptly.

A smile hovered at the corners of his mouth. "But you have made me wait so long. I think I will be arrogant as my grandmother says. Perhaps I will not do it until you beg me," he said.

Standing up, Casey took the two steps necessary to bring her to his side. Then, not touching him, she leaned over and touched her mouth to his. His mouth moved under hers, parting softly so that she felt the edges of his teeth against her lips. He sighed. "Very well," he told her. "I will do as you wish."

Pulling her unexpectedly into his lap, he gently tugged on the sash of her bathrobe so that it fell open. Delicately he touched her breasts, stroking each one before closing his lips around first one erect nipple, then the other, tugging slightly, sending bolts of electricity shooting downward to her groin. Reaching to her shoulders, he slid the robe away from her, so that she was naked against him. There was something incredibly exciting about being naked in his arms while his body was still covered. There was a roaring in her ears that had nothing to do with the nearness of the ocean. Tangling her fingers in his thick, crisp hair, she held his head hard against her breast, straining to get closer to him.

After a moment he stood, lifting her with him, looking down at her, his eyes hooded now with passion, almost somber as he gazed at her. After laying her gently on the bed, he pulled off his own robe and let it drop to the floor.

His body was beautifully formed, toned by the physical work he did, suntanned everywhere except for the white strip where his swimming trunks had covered him. "I do admire a good suntan," Casey murmured enviously. She had never dared expose herself to the sun without a covering of sun block. "At least I don't freckle like most redheads," she said to comfort herself.

Michel laughed, then lay down beside her. "I wish that you had freckles. Hundreds of freckles. If you had freckles, I could kiss every one."

The bed was down filled. It received their bodies and cradled them gently. Raising himself on one elbow, Michel looked at her body, lazily touching her here and there with sensitive fingers.

The silk-clad lamps on either side of the bed lit their bodies with a clear soft light; but Casey, who had always been shy, felt no shyness at lying there, so open to his gaze. And to her amazement, her father had nothing to say in her mind. There was only blessed silence, except for the slight rasp of her breath and Michel's, as long-banked excitement began to pulse toward release.

Yet still they restrained themselves. It was as if they had all the time in the world and could not bear to hurry. Or perhaps that they had so looked forward to this consummation that they were afraid to proceed too fast, in case the reality did not live up to the anticipation. No, she thought. She had no fear of that.

Seven hours until dawn, she thought contentedly.

"I wish to touch every part of you," Michel said.

"Okay," she agreed. "As long as I get equal time."

"Am I not a gentleman?"

As he caressed her, she let her gaze follow his movements, loving the suntanned elegant fingers that showed up so clearly against her own creamy skin; loving, too, the feel of them as they stroked and touched her breasts, her abdomen, the soft patch of hair between her thighs.

"I had thought it would burn," Michel murmured.

"It does," Casey whispered back.

He smiled, but did not pause in his exploration, now following with his mouth in the path of his fingers, pressing soft, delicate kisses on her flesh, touching her gently with his tongue.

How long could she lie still under his ministrations before she went mad, she wondered, and then realized no one had told her she must not move. Putting her arms around him, she rolled with him on the billowing mattress until he was on his back and she was leaning over him. Now it was her turn to explore, and she took her time about it, lovingly learning the shape of his ears with her tongue, the rasp of whiskers against her cheek, the prickling of dark hair against her breasts and thighs. Eagerly she searched out all his secret places and made them known to herself, her kisses becoming harsher, harder, more erotic as she learned.

And now Michel's patience was also exhausted. Pulling her tightly against him, he kissed her with a mouth that had become charged with steel. She thought that she would never get enough of his mouth; she could not let it move from hers, not even so that she could take a breath. It was a while before she realized that the sounds she could hear—the small, incoherent excited whimperings—were coming from her own throat. In her mind, an image formed of the blue irises Michel had sent her, the tight buds slowly unfurling into full and glorious bloom.

Michel was beneath her, beside her, over her, his body arching, her own arching to meet it. And then he was entering her with the slowness of a man who knew how to relish the moment. There was a sudden vast stillness all around as she shaped herself to him and found that she had surely been made for him. Then her arms went around him again and she was clinging to him as he lifted her and held her and thrust into her.

He was murmuring something in French at the moment when fireworks exploded inside Casey's head and the pressure that had filled her body was released. He called out something else in his own language as his body lost its rigidity and settled slowly down over hers.

Casey's arms tightened around him as she smiled ruefully, thinking of Fumiko. Whoever was directing that little voice in her mind that kept knowing stuff in advance should get on the job and whisper in Michel's head that at a time like this he should say something she could understand—*I love you,* for example.

"*Je t'aime,*" Michel said, right on cue.

Casey was abruptly terrified.

"Something is wrong?" Michel asked, apparently sensing her change of mood.

She turned her head into her pillow.

"Talk to me, Casey," he insisted, taking his weight off her, but still leaning over her, his muscular shoulders clearly outlined against the lamplight. "It is because I tell you that I love you? How can I not love you? You are a dear, wonderful woman."

"You did it again," she said, her voice muffled.

Gently he touched her face, stroking her cheek with his thumb until she turned her head and looked up at him. "What did I do?" he asked.

"You read my mind. Fumiko told me *Je t'aime* meant 'I love you,' so when you started talking in French, I wished you'd say something I could understand, like 'I love you,' and you did."

He raised his dark eyebrows. "You have discussed me with Fumiko, have you?" He chuckled. "I'm sorry, Casey. I see that you are disturbed, but I see no reason why. If you wanted me to say 'I love you,' why should you object when I do say it?"

"You don't understand. You don't know . . ."

"I know that I love you."

"Why?"

He laughed, cupped her face in his hands and kissed her lightly. "Who can tell all the causes of love? Perhaps because you loved me when I was just a shuttle-bus driver."

"I didn't say I loved you," she pointed out.

His whimsical grin gave a wry cast to his face. "I have been meaning to speak to you about this omission, *chérie*."

"It's too soon, too quick," she protested.

His mouth closed over hers, becoming urgent, his arms tightening around her as his breath filled her. Her whole body seemed to ache with a piercing sweetness as her lips responded to his, touching, parting, touching again. There was a tightness, a warm, heavy congestion between her thighs that begged for release; needed release. Desperately she clung to him as he slid easily into her and began once again to make love to her.

"You love me," he said confidently moments after the sought-after release had reduced her to a helpless, satiated, spineless creature without enough energy to blink an eyelash.

"I love you," she agreed on a long sigh.

He hugged her tightly. "*Alors,* nothing else matters, *n'est-ce pas?*" His gaze roamed tenderly over her face. "It is enough that we love each other. I do love you, Casey," he said, his eyes darkening as he looked down at her. "I have loved you from that very first evening when I looked at you through the car window and smelled your perfume. I knew then you were an enchantress and I know it now. You have bewitched me, *ma chérie.*"

She hoped he would mistake the tremor that went through her for the residue of passion rather than fear. He had just confirmed her deepest fears, but how could she confess about the perfume now? He would think she was crazy; or else he would begin to wonder if some outside agent *had* been responsible for his falling in love with her. Either way, he might decide this relationship was not such a hot idea. She sighed as Michel released her.

You've made your bed, now you have to lie in it, her father said.

Which was pretty funny, considering where she was at this moment.

So if it was so funny, why wasn't she laughing? And why, in this moment after a declaration that was supposed to bring total happiness to anyone's life, was she so suddenly sure that somewhere on the limitless horizon outside the cabin a dark cloud was hovering, just waiting for a chance to drift in to shore?

CHAPTER EIGHT

IN THE MORNING, they came together before they even opened their eyes, Michel's hands moving over her naked body from behind, stroking her breasts, her abdomen, her thighs. So quickly had the touch of his hands become familiar to her, she marveled, as she welcomed his caresses and returned them.

Dawn was lighting the eastern windows of the cabin, casting a rose-pink glow across their bed, touching their flesh with warmth and magic. Casey could hear the muffled roar of the ocean through the window they had left slightly open, the occasional mewling sound of a seabird. They didn't speak as they made love. It was as though the hush of morning should not be interrupted. But still they communicated, with sensitive fingers, and tender mouths and glances.

Afterward, they ate mushroom omelets at the table in the bay window before going down to the beach to wade at the ocean's edge.

Surely sea breezes had never smelled so refreshing, Casey thought. Surely the water splashing around their ankles was cleaner, clearer and more sparkling than any seawater had a right to be in this industrialized twentieth century.

Whatever had brought them together didn't matter now, she decided. She was committed. She was loved and she was in love. It was a beautiful morning. There was no reason at all for her to worry about dark clouds hovering.

After lunch they lay on their backs in the dunes, watching the dragon kite Michel had bought at the lodge gift shop. The kite swooped and soared and shook its long tail high above their heads—requiring only an occasional jerk on the string to keep it in motion. The Highest-Flying Kite in the History of the Universe, Michel had dubbed it.

"*Grandmère* and I used to fly kites when I was little," he murmured, sounding sleepy. "There was a big meadow not far from our château—" He broke off.

There was a silence, then Casey said, "I thought the French word for house was *maison*."

"Yes. That is correct."

She raised herself on one elbow, looking at his face. "Château means castle, doesn't it?"

"Or country residence. Manor house."

"You're telling me you lived in a manor?"

He sighed, then grinned ruefully up at her. "I suppose it is time I made a complete confession."

"Perhaps it is."

Such a chilly note in her voice. He sat up and started winding in the kite string. All along, he had known he would have to tell Casey the truth, but he had kept delaying it.

"You will not become angry and 'go to your room'?" he asked, after he had packed the kite away, hoping to make her smile.

"I'm not guaranteeing a thing," she said.

He sighed. "Well, then, I must take my chances. Yes, I did live in a manor house. The château is southwest of Paris. My mother's family has lived there for one hundred and seventy-four years."

"Your family is rich," she stated flatly.

"Now, more than ever," he said. "Before, there was much land and tenants. And for more than fifty years my grandfather has manufactured automobiles. As they become old enough, my mother's brothers worked for him, and now their sons also. There is a factory in Tours, and another in Le Mans—you have heard of the race there, no doubt?"

A frown creased her forehead, but she didn't comment. He ran a hand through his hair, worried about the way this conversation was going. "My mother's father founded the company and named it for his family name. Perhaps you have heard of it. His name is Jean-Paul Rapide."

"There was a report on the new Rapide sports car in the *Seattle P-I* a while ago," Casey exclaimed, sitting up abruptly. "It's supposed to be the most luxurious sports car ever made. People are raving about its brilliant engineering. 'Rapide-mania' the newspaper called it."

"Yes. It has proven very popular in the United States," Michel replied.

Casey stared at him, looking totally overwhelmed. "I guess I conjured up a prince, after all," she said finally with a funny little half-sad smile. She had pulled her knees up under her chin and was clasping them with both arms. "Not the son of a monarch," she went on. "But a prince of industry."

"Conjured?" he queried.

"Private joke," she responded, with no sign of humor in her expression.

There was a coolness between them that had not been present at any time during the past four weeks, not since he had let her believe he was only a shuttle-bus driver so that he could surprise her with the truth. "You are full of surprises," she said rather stiffly. "I take it you lied when you told me you had to take the job driving a shuttle bus to support yourself while you finished your studies?"

"I told you the truth," Michel replied. "It is very complicated, Casey."

"Try me," she said drily.

"Very well. I will begin at the beginning. It was expected that my father would go into the family business when he got out of the air force, you see. He was an orphan, with few ties to the United States. But he died before his release." He paused for a moment, wondering as he had wondered before, how different his upbringing might have been if his father had lived. Would his father have respected his desire to live his own life? "When I graduated from university, naturally Grandpère expected that I join him in the company."

One word echoed in his mind. *Naturally.* Grandpère had never considered any possible alternative, had not heard any of Michel's protestations, or if he had, had ignored them. Michel sighed. He had gone over the old quarrels with Grandpère often enough. It did no good to wish now that their parting could have been more amicable.

"After graduating with a degree in engineering," he continued, "I worked for Rapide, for my grandfather—as he expected. But it was so boring, Casey. I like cars, yes. To work with my hands, yes, I might have enjoyed that. But it was decided my skill was as a draftsman, a designer. So I sat at a desk all day, designing parts for the automobiles." He could not repress a small reminiscent shudder. "To make it all bearable, I took a job on weekends and holidays, working for a landscape architect. My grandfather did not approve. He kept telling me I should be *sage,* which literally means wise, but in his mouth means I should do as he tells me. However, I was a grown man. Grandpère could hardly forbid me to take a second job, especially as I was still working full-time for him."

Hands still clasping her knees, Casey was watching a flock of sandpipers soaring and wheeling above the water's edge, but he was pretty sure she was listening carefully. He wished he knew what she was thinking. Sometimes it seemed he could read her thoughts as clearly as though they were his own; but her mind was closed to him now. There was something very rigid in the set of her shoulders, something rejecting about her stillness. "Are you impossibly angry with me, Casey?" he asked.

She hesitated, her lips compressed. "Not angry, no. Just shaken. It seems as though you keep changing into someone else. A pass of the hands and a flash of light and you change from shuttle-bus driver to landscape architect. Another pass and you are a member of a wealthy manufacturing family. What will the next pass bring? Your grandfather is a baron, maybe? Your grandmother's the Queen of England?"

"You know everything about me now," he said firmly. "I am Michel Gervais Smith, landscape architect. This is the only identity you need to consider."

She sighed. "What brought about the parting of the ways?"

He wished he could take her in his arms and kiss away the stiffness that had come over her. But he had the feeling that would be entirely the wrong thing to attempt. All he could do was carry on and hope the air between them would eventually clear.

"Three years ago, my grandfather decided he would retire when he reaches eighty years, which will be next year. It was his wish that I begin training to become chief executive officer of Rapide Corporation. I did not want to do this—so there were many arguments, not only between us, but with the whole family. My cousins and uncles do not like it that Grandpère favors me. Favored me. I must use the past tense, I am afraid. There was a big quarrel when I left."

He sighed. "I had seen what had happened to Grandpère himself, you understand. So much responsibility, so many meetings, so many arguments. He is not an even-tempered man. Much stress all the time. He rarely takes the time to smell the roses."

A reluctant smile tugged at the corners of her mouth. "So you decided to take time to smell them yourself?"

"As I told you before. By then I had thirty years. So I came to this country. I became a shuttle-bus driver, because the money I was earning from Harlan and Fawcett was not enough to support me and pay for my studies, and I did not wish to use any of the money I acquired from Rapide. One of the things Grandpère said to me when I left was that I would find out I was nothing without the family. So I wished to prove myself capable of supporting myself. I did not use my savings from my former salary, nor the income from my shares. Except for my Porsche, of course. I had to have an automobile."

"Of course," Casey agreed. He sensed she was agreeing tongue in cheek, thinking of her own old Volkswagen, perhaps.

"The Porsche is an admirable car," he explained to her.

"I'm sure it is."

The coolness was still there. It was as though she were disappointed in him. Perhaps he should try a lighter touch.

"You asked me if I had come close to marriage," he reminded her. "I can tell you now that my family kept choosing young women for me—with my two jobs I had little opportunity to make a date of my own choosing. But I am stubborn enough not to be pushed into anything. So there was no wife."

He shrugged, smiling at her. "I have escaped from a very rigid life-style, Casey. One in which many decisions were made for me. For now, I am enjoying my freedom. But no doubt, once I have established my independence, then I will marry a suitable young woman of whom my family would approve."

She brought her gaze up to give him a surprised glance. "You need your family's approval?"

A typically American response. It was difficult for Americans to accept the feudal nature of older European families—which was more than a little exaggerated in his family.

"The family is very important in France," he explained to her. "I may be a rebel, but I am not a—what do you say—a maverick." He looked at her closely. "You are upset with me?"

"I guess I must be." She shook her head. "Go on, Michel, please. Tell me the rest. Tell me what influenced you to give up everything so you could smell the roses."

"Well, it began long before I was thirty. When I was sixteen, my whole family, including my mother, went away for a long vacation to the south of France with Grandpère and Grandmère. I was recovering from a broken leg. I had fallen from my horse. So I was left at home with only the servants."

"Servants," Casey echoed.

"I'm afraid so," he admitted. Why did he feel the need to apologize?

"Go on," she said tersely. "I'll try not to interrupt anymore."

"I was very bad, I am afraid," he told her, to make her smile. It didn't work. He sighed and labored on. "I had always hated the château gardens, you see. Oh, they were so rigidly formal, every little hedge and bush clipped just so, every rosebush standing at attention, every path going directly north to south or east to west."

He shrugged. "So this is what I did. While my family was away, I engaged the help of the chauffeur and two stable-hands and together we ripped out walls and plantings and took up all of the paths. Then I made a garden such as Bacon described."

"Bacon?" she queried.

"Sir Francis Bacon. English philosopher and statesman, sixteenth-seventeenth century. He wrote that there should be wild places in a garden and that a garden was the greatest refreshment to the spirit of man." He grinned hopefully at her. "I'm sure he meant to include women. What use is a garden without a woman in it?"

"What did your new garden look like?" Casey asked. Ah, she was looking at him with renewed interest, her bewitching green eyes fixed on his face, her expression much softer now. Was she attracted by the sixteen-year-old who had loved gardens? Perhaps.

He leaned back against the sand dune. "We found old used bricks and made walkways," he told her. "We created rolling lawns between stands of existing trees. In the flower beds, we planted delphiniums and hydrangeas, Campanula, peonies, hellebores, islands of shrubbery in beguiling combinations of color, blossoming trees, old-fashioned roses. It was wonderful, Casey, so natural looking, like a park, though it was actually carefully controlled as to color and size of plants and the positioning of each.''

"And what happened when your mother came home?"

He grimaced and sat up straight again. "Unfortunately, Grandpère and my uncles arrived first. I was given a whipping, the stablehands were sacked, and the chauffeur was severely reprimanded.''

"They destroyed your garden?"

He shook his head. "They wanted to, but fortunately my mother and Grandmère returned in time to save it. Grandmère loved the garden. My design is still there, mostly unchanged. Even my uncles came to admire it eventually. And Grandpère also. All the same, Grandpère did not approve of my actions. It was the fact of my doing it myself he could not forgive. It was not suitable for a son of the Rapide family to dig in the ground like a common laborer." He sighed again. "There was also the suggestion that it was not quite...manly to have such an interest. Grandpère, you see, had never worked in a garden. He did not know how much muscle is required.''

"Why didn't you tell me about your family right away?" Casey asked.

If he was to remove that stern look from her face he must be perfectly honest, no matter the possible cost. He looked at her directly. "I have found it is best not to reveal too much about my family too soon."

"To women, you mean? In case they decide you are a good catch?"

He winced. "Something like that, yes."

Okay, she was mad because he'd deceived her. Most women were when they found out about his family. But most had forgiven him when they discovered how wealthy the Rapide family was. If Casey was one of those it would be his turn to be surprised.

She surprised him in a different way. After obviously pondering the subject for a few minutes, she nodded and said thoughtfully. "I can see why you'd feel the need to be cautious. Yes." She looked at him levelly. "Thank you for telling me about them now."

"But you do not approve of them?"

"Why would you think that?"

"Because the temperature on this beach has dropped several degrees while I was talking about them, even though the sun is shining directly down on us. I keep getting the feeling you are going to stalk away from me again and I will have to get down on my knees in the sand to beg you to come back."

Several emotions struggled for dominance over her clear face, finally settling on a sort of rueful humor. "Okay, I suppose I do owe you an explanation."

She took a deep breath. "Have you ever heard the expression 'the wrong side of the tracks,' Michel?"

He nodded.

"That's where I grew up—on the east side of town. When my father was ordained, he had the choice of several well-to-do churches, but he preferred to establish himself where he could do the most good. He operated a mission in the poorest district. His congregation was composed of street people and derelicts and people down on their luck. One of his favorite biblical sayings was this: 'It is easier for a camel to go through the eye of a needle, than for a rich man to enter into the kingdom of God.' He believed it and practiced it. We were terribly poor, which to my father was synonymous with virtuous. However, as I told you, he and my mother wanted me to have a good education. When I was eleven they decided I must go to a private school, Cornforth's Academy, on the other side of town—the rich side of town. My parents were such good people, Michel, such Christian people, it never occurred to them that the other children, the rich children, would know where I came from.''

''They were cruel to you?''

''Of course. Their parents, too. They didn't really feel I belonged there. I might carry germs from all those dreadful people my father mixed with. They decided on my very first day that I was not...suitable. And they never changed their opinion. I was ostracized the entire time—when I wasn't being jeered at. One of the problems was that my parents couldn't afford the official custom-made uniform, which was a navy jumper and a blazer with red and gold cord around the edges. My mother made my jumper and bought a cheaper version of the blazer. She twisted the cord and sewed it on herself. It never did look right, of course. And kids dearly love having someone around who doesn't look right, someone to jeer at, someone they can feel superior to. Human nature, I suppose.''

There was bitterness in her voice, for which Michel could hardly blame her.

''I tried to tell my parents that I didn't want to stay in the school, but they would not budge. I didn't have the heart to tell them how badly the kids treated me—they had sacrificed so much to raise the money. So all I could do was struggle on through, trying not to mind that I was a misfit.''

"So when your parents were killed, you left at once?''

She shook her head. The breeze had increased, Michel noticed. Casey's hair was tossing around her shoulders. He wanted to caress it, but did not think she would welcome his touch at the moment, not while she was reliving the unhappiness of her past.

''I wish I had quit," she said. "It would have been less humiliating. But I felt convinced that Mom and Dad would have wanted me to stick it out to the end. I was prepared to do just that, but the last quarter's fees were due and the courts hadn't decided yet if our house could be sold to pay my expenses. I asked the school administrator to hold off awhile and I'd pay him as soon as I could, but he refused to wait. I knew that he'd waited twice as long for wealthy parents to pay their fees—wealthy people, it seems, are sometimes absentminded about their smaller bills—but I knew if I reminded him of that, it wouldn't make any difference. I figured out later it was one thing to let a poor child in when her father was a respected minister, but when the child became an orphan there was no real reason for keeping her on.''

"Prejudice isn't restricted to race," Michel murmured, turning his head to look at her.

"Exactly," Casey said.

He nodded, then pounced. "Knowing that, how do you justify being so prejudiced yourself?" he asked.

"Me?" She was highly indignant. Then her face fell. "Oh. Yes. Judging you by your family.''

"After I have told you how hard I worked. After I have shown you my garden that I made with my own hands."

"Michel, I'm sorry. I appreciate what you are saying, and I know you can't help who you are or which family you were born into any more than I can. But I still feel uneasy around wealthy people. I know it's a hang-up, but I can't seem to shake it. I can't identify with any of my wealthier friends—I have to like them in spite of their assets."

"So, can you not like me in the same way?"

"Of course I like you, Michel."

He pulled her down to lie on the sand, cradling her head against his elbow so the sand would not get into her hair. "And love?" he asked. "Was that only the heat of the moment last night? Can you not speak to me of love in the light of the day?"

She met his gaze, her eyes reflecting the sky so that they appeared cloudy, not as clearly green as usual. "I love you, Michel," she said softly. "You know I do."

The admission should have revived his flagging spirits, but there was a note of doubt in her voice that worried him mightily. He kissed her, hoping to rekindle the passion they had shared such a short time ago. She returned the kiss, but there was a sadness in it—almost a feeling of finality.

CASEY WAS HANGING THE clothes Fumiko had received on consignment when Skip walked into her shop on Monday morning.

"How was your weekend?" he asked.

She picked up her small steamer and started steaming out a few wrinkles in the Diane Freis two-piece she'd just hung. "Fine," she said, wondering if there was any particular significance in the question.

"Heard you went off to the beach with 007."

She had taken Michel to Skip's restaurant for dinner a couple of times during the past month. Skip insisted he looked exactly like Timothy Dalton, the actor who had taken over the James Bond role when Pierce Brosnan had been unable to accept it. "Fumiko told you, I suppose?" she asked flatly.

"Who else." He stood appraising her, rocking from his heels to the balls of his feet, whistling tunelessly under his breath, his hands in the pockets of his gray sweats. "Looks like it was a flop," he said at last.

"I had a great weekend," she stated firmly, keeping her gaze fixed on the garment's animal print.

"Uh-huh. So where's the light that should be shining in those green eyes? Where's the glow to the skin? Why isn't the red hair crackling with vitality?"

Switching off the steamer, she set it aside. Skip always had been able to see through her. Not looking at him, she smoothed the ruffles on the front of the peach-colored blouse she was wearing with her long black skirt. It had come in on Saturday and she'd decided to claim it from the vintage rack for herself.

"You going to come clean to your old buddy?" Skip asked. "Or am I going to have to stand here all morning needling you?"

She smiled ruefully. "You'd do it, too, wouldn't you?"

"Damn right. Came in here to get some gossip about some raging love affair. Fumiko said it looked like love to her. Came to find out for myself."

Feeling self-conscious, she looked down at the floor.

"What's this demure-maiden impression supposed to mean? It *is* love?"

"Yes, it's love," she admitted with a sigh.

To her surprise he scowled.

"What now?" she demanded.

"You haven't known him long enough to fall in love. Wasn't four weeks ago you still weren't sure he was a con man or not."

Had my doubts two days ago, she thought, but didn't say so. "He's not a con man," she said firmly.

"All doubts resolved?"

"On that score? Every last one."

"This love of yours—it's requited, as they used to say in old romance novels?"

"What do you know about old romance novels?" she teased, hoping to lighten the atmosphere.

He grinned at her. "Brenda used to leave them lying around. I'd pick them up sometimes, figured I'd learn something about women."

"And did you?"

He scowled. "Not enough, apparently. But enough to know you're avoiding my question."

"Michel has declared himself, as Fumiko puts it, if that's what you mean."

The scowl deepened. "You be careful, young Casey," he said. "He seems like a good guy, what I saw of him. But you just remember they don't call it falling in love for nothing. Falling often precedes a crash landing."

"Oh, Skip, don't you say things like that."

"You afraid I'll put a whammy on you?"

Her nervousness increased. "Don't say things like that, either."

His eyes narrowed. "So I was right. Trouble in paradise. What you worried about now? And don't tell me you're not worried. You tell me you're in love and Mr. Smith's in love, but you look like your best friend just died. Something sure as hell doesn't add up. So what is it? What's bugging you?"

"I just found out Michel has a rich family."

Skip's eyebrows lifted. "Definitely a drawback."

"His family owns the company that makes Rapide cars, Skip."

Skip whistled. "That's rich, okay." He looked at her closely. "I get it. Cassandra Templeton, born to poverty. You're afraid you don't fit in with company like that?"

She nodded. "One of the things he mentioned was that he'll eventually marry a girl his family will approve of." She laughed shortly. "I'm not rich enough for *Justin,* so I guess I'd hardly qualify in the Rapide family's eyes."

"Family's thousands of miles away, Case. What does the family matter if Michel loves you?" He looked at her closely. "You don't believe he loves you?"

"I don't believe he loves me for myself."

Skip made no effort to hide the fact he was totally bewildered. "What you think he loves you for, then?"

"The perfume," she blurted out.

Immediately she could have bitten her tongue, but the words were out now, and there was relief in that. She needed to talk to someone.

Skip looked blank for all of ten seconds, then he frowned. "Does this have anything to do with that so-called magic perfume you told me about? Stuff some old biddy gave you at an antique show?"

"Inga was not an old biddy," Casey said indignantly.

"I'll be damned." He stared at her with disbelief. "You *are* talking about that perfume."

She nodded. "I used it," she said awkwardly. "The day I told you about it. Later that same afternoon. And right after I used it, Michel came into my shop."

He was still staring at her. "What the hell are you trying to tell me, Case?"

She let out a long breath and averted her eyes. "I'm afraid that's what attracted Michel to me."

"So? I've been turned on by perfume myself. Brenda uses Obsession. Great stuff. Gives me all kinds of lustful ideas."

"Perfume wears off, Skip."

His eyebrows climbed again. "And love dies? Is that what you're thinking?"

She nodded miserably. "I've got this horrible feeling it's doomed, this thing with Michel. It's like a cloud hanging over my head. A dark cloud. And so far, whenever I've thought something in connection with Michel, it's happened. So maybe I'm right." She glanced at his face. "What do you think?"

He shook his head, then walked over to her and put his large hand against her forehead. "Don't feel like you've got a fever," he said.

"You think I'm crazy?"

"I'm striving to be charitable, Case," he told her. "But when someone whose sanity you've always respected starts believing in magic perfume and babbling dark clouds and thoughts coming true, your own m_____ and says, 'Say *what?*'"

She _____d. "I guess I should have known you wouldn't understand," she said.

"Guess you should." He shook his head. "Look, Case, forget what I said about crash landings. Cynic's my middle name. You love Mr. Smith. Mr. Smith loves you. That's good enough for now. Just hang on to that and don't question where it came from."

"But . . ."

He held up a hand as if he were stopping traffic. "Don't say one more word about dark clouds or magic perfume. I don't want to have to get you committed to Western State."

"You do think I'm crazy."

He laughed, then kept on laughing. "Come on, Case. This is me, The Grange, remember? Get off it."

"Okay," she said gloomily. "But you just wait and see. Something bad's going to happen. I can feel it."

"Worst thing's going to happen, I'm going to invite you to dinner tonight. That's why I'm here. Seems to me you need a good dinner, bring you down to earth. Going to have some great salmon steaks fresh off the boat—stuffed with onion and garlic and lemon, and grilled over charcoal—served with broccoli, little new potatoes. Some of chef Patrick's own tartar sauce."

Skip's restaurant specialized in seafood, which Casey loved. Regretfully she shook her head. "Barbara Harriman's giving a baby shower for Justin's sister tonight. I promised I'd go."

"Justin going to be there?" Skip asked in what was apparently supposed to be a casual voice.

Casey gave him an exasperated look. Justin hadn't even called her since she'd broken off with him, which Skip well knew. She wasn't so much disappointed in Justin as she was in her own judgment. She'd thought he might at least have checked up on her for friendship's sake. But apparently he hadn't even missed her.

She contented herself with saying "It's a ladies-only shower."

"Good." He turned to go.

"I'm sorry I can't make it for dinner, Skip," she said.

He shrugged, but she could see he was disappointed. Feeling so strung out herself, she was more sensitive than ever to the air of loneliness that seemed to hang over him. She was definitely going to ask Barbara about her lobbyist friend tonight.

"How about tomorrow?" she asked.

He hesitated in the doorway and turned around, his eyes narrowing. "No date tomorrow, either? Is that what all of this gloom and doom's about? What happened? Mr. Smith didn't respect you in the morning?"

She made a face at him. "Michel's busy all week."

"He's still driving the shuttle bus?"

"He's through with all part-time jobs. He's got a couple of potential clients. One possible job is for a roof garden on the new Cartwright Tower—quite a challenge. I'll tell you all about it when we jog tomorrow," she added, seeing that someone was about to enter the shop.

Skip moved out of the way, to reveal Michel looking devastatingly elegant in a beautifully cut, navy blue blazer and gray slacks with a striped white shirt and red tie. The cloud that had been hanging over Casey lifted as delight warmed her from the inside out. She hadn't expected to see Michel until later in the week.

A second later, as the two men shook hands, the cloud returned. Michel's face was set in a very grim expression. He was making an attempt to smile at Skip, but the strain in his face was in marked contrast to his usual whimsical grin.

"Something's wrong?" Casey asked.

"I am afraid so," Michel answered mournfully.

Casey's heart sank. Once again her thoughts were being interpreted into reality. The dark cloud was hovering right over her head now.

"Leave you to it," Skip said tactfully, and left at once.

Casey went to Michel immediately. "What is it?" she asked. "Did the police come after you again?"

He shook his head, then put his arms around her and held her very tightly for a moment. "I have received a phone call from home," he murmured against her hair.

Casey's stomach tightened into a knot.

Setting her away from him, Michel looked down at her solemnly. "Grandpère has had a heart attack," he said flatly. "My mother telephoned while I was away with you and left a message on my answering machine. I knew at once what it must be—her voice sounded so unnatural. I tried to call back but there was some difficulty on the overseas lines and I could not reach her until this morning."

"He's not—"

"No. Evidently it was a fairly mild attack and there is no apparent damage to the heart itself, so the doctors do not see a need to operate at this time. Grandpère is strong, Casey, but you understand he is an old man, almost eighty years. I am afraid—"

"You're going to see him, aren't you?"

"I must, Casey. You understand that even though we have been estranged, Grandpère is still most important to me. Even if we have disagreements in our family, we still care very deeply about one another. The family is like a tree, solid and protective, with roots that go deeply into the soil." He let out a shaky-sounding breath and she saw that there was moisture in his eyes.

"Alors," he said firmly, obviously fighting for control, "I have booked on a flight leaving this evening. My mother said Grandpère has asked repeatedly for me. Even if that were not so—"

"I understand."

"I do not know how long I will be gone."

It was over. He would go home to France and he would never come back. Casey took a deep, steadying breath. How could she be so concerned about herself when Michel was so dreadfully worried? He obviously hadn't slept all night. A thought occurred to her. "What about the police?" she asked. "I mean, aren't they going to be suspicious if you disappear—"

"I called Sergeant Bennett this morning," he explained. "No one had said I must not leave town, but I did not want to find out later that it was so." He shrugged. "He said I am free to go wherever I wish, but that I should get in touch on my return so he can report progress to me." He frowned and shook his head. "This is not a friendly man. Very gruff."

Something clutched tightly in Casey's throat. What if Michel decided this was not a friendly country and he'd rather not come back? What if his mother persuaded him his duty lay with his grandfather? No, she was being silly. He had a business to return to. A new office. A couple of potential clients. *Potential.* No contracts yet, her traitorous brain reminded her.

"The police have to realize you can't possibly be guilty," she said.

"I am afraid that is wishful thinking, *ma chérie.*" He held her close again for a moment, his lips to her forehead.

"What's going to happen with the Cartwright Tower and the other job in Bellevue?" she asked when he released her, then wished she hadn't. He was going to think she was putting up barriers, trying to persuade him not to leave.

He managed a small smile. "It is all right. I have to prepare detailed renderings of the finished landscaping and I can do that while I am away. I have already surveyed both sites. And Richard Harlan has promised to get behind our landlord and make sure he proceeds with my office."

He looked at her solemnly. "I must go, Casey. I have many preparations to take care of."

"I know." She sighed. "I'll miss you, Michel." The understatement of the year, she thought. Since he had burst into her life she had lived for every moment they had spent together. The thought of being without him . . .

"And I will miss you." His fingers cupped her chin, his thumb lightly stroking her lower lip, causing her breath to get tangled up in her chest. "I will think always of our weekend together," he said softly.

That sounded terribly final, she thought even as he put his arms around her and kissed her very lovingly and thoroughly, his mouth warm on hers, his breath sweet in her mouth. Then he tore himself away and walked out hurriedly without looking back.

The empty shop seemed to echo all around her. And Monday was rarely a busy day. It stretched ahead endlessly. That was the trouble with touching the heights, she thought; it was such a long way down the other side to the depths. At least with Justin she hadn't felt she was living on a roller coaster, ready to hurtle downward into freefall any minute.

What did she really want? she wondered.

To be with Michel always, the answer came back.

Sarah smiled in her usual sweet way, but her round face looked pinched as though the heat were getting to her. "Sure can," she said. "People are pretty generous, Casey. You'd be surprised. Might be more so if I could play a fiddle or a trombone like the guys that hang around Pike Place Market—but I never could carry a tune."

"I meant from the state or the city," Casey explained.

"I know what you meant," Sarah responded with a sigh. "Don't think I didn't try that route. Found me a real nice place to stay—free room, food, medical care, lots of company. Only problem was the pressure. Nice people there, but all the time pressuring me—not in so many words, you understand—but still and all, what they were saying was 'Better you give up this child.'"

"They can't make you give away your baby," Casey protested.

"I know that. Nobody came out and said I should. Counselors just told me how many people are waiting to adopt a child, how many people have nice homes, lots of money to educate a child, told me how many people can't have children, would be happy to take mine. Doing them a terrific favor as well as making sure of a better life for my baby, if I just happened to decide to give her up." She shrugged. "I thought I could hold out until the baby was born and I could get out of there, but then at three o'clock one morning I caught myself thinking maybe they were right, maybe it would be better for my baby if I gave her away. And that scared me so much I hightailed it out of that place soon as the sun came up." She frowned. "I never did have anyone to love, Casey. Maybe this baby's my only chance." Her face tightened. "I'll find a way to take care of her. Never you fear."

"Her?" Casey queried.

Sarah grinned. "Haven't had no test, but I *know*, right deep inside, I know this is a girl. Got a name picked out already—Amanda. Nice, huh?"

"That's a pretty name," Casey agreed. Her legs were going to sleep. She stood up, fumbled in her purse and put a five-dollar bill in Sarah's can, ignoring her protests. "You're still staying with your friend?" she asked.

Sarah's gaze shifted as if she didn't want to meet Casey's eyes. "You have a place to stay?" Casey persisted.

"Don't worry about me, Casey," the girl said. "Me and Amanda are doing just fine."

Casey glanced at her watch. She was already late for the shower. "I'll see you again," she told her.

Sarah's singularly sweet smile lit up her round face. "I'll be here," she said.

THE CONTRAST WAS so great that Casey was disoriented for the first half hour. Marilyn Kendrick, née Boyd, was dressed in a pale blue silk crepe maternity suit that had designer written all over it. Her pretty face, so like Justin's, was beautifully made-up and glowing with health. Her straight blond hair was newly washed and swung when she moved her head. Her fingernails, like those of the other women present, had been recently manicured, coated carefully with rose-colored polish to match her lipstick. She looked cared for, indulged, loved, as surely every pregnant woman had a right to be.

She was going to have to do something about Sarah Bailey, Casey decided.

It was one of those showers where everyone had to play games—not one of Casey's favorite occupations at the best of times, but at least it beat the small talk during dinner about recent trips to Vegas and Hawaii and cruises to the Cayman Islands—conversation in which she could not possibly join. All the same, when she was feeling bereft and worried about Michel, concerned about Sarah Bailey, it seemed inane to spend time trying to remember which baby-care items had been on the tray before it was whisked out of sight, what baby-related words could be formed out of the indecipherable anagrams listed on a piece of paper.

Casey wished she hadn't come.

Where would she rather be? she chided herself. In her own studio apartment staring at the paneled walls?

No, she'd rather be wading with Michel at the edge of the Pacific Ocean, or flying the dragon kite with the long, long tail—the Highest-Flying Kite in the History of the Universe.

Thinking of Michel, she could feel his naked body against hers, his mouth kissing her warmly, passionately, his hands touching her in intimate places. There was such a vacant space in her life, suddenly. Was it all over?

"Are you okay?" Barbara Harriman asked as the other women started gathering gifts to lay at Marilyn's feet.

Casey managed a smile. "Time of the month," she said. It was partly true, her period had started around midafternoon, but it didn't ever affect her badly as it did some women.

"Heard you had a new boyfriend," Barbara murmured, sitting down next to her. "Frenchman? Shuttle-bus driver?"

From Marilyn via Justin, no doubt. Out of sheer cussedness, Casey was tempted to let Barbara go on believing Michel was a shuttle-bus driver. But that wouldn't be honest, and Barbara was her friend. "The shuttle-bus driving was temporary," she explained. "He's actually a landscape architect with Harlan and Fawcett."

Barbara's slim eyebrows arched. "They did the Attwater grounds in Bellevue. Very pricey." She looked impressed. "How come Justin didn't tell me all that?"

So she'd got the word directly from Justin.

Casey laughed shortly. "I didn't find it necessary to tell him," she admitted. "He was acting rather snobbish at the time."

She'd expected Barbara to laugh, too, but the other woman just nodded vaguely, apparently preoccupied. She was looking very thin, Casey thought. Perhaps because she was wearing a black silk jumpsuit. No, she was thinner in the face, too.

Barbara was on a perennial diet she'd crafted for herself. She starved all week, ate whatever she wanted to on weekends. It worked for her, she'd insisted to Casey often. Casey wasn't sure how anyone could exist on the small amounts of food Barbara ate during the week, but she'd always seemed pretty healthy before. Tonight her narrow face looked sallow and there were lines in her forehead that hadn't been there before. Her mass of curly auburn hair had lost its shine. She and Marilyn were the same age—twenty-nine—but Marilyn, pregnant as she was, looked far younger tonight. "Are *you* okay?" Casey asked.

"Mentally or physically?" Barbara asked with a wry smile.

There *was* something wrong, then. "Either or," Casey said.

"Physically, great," she answered. "I even lost some weight without trying. Mentally—about to become relieved, I think. Lyle and I have filed for divorce, Casey."

She had lowered her voice, so evidently her other friends didn't know about this yet. Probably she hadn't wanted to cast a blight on Marilyn's shower. Barbara was like that, which was one of the reasons Casey liked her so much.

Shocked, she stared at the other woman. She would have said Lyle and Barbara Harriman were set for life. The marriage of the handsome and wealthy, young state senator and the equally rich, always beautifully groomed and dressed descendant of one of the state's original timber barons had seemed made in heaven when the wedding took place five years earlier. And whenever Casey had seen the attractive couple—which, granted, had usually been at one or another of their fabulous parties—they had seemed devoted to each other. She had a photograph of them in an album at home—the two of them in evening dress, standing together in front of that marble fireplace over there in this very same penthouse, champagne flutes raised, wishing their guests a Happy New Year, Lyle's tuxedo-clad arm around Barbara's bare shoulders, their faces radiant with well-being. The Beautiful People personified.

It is easier for a camel to go through the eye of a needle, than for a rich man to enter into the kingdom of God, Casey's father intoned. He had never missed an opportunity to rub that one in, Casey thought.

"No babies," Barbara explained. "Lyle wants sons to carry on the family name, to follow him and his father and his father's father into politics. Doctor says I can't have any babies. So, goodbye Lyle."

Her voice was bitter. For which Casey couldn't blame her. Lyle and his father and his father's father. The words reminded her of Michel and his family. The dynasty syndrome was alive and well in many countries, she reflected.

How difficult this shower must be for Barbara, watching Marilyn's obvious happiness and excitement as she sat there surrounded by gifts.

"I'm sorry, Barb," Casey murmured, wishing she could think of something comforting to say.

Barbara shrugged. "There was a lot of other stuff going on," she said flatly. "Tamara Stevenson, for one."

Tamara Stevenson was a local photographic model, twenty-two years old, nubile, usually posing wearing fabulous furs or leaning on the hood of an expensive sports car. She had helped raise money for Lyle's last campaign, Casey remembered. At the time she had wondered why—Tamara hadn't seemed too politically aware.

Barbara's thin hand touched hers lightly. "Don't start worrying about me, Casey. I'm a survivor." Standing, she went over to Marilyn's side. "Let's get this show on the road," she said brightly. "Leslie, how about you make sure the cards and gifts stay together. Dorrie—you get to make the ribbon bouquet."

The gifts seemed endless—designer-made baby togs, an engraved sterling-silver spoon and cup, the very best crib-sheets and receiving blankets, a car seat, a stroller, a white wicker cradle lined with satin—everything any new baby could possibly need for the first year of life. Maybe she should ask for a doggie bag, Casey thought—she could carry off a few items for Sarah Bailey. No one would even miss them amongst all this wealth of generosity.

Casey's own gift almost moved Marilyn to tears. It was a christening gown, wonderfully hand-embroidered in white on white. She'd bought it at the same antique show where she'd run into Inga and her magic perfume. Maybe she should try to track Inga down and see if she had any magic potion that would bring Sarah her heart's desire, she reflected. It was so little to ask—just a home and enough money to raise a daughter.

"Thank you, Casey, it's beautiful," Marilyn said, her blue eyes, so like Justin's, shining with affection. Earlier, Marilyn had seemed to feel uncomfortable in Casey's presence. It was the first time Casey had seen her since she and Justin had broken up. But now, when Casey went over to her to give her a hug, she was her friendly self. "I'm sorry I'm not going to get you for a sister," Marilyn whispered.

Even though you were in agreement with Justin about the need for a rich spouse? Casey thought drily. But she wasn't going to say anything of the sort. The Boyd plan seemed to have worked in Marilyn's case, anyway; Marilyn seemed serenely happy. Casey smiled at her. "We can still be friends, right?"

"Right," Marilyn said firmly. It was evidently okay to have a friend who wasn't rich.

That awkwardness over, Casey remembered her other mission tonight. Taking Barbara aside as Leslie and Dorrie cut the cake and began serving coffee, she asked, "What was the name of that really pretty black woman who was at your Christmas party? She said she was a lobbyist for some consumer group. I was hoping she'd be here tonight.''

"Kristi Wentworth?"

"That's the one.''

"She was invited, but she's in the other Washington this week. You liked her? She's one of the brightest women I know. Intimidates me, though. Only woman I ever met who understands world economy.''

Casey laughed. "That would intimidate me, too. But I wondered—is she single?''

"Sure is. And wishes she wasn't.''

"Really? I might just know somebody.''

Barbara grinned. "That's our girl, Casey—always working to make people happy. Who's your candidate?''

Not wanting to tamper with Skip's privacy, Casey answered vaguely. "He owns a restaurant in town.''

Barbara nodded. "That would do it. Kristi's looking for somebody solid. Needs someone to support her habit, she says.''

"Her habit?" Casey echoed, feeling alarmed.

"Born to shop," Barbara said with a grin.

"Oh." Casey was relieved and disappointed at the same time. The last person Skip needed was someone to spend his money. Brenda had already fleeced him out of enough of his hard-earned capital. Scratch one lobbyist from the field, she thought.

"You want me to have Kristi give you a call?" Barbara asked.

Casey shook her head. "I'll call her," she replied, knowing she wouldn't.

SHE COULDN'T GET the difference between Marilyn Kendrick's pregnancy and Sarah's out of her mind.

Tossing and turning all night, she kept contrasting Marilyn's blue crepe suit with Sarah's T-shirt and jeans; Marilyn's flushed and beaming face with Sarah's sweet but strained expression. She should have taken up a collection, she told herself. All those wealthy women...

She had eaten too much, that was the problem. Her stomach had never accustomed itself to rich food. There had been times during her childhood when there wasn't much food at all. Whenever she did overindulge, she was reminded of the gnawing ache of a stomach that hadn't received quite enough nourishment. Sarah would know that sensation, she felt sure.

What a contrast between that laden buffet table tonight and Sarah's lone paper bag containing two carrots, a potato and a cabbage.

It wasn't fair. It never had been fair.

THE SUNSHINE THAT HAD blessed the Puget Sound region for several days was gone the following morning. Casey awoke feeling bleary-eyed. There was emptiness all around her—not just in her physical space, but in the knowledge that Michel was no longer in the city, not even in the country.

She had to stop thinking about him for a while, she decided, pulling back the covers and setting her feet firmly on the planked wooden floor. She couldn't do anything about Michel's absence, so she just had to accept it and carry on with her life. And the first thing she had to do was go jogging with Skip. Some exercise would make her feel better; it always did.

The shop was fairly busy that morning. There were several conventions in town and some of the women had decided to spend the cloudy morning shopping for bargains. Casey didn't have time to think of Michel, but about midmorning a drizzly rain started falling and she began to worry about Sarah, instead.

At noon she impulsively locked the shop and drove up the hill. Sure enough, Sarah was sitting in her old spot, pulled back under the store's overhang, as close as possible to the wall, her back resting against a duffel bag. She was wearing a blue denim jacket over her T-shirt. It was as clean as the rest of her, but it had definitely seen better days, and there was no way it would close over her belly.

Casey tapped her horn and signaled Sarah over, wincing as the girl lumbered stiffly to her feet. "Hey, Casey," Sarah greeted her. Her voice was cheerful enough, but her wide smile didn't quite reach her eyes.

"I want you to come with me," Casey said.

Sarah studied her face for a full minute, then replied, "Okay," and went back to get her coffee can and the duffel bag and the square of blanket she usually sat on.

"Where're we going?" she asked as Casey drove down the hill.

"My place," Casey said. "I couldn't sleep last night for worrying about you. I want to make sure you get at least one good meal in you today."

Sarah chuckled. "I'm not going to argue with you. Food sounds pretty good to me anytime."

"Did you have breakfast?"

She nodded. "Oatmeal and banana. Big glass of milk. I told you I'm feeding this baby right."

"Where did you have it?"

"Little café I know."

"You didn't have anywhere to cook?"

Sarah stole a glance at her. "Been doing some high-powered guessing, haven't you?" She let out a long breath. "Okay, Casey. Yes, I'm back on the street again. My friend's boyfriend decided he wanted his privacy back."

"When?"

"Sunday."

"Why didn't you tell me yesterday?"

"Not your responsibility, Casey."

"Of course it is. Nobody should have to sleep on the street."

"I slept in a shelter," Sarah said. "Anyway, lots of people sleep on the street, you know. You going to take in all of them? Winos, too?"

Casey grinned wryly. "I would if I could, believe me."

Sarah patted her arm. "You're good people, Casey. And I like that you're going to feed me lunch. But I don't want you worrying about me anymore. Okay?"

Casey didn't answer. And she didn't say a whole lot as she heated some of her homemade vegetable soup and French rolls in her tiny kitchen area. Sarah did most of the talking. "This is a nice apartment," she said first, looking around. "Even if it's only one room, it looks like you could swing a fair-size kitten in here. Maybe even two." She shook her head. "You should see my friend's place. Nine-by-twelve, kitchen included. Share the john down the hall. Not clean." She made a face. "Anything I like, it's a clean house." She nodded approvingly, still looking around. "This is one of those old buildings got restored, huh? Would you look at that paneling! Do you light fires in the winter in the fireplace?"

Casey shook her head. "My landlord worries about the chimneys, so we're not allowed to actually use the fireplaces."

"Well, it looks pretty, anyway. I like the way you've furnished the place, too. Always did like blue and white together. You live here alone? No husband?"

"No husband," Casey replied.

"Boyfriend?"

Casey's stomach tightened, thinking of Michel. "He's out of town right now." Where are you, Michel? What are you doing right now? Please come back soon. Please come back.

"Nice guy, I bet," Sarah said.

"Yes."

Sarah nodded. "He send you those blue flowers?"

"The delphiniums, yes. Michel grew them himself. He designs gardens. A young man who lives in Michel's apartment complex brings the flowers to my shop regularly."

Sidney was a nice guy, too, she thought abruptly. Maybe she should introduce him to Sarah. Maybe... She sighed. Sidney had all he could handle, putting himself through university.

"You sleep on that pretty daybed?" Sarah asked.

Casey shook her head. "The sofa's a pull-out couch."

"Nice furniture," Sarah said again. "I guess you like old stuff, huh?"

"They're mostly antiques, yes," Casey explained. "I spend a lot of time at flea marts and antique shows looking for vintage clothing and jewelry for my shop, so I pick up bargains in furniture when I see them."

"Must be fun, huh, going to shows like that?"

Casey nodded. "I meet a lot of interesting people. Some dealers travel up and down the West Coast, going to all the shows. You should hear the gossip that goes on."

She frowned, aware that something she'd said was important for some unknown reason.

"Never did think I liked antiques," Sarah murmured. "Used to think all I ever wanted in life was a white leather sofa. Saw one once in The Bon—prettiest thing. But this stuff is real homey. Can I try the rocker?"

"Be my guest," Casey said vaguely, still pondering.

Sarah took off her shabby jacket and rocked for a while in silence, then laid her head back against the rails and closed her eyes. When the strain left her face she looked about fifteen years old.

Dealers. Traveling up and down the coast. Hearing all the gossip. Reading the local newspapers. Talking to customers. What if they heard about some young punk who was fleecing senior citizens, pretending to treat carpenter ants? Casey knew at least a dozen nomadic dealers. She had their business cards.

"Feels good," Sarah declared, opening her eyes. "Feels right for Amanda, rocking like that. Soothing, maybe. Not that I mind her kicking. Least when she's kicking I know she's healthy."

"You don't have any family who could take care of you?" Casey asked as she ladled steaming soup into bowls. What if she called the dealers she knew? Asked them to keep their eyes and ears open?

Sarah shook her head, her cluster of braids swinging, her face closing. Okay, Casey thought, you've a right to your privacy, I agree.

"Let's eat," she said, and found to her surprise she was hungry herself. Having thought of a possible way to help Michel, she felt optimistic again. What if he called her and she was able to tell him she'd cleared his name? Then he'd be sure to come back. She began to feel excited. Her soup tasted as good to her as it obviously did to Sarah. Sarah passed over her bowl for two refills and went through three rolls before pronouncing herself satisfied.

"That's the best soup I ever tasted in nineteen years," she said extravagantly.

"That's how old you are?"

"Going on twenty. Come January." Her face looked rounder than ever, Casey thought. It was as though the simple meal had filled her out.

"Well," she announced after she and Casey had finished their coffee, "guess I'd better be getting back to my beat."

She stood up and pulled on her jacket.

"It's still raining," Casey said after glancing out the window.

"People go shopping, even when it rains," Sarah pointed out. "I have to stay with it, Casey. Only two-and-a-half more months to go."

Casey looked at her. Her face had assumed its pinched look again. There was no way Casey could possibly send her back out to the street—shelter or no shelter. Having lost sleep over her, having fed her, she was committed.

"You can stay here," she blurted out.

Sarah looked at her as if she'd suddenly grown two heads. "What did you say?"

"I said you can stay here, live here. Until after the baby's born and you can get a job and get back on your feet. I can't bear to think of you sitting on that sidewalk. I know there's not much room here, but we can manage. I'm gone most of the day, anyway."

Sarah was staring at her, openmouthed. Feeling awkward, Casey babbled on. "You could have the daybed. It's a fairly firm mattress, but comfortable enough. About the only problem you might have is with the shower. The shower head is shot, so the pressure's abysmal. It's hard to get shampoo out of your hair. I've reported it to the landlord, but he's not the swiftest when it comes to repairs."

"But I have to go begging," Sarah said faintly, finally finding her voice. "It takes a lot of money to have a baby, Casey. I don't have nearly enough saved up yet."

"We'll get the money some other way," Casey told her firmly. "We'll work it out together."

Sarah put down the duffel bag she'd picked up and looked slowly around Casey's apartment, her gaze lingering on the mullioned windows and the high ceiling. Then she looked at Casey. "You mean it, don't you?" Her voice was a whisper.

Casey nodded.

Sarah sat down heavily on the rocking chair and looked at her again, her brown eyes shining with something that looked suspiciously like moisture. A moment later, her shoulders slumped as she buried her face in her hands and burst into tears.

CHAPTER TEN

IN THE GRANGE RESTAURANT'S early days, Skip and chef Patrick MacMurray had spent months developing the ultimate clam chowder. Now they proudly advertised it as the best in the West. To be sure it stayed that way, Skip and Patrick always supervised its preparation personally. They were doing so on Friday morning when Skip's old friend Luther Everett walked into the kitchen.

Skip felt as though someone had poked him with an electric cattle prod in some vital spot, jolting him from toes to scalp. The last time he had seen Luther was the day before Brenda left town with him. He had not really expected to see his onetime best friend again. "What's happenin', Luther?" he asked warily as he came around the end of the kitchen island.

Luther held his hand out but Skip, wiping his own hands on a dish towel, pretended not to see it. There were limits, after all. "What you needing from me this time?" he asked. "Don't have any more wives to spare."

Luther winced. He was two years older than Skip, almost as tall but slender, rangy rather than muscular. He looked a little baggier under the eyes than he used to, Skip noticed, and he'd developed a bit of a stoop—his posture wasn't nearly as upright as it once was. He'd lost some hair, too. Living with Brenda could age anyone.

"Can we talk?" Luther asked.

Skip led the way to the bar. He didn't usually drink before evening, and then moderately, but sometimes an exception seemed called for. "Make it short," he said grimly, gesturing at a table. "Got work to do." He gathered up a couple of cans of Rainier from the bartender, turned a chair around, straddled it and took a healthy swig of beer. "So, talk," he commanded.

Luther popped his own can open, but didn't drink, just cradled it between his palms as if he needed to cool them off. Sweating, maybe. "Heard from Brenda you've been providing money right along," he said.

Skip raised his eyebrows. "You telling me you didn't know?"

Luther shook his head. "She told me she had this special savings account for emergencies."

Skip laughed shortly. "Well, guess there was some truth to that."

Luther obviously didn't want to meet his eyes, but forced himself to do so. He never had lacked courage. "Made me feel . . . small," he confessed.

Skip nodded.

There was a silence. Once upon a time, he and Luther could spend hours rapping over a can of beer—swapping Vietnam stories, woman stories, sports stories—Luther had played baseball in college until a bum elbow sidelined him permanently. One of Skip's sweetest memories was of twenty-year-old Luther making it look easy to throw a ball at ninety-some miles an hour to a seventeen-inch plate, sixty feet away.

Now there was constraint between them. Which was hardly surprising. "I want you to know it won't happen again, Grange," Luther said.

"Uh-huh."

"And I fully intend paying you back the money you gave Brenda since we..."

He seemed to be searching for a phrase. Skip was happy to supply one. "Since you stabbed me in the back?"

Luther's skin took on a darker tinge but he didn't try to defend himself. "Also want you to know I'm employed again. The savings and loan I worked for just got revamped into a bank. Manager wants me back as his assistant. Might make manager myself, someday, he says."

"Good news," Skip replied flatly.

Luther's eyes shifted. "Guess I couldn't expect much of a reception," he said.

"You're lucky I didn't greet you with my fist," Skip pointed out.

Luther sighed. "Might have preferred it."

Skip laughed shortly. "Water under the bridge, Luther, my man. Don't have the passion I once had."

"Well. Guess I just wanted you to know Brenda won't be looking for support from you anymore," Luther said, standing up. He started to turn away, the swung back. "Sure do miss our talks," he added.

He looked miserable as a hound someone had chastised with a rolled-up newspaper. Skip would have expected this to make him feel smug, but instead he felt sad. And empty. He wasn't sure what Luther had come looking for unless it was absolution, but he sure as hell didn't have anything to give him. Too bad. All that shared history. Gone.

"They were good days," Luther said heavily.

"Sure were," Skip agreed. "Over now, though."

"I guess so." He hesitated. "I was sorta hoping you might see your way clear to—"

"Some things you don't forgive," Skip said.

Once again Luther turned away. He'd almost reached the door when Skip thought, oh, what the hell—

"Good luck with the new job, Luther," he called out.

Luther turned and flashed a smile that made him look more like his old self. "Thanks, Grange."

On his way out, he passed Casey coming in. Skip saw Casey do a double take, her green eyes widening. "Wasn't that—"

"Yeah," Skip said. "As I live and breathe."

She sat down, eyeing the beer can he was still clutching. "You okay?" she asked.

Skip considered her question, then grinned at her and set the beer aside. Standing up, he turned his chair around the conventional way and sat down again. "As a matter of fact I feel great," he told her. "Pervaded by a whole new mood of optimism."

The surprising thing was that he'd told her the truth. He felt...relieved, unburdened. Not because Luther had told him he didn't have to support Brenda anymore, but because Luther's visit had somehow shucked him of responsibility for Brenda altogether—even emotionally. Brenda was going to be okay with Luther, after all. And Skip didn't have to dread running into Luther somewhere, didn't have to worry that he'd want to slam his fist into the face of the man who had once been closer to him than any brother. The confrontation was over. There wouldn't be another. A dark period of his life was over. Time to pick up and go on.

"How about you?" he asked Casey. She looked pretty as a picture in one of her old-fashioned getups— an olive-green braid-trimmed gown that swept the floor. But her pretty eyes were shadowed and her mouth had a twist to it on one side as though she were biting it.

He hadn't seen Casey since they'd jogged together Tuesday morning and she'd told him about Michel's grandfather. He still wasn't sure what he thought about Michel taking off like that, right after his weekend with Casey. He didn't *seem* like the type who'd lie about his grandfather being ill; but then, as Skip had told Casey earlier, "cynic" was his middle name.

Casey had canceled out their Tuesday dinner date at the last minute, he remembered abruptly, and she'd called and begged off jogging on Thursday without giving a reason. Come to think of it, that was unusual behavior for Casey Templeton. He leaned forward. "You hear from Mr. Smith since he took off?"

She nodded, her face lightening. "He telephones every day. His grandfather's coming along fairly well." She gave him a fair approximation of a grin. "He sends flowers every day, too. He asked the young man I told you about, Sidney Arundel, to bring me a bunch a day without fail."

"So, why aren't you looking on top of the world?"

She shook her head. "Michel told me this morning it was the strangest thing being home again, as if all the strings he'd left behind had wound themselves around him all over again. He's even thinking full-time in French again, he said—he'd gotten so he was thinking part of the time in English." She sighed. "Ever since he left, I've been convinced that he won't be coming back."

Skip discarded the wisecrack about the dangers of clairvoyance that came to his mind. Women in love were too vulnerable—especially when they were in love for the first time.

Getting to be a philosopher in his old age, he decided; then scolded himself. Hell, he wasn't old. He was only thirty-nine. And since Luther's visit, he was beginning to feel more like twenty-nine. "Get you anything?" he asked. "Coffee, maybe?"

She nodded, still chewing on the corner of her lip. "What else, Case?" he asked after he'd signaled the bartender to bring over a coffeepot.

"I need some advice," she said. "I went to Justin yesterday, thinking he might be willing to help. He's teaching summer school, so I caught him in a break between classes. I remembered he had this ongoing savings plan and I thought maybe he'd float me a loan, but he said no."

"You were surprised?" Justin Boyd was a five-percent tipper, he remembered. His waitresses had told him that. The generosity of a man's tips told a lot about him. So did the lack thereof.

Casey smiled wryly. "Not really. But I didn't know what to do, so it seemed worth a try. 'Neither a borrower nor a lender be,' he said. Told me that was his motto." She sniffed. "Justin's a lot like my father was, you know—he had a quote to back up every stand he took."

"Can't imagine you having money trouble," Skip said as he poured coffee for both of them.

"Well, I can't go to the bank manager. I'm meeting all my payments, of course, but I'm not exactly showing a huge profit. I make enough to support myself, though," she added with a certain amount of pride.

"Then what's the problem?"

"Sarah. Sarah Bailey." She took a sip of coffee, then put the cup down and met Skip's questioning gaze. "I don't want a lecture, Skip. I already had one from Justin. I'm too inclined to take in strays, he said. Then he very pointedly asked about Michel. When I told him Michel had gone back to France temporarily, he said I shouldn't expect anything to come of my relationship with Michel; he was obviously just using me and I'm always too willing to be used." She laughed. "He made me so mad, I told him the Good Samaritan story. He wasn't impressed."

"Refresh my memory."

"The Good Samaritan? It's in the Bible. One of my dad's favorites. It's the story of a man who comes down from Jerusalem to Jericho and falls among thieves, who beat him up and leave him at the side of the road. A couple of people approach, but cross the street to avoid responsibility. But then a Samaritan comes along and takes the injured man to an inn and takes care of him. So now, Good Samaritan has come to mean someone who comes to the aid of a stranger."

"Has a certain familiarity to it."

Casey gave him her fondest smile. "It should do—as long as I've known you, you've lived by it."

He felt immensely flattered by what she'd said, but still not too clear about her problem. "Who's the Good Samaritan in this case?" he asked.

"Oh!" She blushed endearingly. "I guess I haven't really explained, have I? I've, well, I've taken someone in."

"Another stray as Justin would say?"

"Sarah Bailey. But she's not the problem," Casey said earnestly. "I really enjoy having her. She scrubs my apartment until it shines every day, has dinner on the table when I get home.'' She laughed. ''Well, to tell the truth, she's not much of a cook, but we're hoping she'll improve with practice. But she's always cheerful and it's fun to be around her. We've stayed up late every night since Tuesday, when she moved in, talking about ourselves. It's like having a sister.''

''Who is Sarah Bailey and where did you find her?'' Skip asked, noticing that no real information was forthcoming.

''Well, actually, she was on the street and—''

''She's a hooker!''

The bartender's head had come up. Skip shot him an apologetic grin and lowered his voice. ''You're telling me you took in a prostitute?''

''No way.'' Casey's cheekbones had flared with color. ''Sarah's a good girl. She's just been unfortunate. And she's an orphan, Skip. When I met her, she was... begging.''

''She can't work like the rest of us poor slobs?''

''She's pregnant.''

''Uh-huh.''

''Don't be snide, Skip.''

He spread his palms open on the table. ''What did I say?''

''It's not what you said, it's the way you always say *uh-huh,* flat like that. It means you're thinking the worst. I know you, Skip.''

''Okay, I'll think the best. Poor Sarah's husband died after making her pregnant?''

''She didn't have a husband. There's no man involved.''

''It's an immaculate conception?''

Casey glared at him. "She doesn't want the father to know about the baby. She doesn't want him to have any part of Amanda." She cleared her throat in an embarrassed way. "Sarah's sure it's a girl, wants to call it Amanda."

"I'm beginning to get the picture. Sarah can't get a job because she's pregnant, so instead of going to the state or the city for help, she goes begging on the street. And along comes Casey Templeton, prize sucker, mainstay of the local wino population."

"I am not."

"Who else donates as much money to their cause?"

"They must spend *some* of it on food."

"Uh-huh. As I was saying. Mainstay of the winos, rescuer of Frenchmen who get hauled off to jail—"

"Michel was innocent."

"And where is he now?"

"I told you I already had a lecture. I don't need another one," she said, green eyes flashing. "You're as bad as Justin." She stood and for a minute Skip wasn't sure if she was going to hit him or just walk out.

She did neither. She sat down again.

"That's hitting below the belt," Skip told her sternly.

"I know. I'm sorry. I didn't mean it. You're right about me—Justin's right about me. Sometimes I'm pretty dumb. But not where Michel is concerned, nor with Sarah. I just don't know what to do about Sarah, Skip. I can support her okay. I think I can even manage the baby after she gets here. It's the cost of *having* the baby that's the problem. Sarah might even have to have a caesarean. I just don't have the money. That's why I came to you."

"Ah—now we're getting somewhere. You don't really want my advice, you want a donation."

"I do not." Indignation turned Casey's normally creamy complexion to a shade compatible with her hair. "I was hoping for a loan," she said hesitantly.

"For Sarah."

She nodded. "If you can't help, Skip, just say so. I know you've had a lot of expense with Brenda lately. So if it's not possible, I'll quite—"

"As it happens, I've just had a promise of a debt to be repaid. So I'll think about your proposition."

Her whole face brightened. "You will? Oh, Skip, you're such a dear. I just knew—"

"Hold the applause until I reach a decision," he warned.

She stood and came around the table to hug him. "Thank you, Skip," she said in a voice filled with relief. "I'll check back with you, okay? I have to get back to the shop."

Skip sat where he was for a while after she'd left. He shook his head. That girl had the biggest heart in all creation. Taking on a pregnant woman, of all things.

He frowned. What kind of woman was this Sarah Bailey, anyway? Was she taking advantage of Casey? Probably. Was she even really pregnant?

He glanced at his watch. No time like the present to find out. Casey had returned to her shop. He'd just take a look at Sarah Bailey for himself.

SHE WAS PREGNANT, all right. Belly out to here. Homely little barefoot black kid in a bloated T-shirt and blue jeans. Casey hadn't mentioned that she was so young, or that she was black. Of course, Casey always had been color-blind where race was concerned.

"Casey didn't tell me you were just a kid," he said, caught off guard.

The girl's face lit up with a thousand-watt smile. Quite suddenly she wasn't homely anymore. "You're a friend of Casey's?"

"Skip Granger."

"Come on in," she said promptly. "Casey's told me all about you," she added as she gestured him to the couch and sat down in Casey's small rocking chair. "You own the restaurant next to her shop, right?"

Skip nodded. "You ever been in?"

She shook her head, setting a couple of dozen dangling braids to jiggling. Skip had never cared for that particular hairstyle, but on this girl it looked terrific. "At your prices?" she asked. "I've read your menu in that box on the wall. Everything sounds good but, man, it's expensive."

"Worth it," Skip said.

She grinned. She had a wide mouth. Too wide for beauty. Except when she smiled.

"How old are you?" he asked.

"Going on twenty."

Going on twenty. And begging on the streets. There ought to be a law. Probably was.

"How'd you get in this condition, anyway?" he asked.

A sassy look appeared in her brown eyes. "The usual way." Almost immediately she looked contrite. "I'm sorry. I shouldn't be teasing a friend of Casey's."

She was deliberately avoiding his question. He let it pass for now. "Casey says you don't have any folks."

"Never did have a daddy around. Mom died when I was six. Cancer."

Her tone was matter-of-fact, but there was a little-girl-lost expression on her face. "What happened to you then?"

"What is this? Third degree?"

"Just answer the question, kid."

"I'm not a kid. I'm a woman. A mother-to-be."

He had to admit there was a certain dignity about her when she drew herself up like that. "I'm interested, okay?" he said. "Humor me, why don't you."

She gave out with a long-suffering sigh. "My mom's sister took me in. She and her husband didn't have any children."

"They treat you right?"

"Aunt Mamie was good to me."

"Uncle?"

She paused before answering. "Not so hot."

"So then what happened?"

"When I got pregnant, I left home. Left town, too. Had a job as a waitress, figured I could get another one anywhere. And I did. But then I kept getting sick. Barf-type sick. Restaurants don't go much for help throwing up. Bad advertising. Guess you'd know that."

"They fired you?"

"Like a shot. Worked in a department store a couple of months, but kept missing because of getting sick. Early months I had this theory that Amanda was suffering from motion sickness. Every time I stood up, I threw up. Anyway, the department store fired me, too. So then I went to this home where they said they'd take care of me. Which they did—except they kept making it seem like a good idea to give my baby up to somebody else."

"You don't want to do that?"

Her hands immediately went to her swollen abdomen, as though she wanted to protect the child inside. Again Skip made a mental note of her innate dignity. "This is *my* baby," she said simply.

Skip felt himself softening. It was easy to see why Casey had taken this child in. There was a pride about her that was admirable, and a sweetness, an innocence that was endearing. He was almost tempted to adopt her himself. Okay, Case, he told his friend silently, you've got yourself a loan.

"You still didn't tell me how you got in this condition," he pointed out. "I know it doesn't seem to be any of my business, but Casey came to me for help and I'd like to be sure—"

"I'm not some blowsy little hooker playing Casey for a sucker?"

"Obvious to me the minute I saw you that you're not a hooker," Skip said sternly. "Let me put it this way," he added as she grinned apologetically. "Have you told Casey how you got this way?"

She shook her head. How long would it take to put together all those braids, he wondered. Did she have to do that every day, or were they washable as they were? Must be. She was certainly clean. Every part of her shone as though it had been scrubbed. She smelled clean, too. No makeup. Quite a contrast to Brenda. Her dressing table used to be covered with pots and tubes and boxes and brushes. Eye shadow in every color of the rainbow. Enough lipsticks to paint a mural on the side wall of a public building.

"I already told you how I got to be this way," Sarah said quietly after a minute's silence.

He frowned. "You most certainly did not," he began, then saw the pain that was showing in her eyes and caught on. "You said your uncle's treatment of you wasn't so hot."

She nodded.

"He..." Skip couldn't put it into words. Imagining it was bad enough.

"He suddenly noticed I wasn't a child anymore," she said quietly, looking down at her own clasped hands. "Suddenly realized I wasn't related to him except through his marriage. And he'd been supporting me all those years, figured he had something coming in return. Tried to fight him off, but he was bigger than me. That's what it comes down to for women, Mr. Granger. Men get to be bigger, stronger."

"You go to the police?"

She shook her head. "My word against his. He was a respected businessman. I was a nothing. Besides, I didn't want to see his face again, or any other part of him. Didn't want to break my Aunt Mamie's heart, either. I just wanted out of there. So I left. Came to Seattle. Got a job. You know the rest. Took me a while to adjust. There I'd had me a home, friends, a job, loose change in my pocket. All of a sudden I had nothing. Except Amanda."

Skip felt sick. There were times when he despaired of his own sex. Times when he was pretty upset by the opposite sex also, he conceded. Had to keep remembering there were good people on both sides—though it did sometimes seem like the bad people outnumbered the good.

"You want to keep this baby even though—"

"This baby didn't do anything bad, Mr. Granger. This baby has a right to live. This baby is mine."

Her courage and dignity were awesome. Some kind of woman, Skip thought admiringly.

"I'm starved," she announced abruptly. "You want me to fix you some lunch?"

Skip grinned. "Casey told me you're not much for cooking."

She laughed. He sure did like the way her whole face lit up when she laughed or smiled. As if she had her own private lighting system operating from inside. "Got some canned tuna," she said. "Anybody can slap tuna between two slices of bread."

Skip winced and stood up. "You lead me to the tuna," he told her. "I'm going to teach you how to make the best tuna-salad sandwich in the world."

CHAPTER ELEVEN

THERE WAS A HAZE of heat over the flower garden and
Michel was beginning to perspire, but he was much
happier working out here than he was sitting around in
the house. All of his uncles and aunts and some of his
cousins had descended on the château for the weekend—as if his grandmother didn't have enough on her
mind. They all kept creeping in and out of rooms looking lugubrious, asking each other, "How is Grandpère
now, then? What is the latest word?" all of them looking at Michel when they thought he wouldn't notice,
raising their eyebrows at each other, wondering if he
was home to stay.

America seemed very far away.

The roses were glorious, he thought, trying to cheer
himself up. A few years ago, he had planted this area of
the garden with fragrance in mind, and it had been
maintained in the same fashion, with lemon-scented vi-
burnum, woolly thyme creeping between the paving
stones, clove-scented Hesperis. And over all, the rasp-
berry-scented bourbon rose—"Zephorine Drouhin"—
dominated. He had introduced the thornless climber
himself, and now it blanketed the trellised arch over the
walkway, reminding him of the roses Casey had admired on their trip to the San Juan islands.

The pink cabbage roses were also unsurpassed for
scent. He inhaled deeply, as he tidied the ground around

them. Again he was reminded of Casey. The very air seemed to speak her name. But her perfume had a deeper note; spicy rather than sweet. Casey, he thought. Sweet, sweet Casey. She seemed very far away also. Part of another life, another dream. He had a sudden mental image of her lying in his arms in that oh-so-soft feather bed, her creamy skin glowing under the lamplight, her hair flaming in wild disarray over the pillows, her bare breasts inviting his touch, his mouth.

"What are you doing, Michel?" his mother asked.

Michel started guiltily and got to his feet. As far as he knew, his mother couldn't read his mind, so what he was doing was fairly obvious. It followed, then, that Jeanne was expressing disapproval rather than curiosity.

"I'm weeding, *Maman,*" he answered mildly.

"We employ several people to take care of such tasks," she pointed out. "If the flower beds need attention, then it is obvious the head gardener should be informed."

Michel sighed. "It is perhaps more that I need to weed the garden than that the garden needs to be weeded," he said. He stepped carefully over the border plants to join his mother on the old brick path. She was looking lovely as always in a white linen dress and a wide-brimmed straw hat. At fifty-five, she looked more like forty. She had been well taken care of, always, and had taken care of herself, protecting her complexion, watching her diet, buying the prettiest of clothes.

"You are worried about your grandfather?" she asked.

"Aren't you?"

"Extremely. He has not been the same since you left, Michel." There wasn't a hint of reproach in her voice, but the pressure was unmistakably there.

They started walking along the path to the house, Michel stopping at a faucet to wash his hands. "According to the doctors, it is Grandpère's life-style that brought on the heart attack," he said carefully. "He has never been the calmest of men. He adores rich foods. And he has always, as long as I can remember, worked far too hard."

"He is a perfectionist, yes," Jeanne murmured. "But I was not blaming you for his heart attack, my son. I was thinking that now we have been warned, it is up to us to guard his health, to give in to him instead of arguing with him."

"You mean you want *me* to give in to him," Michel said grimly. "You've given in to him ever since my father died."

"Not at all. I wanted to come back home even before I lost your father. I missed my family very much."

Michel wondered, not for the first time, if his parents' marriage would have lasted if his father had lived. Possibly not. From what he had heard of Conrad Smith, he would not have willingly signed his life over in the service of Jean-Paul Rapide.

"You had the chance to remarry several times," Michel pointed out. "Just because Grandpère disapproved of every one of the men, you refused to consider any of them."

"I have always respected my father's opinion."

How had *his* father won her? Michel wondered. Actually, he knew the answer. Conrad had eloped with Jeanne without waiting to ascertain Jean-Paul's opinion.

"Besides which," his mother continued, tucking her hand into his arm, "I had your future to consider. Your prospects looked far brighter with my own family than with any possible stepfather."

So now she had given up her own happiness to make his future secure. Why was he even arguing, Michel wondered. He knew it was impossible to win an argument with any member of his family. Were he to accuse his mother of trying to make him feel guilty, he knew she would deny any underlying motive.

"Your grandfather wishes you to take lunch with him," she said now, looking up at him from under the brim of her hat. "I think it would be a nice thing for you to do."

"Sure, *Maman*," he agreed flatly. He had come here to see his grandfather, after all; and it was certain that he loved his grandfather. So why did he feel this tightening of his stomach at the prospect of spending time with him? Grandpère did not simply want to enjoy his company, Michel knew. He did not issue invitations to his sickroom unless he had some purpose in mind. Why was it so difficult at such times as this to remember that he was a grown man with a mind of his own?

Jean-Paul Rapide did not fit the image of an invalid. To begin with, he was a big man—almost as tall as Michel, even broader in the shoulders. Propped up in his massive bed against white-linen-covered pillows, he looked vigorous and virile. Snow-white hair sprang from his temples in crisp profusion and there was nothing weak about the fierce brown eyes or the aquiline nose.

His big hands were the only part of him to show his age. Brown-spotted and gnarled, they lay on the white duvet in unnatural stillness. Michel felt a pang of compassion. How Grandpère must abhor being bedridden.

Michel's grandmother was sitting beside her husband's bed, looking down at him. Always slender, she looked frail next to Grandpère—the hand that was lying on top of Jean-Paul's seemed almost transparent. But it was a deceptive frailty; Hélène Rapide was notoriously healthy, and in all the arguments she waged with her husband, she very often won.

"Michel's here," she said to Jean-Paul, lifting her face with a smile to receive Michel's kiss of greeting.

Her smile was as loving, as radiant, as ever. No one had ever had such a beautiful smile, unless it was Casey. Was that what had made him fall in love with Casey—that her smile reminded him of his grandmother? Would she be flattered to know that?

"I'll leave you two alone," Grandmère said, getting to her feet. She was as limber as always—she had never shown any signs of aging as far as her bones and skin were concerned. Only the lines that radiated from her eyes and mouth and the whiteness of her smartly bobbed hair, gave her away. From behind she still looked like a girl.

"No arguing," she commanded her husband, bending over him to straighten the duvet.

"Don't fuss, woman," Jean-Paul told her. The loving look he sent after her retreating back belied the sternness in his voice.

"He's in a grouchy mood," Grandmère said over her shoulder to Michel as she went through the doorway. "Don't let him bully you."

She was right about Grandpère's mood. Jean-Paul spent the first part of their lunchtime complaining about the quality of the meal. The fish was freshly caught and excellently prepared, but it was without the white-butter sauce he so enjoyed. He had also been forbidden alcohol, and for a Frenchman to partake of food without wine to accompany it was a sacrilege.

Sipping his decaffeinated coffee with much grimacing, Jean-Paul finally brought the meeting to order. "It appears I will retire sooner than I expected," he said with a deep sigh.

Michel nodded. "You've earned some rest, Grandpère," he replied.

Jean-Paul glared at him. "Rest?" he repeated harshly. "There will be time enough to rest when I am dead and buried. I do not intend to stagnate, Michel. I merely mean that I am ready to step down from my position. Someone else must push all the buttons. But naturally I will keep a wary eye on the operation of my company."

"Naturally," Michel agreed. He must be agreeable when possible, he told himself. Grandpère was obviously leading up to something—and he was pretty sure what the something was. He'd best save all arguments for when they were really needed.

"So, I must make some decisions. Who is to take my place?"

"Uncle Pierre seems the obvious choice," Michel said, naming his mother's oldest brother.

"Pierre is almost sixty years old. His blood pressure is higher than mine. He'll be lucky to outlive me. And before you trot out my other sons, allow me to point out that André is more interested in the little mistress he keeps in St. Denis, Marcel does not have the brains for the job, and Jacques is too much a yes-man to succeed at the helm. Besides, Jacques does very well with the publicity end of things. He has the charm for it. This job does not require charm. This job requires a strong man with a good mind, a hard head for business and a lot of experience in the manufacture of automobiles.''

"Any one of my cousins would answer to that description, Grandpère.''

"Your cousins are too young.''

"Charles is two years older than I am. Sebastien is my own age. And they are both eminently qualified. Charles is the one of us who is most like you, Grandpère. He lives for the company.''

"But he is so boring, Michel—so earnest always. And his wife, such a homely woman, so fat now from childbearing. How could she preside when Charles must entertain? Your grandmother—''

"Grandmère is the most beautiful woman in the world,'' Michel interrupted. "She is also the most gracious hostess. You cannot expect any other woman to live up to her. Be fair, Grandpère. Charles is earnest because he cares so much about the business. He can't help it if he's a little—stodgy. A CEO doesn't have to be the life of the party. And his wife is not homely at all. A little rounded here and there, perhaps, but look at Renoir's portraits. Plump women can be attractive, too.''

Jean-Paul snorted.

"You have seven grandsons,'' Michel pointed out. "The other six are all mature men, devoted to their wives and families.''

Jean-Paul pounced at once on this new argument. "They are too devoted.'' He looked at Michel sideways. "You, on the other hand, have no other ties. You could concentrate all of your energy on the business.''

"But I don't want to, Grandpère,'' Michel said firmly. "Besides,'' he added in a lighter voice as Jean-

Paul placed a hand in the area of his heart and grimaced dramatically, "I may acquire a wife and family myself."

"You have an interest in that direction?" Jean-Paul asked.

His hand had dropped away from his heart, Michel noted. Best not to mention Casey yet—the questions would go on too long and Grandpère would get upset. "I have no plans to marry at present," he said carefully. "But one never knows when..."

Jean-Paul had made a dismissive gesture with his right hand. "We are not talking about the distant future, Michel. We are talking about now. I need you, my boy. I let you go when you insisted you must investigate your father's country."

Let me go, Michel's mind echoed. Remembering the battle royal he and Jean-Paul had waged three years ago, he could not recall any precise moment when Grandpère had given him permission to leave. Grandpère had a habit of rewriting history to suit himself.

"So," Jean-Paul said now. "You have investigated. Now it is time for you to come home. I need you to take over. I have built everything myself. Now I want to give it all to you. Surely you must accept it."

"I cannot do it, Grandpère," he answered simply. "If it was the only way—if I was the only one who could possibly take over—maybe I'd sacrifice myself. But it isn't the only way, and I'm not the only one."

"Sacrifice?" Jean-Paul echoed.

"That's what it would be, Grandpère. And I think you know it. I have a new life in my father's country. I look upon it as my own country. My new business will be my own—I will make it myself, carve it out of the ground with my own hands, just as you carved Rapide.

Do you not remember how exciting it was when you began Rapide? Can't you possibly understand how I feel?"

Jean-Paul leaned back on his pillows and closed his eyes. His face seemed pale. He was not putting on an act now, Michel was sure. He really was exhausted. Michel's heart turned over with pity. Looking at this situation from Grandpère's point of view, was it really so much for him to ask that his favorite grandson step into his shoes? How many men would turn down the glittering prizes Grandpère wished to lay at Michel's feet—the château and its grounds, the factories, the wealth, the position as one of the highest-paid executives in the nation. Many men would call him a fool. Perhaps he was. Since he had come home he felt the old ties strongly—ties of familiarity, ties of love. One after the other, his grandfather and his mother had spoken to him of duty and family—words that were hard to resist. In the last couple of days he had thought several times that it would be easier to give in than to hold out against all the pressure. "I'd better go now," he said softly. "I'll come back later when you are rested."

"What is the point of it all?" his grandfather answered bitterly. "If I cannot count on you, who can I count on?"

He had known the pressure would build, Michel thought as he descended the great staircase. But he hadn't suspected that his own will would begin to waver.

"Bonjour, Michel," a female voice greeted him from the foot of the staircase.

He was astonished to see Angèle Bertrand, the daughter of the château's closest neighbor. Angèle's father, who owned an import business, was the son of Grandpère's oldest friend. Michel and Angèle had gone to school together and had been close friends until Michel went to university and Angèle was sent off to finishing school in Switzerland. On their return, their families had pushed them together and they had not been unwilling. They had enjoyed a torrid affair that had burned itself out in a few short months. Then they had gone back to being friends. A year or two after that, Angèle had married and had gone to live in Chantilly.

He caught her up in a hug, lifting her off the floor. Angèle was tall but slender, light as thistledown, with silver-blond hair she wore cropped short in a boyish style that emphasized her perfect features.

"But what are you doing here?" he demanded. "Are you visiting your father? Did you bring your husband?" What was the man's name? Peverell—Gilles Peverell.

"I have been home for some time, Michel," she said, after enthusiastically returning his hug. "Gilles and I are divorced. Surely you knew that?"

Something stirred in his memory. His mother had mentioned something of the sort on the telephone a year or so ago. Engrossed in his new life, the news had made little impression on him. But he could hardly tell Angèle he had forgotten.

"Should I offer my sympathies?" he asked.

She shook her head vehemently. "I'm well rid of him, believe me. Such a boring man, Michel. He thought only about his precious racehorses. I cannot believe I lived with him for nine years. I stayed only because my father was against our marriage and I didn't want him telling me 'I told you so.' Which he did, of course."

She made a dismissive motion of her right hand. "I do not wish to even think about Gilles anymore. He is out of my life forever. I thank God daily that I did not have children. I might have felt obliged to stay with him."

She laughed. He had forgotten what a musical laugh she had. It enchanted him now as it had when they were children together.

Taking his hand, she tugged him across the hall. "Come and have a glass of wine with me in the little salon," she invited. "I know you didn't get any with Jean-Paul. If Jean-Paul is not allowed to drink wine, nobody is allowed to drink wine."

"I'd love a glass," Michel said, taking her arm. "I'm feeling the pressure. Grandpère and my mother are after me to come back into the fold. I'm afraid they are very displeased with me because I keep resisting."

She lifted a shoulder gracefully. "They love you, Michel."

He sighed. "I know that. I just wish they loved me enough to let me live my own life."

"You enjoy living in the wilds of America?"

He grinned at her. "I'm hardly camping out in the prairies, Angèle."

She shrugged, and crossed the room to ring for a maid. Angèle would never believe that the United States was a civilized place, Michel knew. To her, as to so many French citizens, there was only one civilized country in the world, and all of the others were to be pitied and looked down upon.

When the wine appeared, Angèle poured prettily for both of them. She was wearing a very attractive full-skirted blue dress that accented the color of her eyes and the daintiness of her figure. Her long legs were bare and tan, her feet encased in blue sandals. Michel had a sudden memory of his own hands caressing those slender feet. She had loved to have her feet touched, had purred like a kitten when he massaged her toes.

Hastily, he accepted his glass of wine and sat down on an upright chair opposite the sofa where she had seated herself, spreading her wide skirt around her.

"Do you remember the summer we came home from school?" she asked, looking at him over the rim of her glass.

How long her eyelashes were. Were they false? he wondered. He didn't remember them being so long. "It was a long time ago," he said uncomfortably.

She nodded, her eyes fixed on his. They were such a lovely shade of blue, like cornflowers. Or perhaps delphiniums. "What happened, Michel?" she asked unexpectedly. "We had something very special together. I remember as if it were yesterday you saying to me, 'Angèle, you are my angel.' And when we made love—surely you cannot have forgotten how incredible we were together. *Très passioné.* Why did we ever stop?"

He moved uncomfortably on the hard chair. "We were very young, only twenty-two, just out of school." He laughed, trying not to sound as nervous as he felt. *"Mon Dieu,* but that was a long time ago. You seemed incredibly sophisticated to me."

"And you seemed incredibly handsome to me." It was still amazing to her when she thought about it, the way four years' absence had turned her old friend, her old *compagnon,* into a desirable man—an *extremely* desirable man. She sipped her wine, regarding him intently. Even in a plain blue shirt and blue jeans and sneakers he was elegant, sexy. "As a matter of fact, you still do," she added.

"You plan to stay with your father permanently?" he asked, after taking a gulp of his wine.

She chuckled softly. He always had changed the subject when he felt uncomfortable. So, then, if she had the power to make him uncomfortable he was not impervious to her charms. "Have I embarrassed you, Michel?" she asked.

He shrugged. "There's no point in discussing old history, Angèle."

Old history indeed. He had evidently conveniently forgotten that he was the one to break things off between them. After seducing her—well, no, that was not entirely fair—the sudden explosion of passion between them had been as much her doing as his. But afterward—it had not been her idea to let things cool off for a while. That had been his suggestion. She'd gone along with his wishes, expecting that after a few weeks or months he would regain his senses and realize they were meant for each other. But it hadn't happened that way, and to save her pride she had made the mistake of marrying the first man to come along and ask her.

"Have my mother or grandfather said anything to you about me?" he asked her, looking at her very directly.

She shrugged. "Jeanne told me you were coming to visit, of course. She knew I was . . . interested."

His eyes narrowed. Did he suspect that his mother had deliberately encouraged her to make her presence known as forcefully as possible? Did he suspect she was supposed to sound him out, find out if there were any weak spots in his future plans, any way she could persuade him to stay in France.

You have one more chance, Angèle, Jeanne had said bluntly. *Michel is coming home for a short visit. It is our last opportunity to persuade him he should not leave again.*

"It's so nice here in the château," Angèle said softly. "Always cool even on the hottest day. You must miss it terribly."

"I think of it, of course," Michel agreed.

"Naturally. It is your home, after all."

"My home is in Seattle now, Angèle."

"You are never homesick?" she asked, making her eyes wide.

"Well, homesick, yes, of course. Sometimes, but..."

Dare she ask him? Was it dangerous to ask him? She wanted to know, needed to know if there were any obstacles to overcome in her fight to keep him in France. Yes, she should ask him. "Do you have a girl in America?"

He seemed surprised that she had asked him that. But he answered readily enough. "There is someone, yes. Her name is Casey. Cassandra Templeton. She has the reddest hair you ever saw. Green eyes. And a great sense of humor."

He had spoken lightly, but Angèle noted that his smile had a definite affectionate cast to it. Casey Templeton. Her task was going to be tougher than she had thought. But not impossible. Nothing was impossible.

SARAH WAS IN THE KITCHEN area mixing something in a bowl. "You had four phone calls," she said as soon as Casey came in. "I wrote them down on that yellow pad over there."

Casey grinned as she dropped her packages on the sofa bed. "What on earth did I do before I had you as a secretary?" She sniffed the air. "Mmm, beeswax and orange oil. You've been polishing again."

"I'm getting to like your old furniture," Sarah admitted. "How was the antique show?"

"Fair. I didn't buy much, but I did talk to all the dealers, asking them to help out with Michel's problem. They promised to keep their ears to the ground."

"Michel was one of the callers," Sarah said. She was carefully chopping green onions into meticulous slices, her tongue caught between her teeth.

Casey felt the constriction in her chest that appeared these days whenever she thought of Michel or heard his name unexpectedly. Usually it was accompanied by an irrational sensation of dread. Why couldn't she shake this conviction that it was all over, that Michel had gone from her life forever?

Sarah was smiling. "What that man does to the English language!" she marveled. "It never sounded so good. His voice sends shivers all the way up my spine. Sexiest voice I ever did hear. Even Amanda stops kicking to listen when Michel talks."

Casey laughed in spite of herself. "What did he say? Is he coming home yet?"

Sarah shook her head. "Not so he mentioned. He'd called the store first, then tried here. Told him you left early to go to an antique show." She raised her eyebrows expressively. "Wanted to know what you were wearing. Told him you had on your creamy-colored lace dress. Said it was his favorite, reminded him of when you took him home from jail." Her eyes narrowed. "Was he pulling my leg?"

"It's a long story," Casey said. Her spirits had lifted at this reminder of the evening she'd met Michel, but they sagged again as she realized once again how much she missed him. Since he had left, the sunny July sky over Seattle had acquired a haze of gloom. All of the joy and sense of adventure he'd brought into her life had vanished. The flowers he'd arranged for Sidney to bring to her daily were as colorful as ever but they had lost their fragrance. The food she ate had lost its flavor—and not just because Sarah was doing the cooking, either. Falling in love often precedes a crash landing, Skip had said. And here she was, flat on her face in the dust.

She became aware that Sarah was gazing sympathetically at her and forced a smile. "Anything else?" she asked.

"Said to tell you he'll call back tomorrow. Early hours there now, I guess. Said he was going to bed. When he called it was around two o'clock here. Six-thirty now."

Casey struggled to keep her smile in place. Michel would call back, after all. He hadn't missed a day since he left. In fact he'd telephoned early that morning. She was suddenly alarmed. Why had he called a second time? "Did he sound all right? I mean, do you think anything was wrong...his grandfather?"

Sarah didn't answer right away. Something had boiled over on the stove and she was busy making a spot in the sink to move the pan to. "Guess it doesn't matter if you overcook hard-boiled eggs," she muttered, running cold water into the pan. "Can only get harder."

What on earth was she fixing for supper, Casey wondered, but didn't risk asking.

Sarah turned to look at Casey, rubbing her swollen abdomen. "Didn't say, Casey. Just said he'd call back. Oh, yeah—he did ask how I was doing."

She shook her head, smiling. Casey had explained Sarah's presence to Michel the first time he'd called after Sarah moved in. To Sarah's surprise, Michel had been very sympathetic, and had heartily approved of Casey's action. "So many people worry publicly about the homeless," he said. "It is wonderful to me, *chérie,* that you should do something about it."

"He asked how everybody's favorite guardian angel was doing," Sarah continued. "Sounded real...fond."

Fond is a weak word, Michel had told her once.

Sarah had peeled the shells off the eggs and was chopping them into the mixture in the bowl. "Sounded tired, too," she added with a small frown.

Casey sat down in what she'd come to think of as Sarah's rocker and pulled off her boots. The antique show had been a small one but even so, her feet were rebelling. And she hadn't been able to find anyone who'd ever heard of Inga. She was beginning to wonder if the old woman had actually existed. If she hadn't, that had been some hallucination. She wished she hadn't missed Michel. The sound of his voice always reassured her, at least temporarily.

"Need some food to raise your blood sugar," Sarah said. "Come and get it, okay?"

"What are we having?" Casey asked nervously.

"Tuna salad."

Casey stood up and padded into the kitchen. "Looks good, smells good."

Sarah licked the spoon she'd used to stir the concoction. "Tastes good," she said with a surprised grin. "That Skip Granger is some teacher."

"You like Skip, huh?"

The grin disappeared. "Seems like a nice man," Sarah remarked cautiously. "He was around here twice this week. You think maybe he doesn't trust me not to take off with your valuables?"

"What valuables? I'm sure he's just interested in how you are doing, Sarah. Skip's a good guy. And he likes you. He told me when we jogged this morning that he had half a mind to adopt you himself.''

Sarah didn't answer and Casey glanced at her sharply. She was standing very still, both hands cradling her abdomen.

"You okay?" Casey asked as she placed a vase full of Michel's pink and white roses on the gateleg table. Sarah's appearance had improved steadily since she moved in ten days earlier. Her eyes shone clear, their whites pristine. The circles had disappeared from beneath them. Even her cluster of braids seemed shinier. Her skin had acquired a healthy glow. But right now, she looked . . . troubled.

"Amanda give you a twinge?" Casey asked when she still didn't speak.

Sarah shook her head. "Amanda's taking a nap." She frowned ferociously, not looking at Casey, then blurted out, "One thing I don't need is a father. You tell that to Skip Granger. Too used to being my own boss."

She was really annoyed, Casey realized. Had she not liked Skip, after all? She certainly hadn't said much about his visits, and every time Casey brought his name up, she frowned. On the other hand, Skip had said he'd told him her life story, so she must have trusted him—it had taken her another week to tell Casey.

Something else to worry about. If Sarah didn't like Skip, and showed it, Skip might decide not to advance the money to Casey, after all.

MICHEL CALLED at five the following morning. "I have a favor to ask," he announced, sounding a little too deliberately charming.

Casey struggled to get her eyes open. "What kind of favor?" she asked warily.

Sarah sat up in the daybed, looked at her, then lay down again and turned on her side, pulling the covers over her head.

"You sound negative already, Casey," Michel said. "This is not good."

"I always sound negative at five o'clock in the morning."

"It is only five? I apologize. My *arithmétique* must have failed me. Can you say I love you at five o'clock in the morning?"

"I love you, Michel."

"*Bien.* Now say, I will do anything for you, Michel."

"I will do anything for you, Michel," she repeated obediently.

"Now say, I will come to you right away."

"I will—what are you talking about?" She was abruptly wide-awake.

"I want you to come here. Now. I miss you."

"I miss you, too, but I can't just take off into the blue because you think I should."

Sarah sat up again and nodded vigorously. "Go for it," she said in a hoarse whisper.

"Don't think about it, Casey," Michel urged. "Don't analyze why or why not. Please just be impulsive. Come to me."

"I can't—"

"I will pay for your ticket, of course."

"I can't let you do that, Michel."

"Why not? I am the one who wants you to make the trip. Of course I will pay."

"I have a business to run."

"Fumiko?" Sarah mouthed.

"Michel, much as I want to see you, I can't—"

"Ah, you do wish to see me, then?"

"Of course I want to see you."

"Then come. I am having a difficult time, Casey. My mother and grandfather are putting pressure on me to stay, to take over Rapide Corporation. My other relatives are anxiously watching to see what my decision will be. No one, except my grandmother, seems to care about what is best for me." He paused for a heartbeat, then added very softly, "I need someone on my side, Casey. I need you."

He certainly knew the fatal flaw in her character, Casey thought, feeling herself weakening. She had always needed to be needed.

Fumiko would jump at the chance to take over the shop, of course. She was always eager to make extra money. But unfortunately, Casey would be losing money. Could she really afford, really justify... She did have a passport, courtesy of Winston Perry IV.

"Are you thinking it over?" Michel asked. "Please say yes, Casey."

"I'll pay for my own ticket," she said firmly. *With what?* a nasty little voice in her mind asked. I'll charge it, she told the voice. I'll pay it off at twenty dollars a month. *And nineteen-percent interest?* If necessary. If Michel needs me, I must go.

Look before you leap, her father said.

She who hesitates is lost, she answered him.

CHAPTER TWELVE

THE FAMILIARITY OF THE countryside they were driving through teased Casey with constant sensations of déjà vu—an avenue of poplars here, a misty willow-fringed river there, an orchard, a rustic village with a cobbled main street. Even the light radiating into the shadows seemed familiar, luminous.

The light. Of course. She was passing through settings that had inspired painters who had changed the course of modern art. "It's like driving through an art gallery," she said. "Pissarro, Monet, Seurat—all the Impressionists."

"*C'est belle, n'est-ce pas?*" Michel murmured. He glanced at her sideways. The warm intensity of his dark eyes hadn't lessened. Nor had their effect on her nervous system. "You are like the Impressionists, too, when you wear your vintage clothing," he murmured. "Berthe Morisot's *Été*—Summer. With you it is always summer. You even smell like summer—roses blooming in the morning sun."

Oh, he did have a way with words. If only he would lose his sense of smell.

No, Casey's mind exclaimed immediately to whomever it was who listened to such imaginings and translated them into reality—she didn't *really* want Michel to lose his sense of smell. It was just that she wanted him to forget that particular smell.

When he had greeted Casey at Charles de Gaulle airport, he had held her in his arms for so long, she had wondered, though uncomplainingly, if he was ever going to let her go. And then he had lifted his head, sniffing the air and said, "Ah, that special perfume. There is no other perfume like it, Casey."

And of course she wasn't wearing any perfume. The strangest thing of all was that she had been able to smell it, too—that wonderfully spicy, velvet scent—the moment Michel took her in his arms. Which anyone would have to admit was weird.

When Michel took her on a lightning tour of Paris, while he pointed out the Louvre, the Tuilerie Gardens, the Rapide showrooms on the Champs-Élysées, the Arc de Triomphe and the Eiffel Tower, he had kept referring again and again to the way she smelled. "What is the perfume called?" he asked as he steered the Rapide two-seater roadster around a stalled Citroën.

"It doesn't have a name."

He gave her a startled glance.

"I mean someone gave it to me," she amended. "There's no label on the bottle, so I don't know what it's called."

"Well, don't use it up too soon," he said softly. "I cannot imagine you without it."

What if that were literally true? What if the smell faded and he literally couldn't imagine her, couldn't see her?

She was losing her mind. No doubt about it.

The traffic had been murderous in the city, but there was little of it once they had reached the outlying countryside. The Rapide apparently handled like a dream, humming along very smoothly and quietly.

"Does your whole family work for Rapide Corporation?" Casey asked before he could start asking questions about the perfume again.

"Most of them, yes. My grandfather believes strongly in nepotism, which he calls family unity and tradition. You'll probably have gathered that he's fairly authoritarian. All of my uncles work for him, and my cousins. Two of my cousins' wives. Gérard's wife Thérèse is secretary to my Uncle Jacques, who is director of public relations. Jules's wife Adrienne is a mechanical engineer, as he is. They met in school. Now they are both on the executive committee. The other younger women have small children, and my aunts are all at home except for Uncle André's wife, who is in marketing."

"Your mother?"

He shook his head. "Maman has a pension from my father and an allowance from her father—Grandpère. Mostly she amuses herself. She attends art galleries and concerts and fashion shows and she plays bridge."

Smiling at her, he touched her knee lightly and she felt the warmth of it throughout her body. "I am nervous, Casey, wondering what you will think of my family. They will be rather overwhelming for you, I think. Most of them work long hours during the week, so they do not come to the château except for special occasions. However, they have been home more often since Grandpère's illness and they are all due back for the weekend—determined to be here in time for the welcoming dinner party Grandmère has planned. Since I have told the family about you, all of them have been panting to meet you."

"You aren't worried about what they'll think of me?"

His usual whimsical smile warmed his face and made her pulse start behaving erratically. He could not imagine her without the perfume—she could not imagine him without that lopsided smile. "How could they not adore you?" he chided her.

Then he grimaced slightly and inclined his head to one side. "Well, let me be honest here. My cousins and their wives will accept you as well as they accept any outsider, I think—they are all anxious for me to go back to America, so they will perhaps see you as a sort of insurance policy. Grandmère will love you. She is happy that I have found someone to love. My grandfather and my mother, on the other hand, will no doubt be disinclined to take you to their hearts because they do not want me to be distracted in any way."

"Distracted?"

"In spite of all my arguments, they are still determined that I should stay in France and become CEO of Rapide Corporation. That is their single goal: to persuade me."

Are they going to succeed? Casey wanted to ask, but as the question formed in her mind, she realized Michel had turned off the road onto a wide driveway lined with tall trees. "Welcome to my home," Michel said.

The château looked more like a hotel than any house Casey had ever seen. Three stories high, fronted by a stone terrace, its flat facade was enriched with columns and steps and seemed infinitely wide. At least three dozen tall, arched windows sparkled in the sunlight.

"Good Lord," Casey murmured, nervousness clutching at her stomach.

Michel laughed. "Impressive, *n'est-ce pas?*"

"Incredible," Casey said.

As they came closer, she recognized Michel's landscaping from the description he'd given her—rolling lawns, stands of trees, and at each side between the lawn and the woods, the sun-warmed brick walkways, the flower beds, riotous with summer color—the roses.

She held on tightly to Michel's hand as he escorted her through the massive doorway, as if it were a lifeline that could stop her from falling off the edge of the world.

THERE WAS A four-poster in her bedroom, complete with a dotted-swiss canopy and coverlet. A beautiful writing desk—eighteenth century by the look of it—a muslin-swathed dressing table, an armoire and several antique chairs and small tables completed the decor, along with numerous portraits of lovely young women dressed in the fashions of days gone by. Casey knew dealers in Seattle who would kill for the contents of this room.

The bathroom was beautifully up-to-date, she was relieved to discover—as convenient as any American bathroom, with the addition of a bidet. The shower water was hot.

The maid who had escorted her upstairs returned just as she finished applying fresh makeup. "*Mademoiselle* is almost ready to descend?" she asked.

Casey was glad to see her. She had wondered how she would ever find her way back to the living area. This house needed street signs, she'd thought somewhat hysterically as the maid led her through endless corridors.

"Just about," she said with a longing glance at the four-poster bed. She had slept very little on the plane, and the canopied bed looked very inviting. But...the family awaits, Michel had told her when he turned her over to the maid. At least she felt less sticky and grimy after her shower. She had brought one of her vintage outfits with her, more for a feeling of security than anything else, and after a consultation with Marie, she decided to wear the peach ruffled blouse and long black skirt for the evening. She certainly didn't have anything else that was suitable. Evidently this was a very formal family.

Checking in a gilt-framed mirror that her makeup and upswept hair were intact, Casey took a deep breath and signaled Marie to lead the way.

The *famille,* Marie informed her on the way down, had gathered for cocktails on the *terrasse* at the rear of the château. It was such a lovely day, Madame Rapide had decided they should spend time before dinner outdoors.

Casey felt relieved. She had stopped to look in the cavernous dining room in passing, and its Louis XVI clock, chandeliers and Savonnerie rug had intimidated her immediately. Maybe a little Dutch courage would help her to face it later.

It was like being the last to enter the lobby of a theater during intermission, she thought. So many well-dressed people, all talking volubly, standing around or sitting in bistro chairs at glass-topped tables. The nearest group seemed to be having an argument, complete with lots of gesticulation and raised voices.

Right on cue, Casey's father spoke in her mind: *War seldom enters but where wealth allures.* Poor people fight, too, Daddy, she reminded him.

The silence spread out from the first person to see her, causing a ripple of turned heads and abandoned conversation. *"Voilà,"* Michel said cheerfully, elbowing his way through the group that had been the most voluble. He was carrying a little dark-haired boy about eighteen months old on his shoulders. Two other toddlers, both girls, clung to his hands. "Some of my cousin Charles's children," he explained, then passed the little boy to a plump woman standing nearby. The little girls insisted on being picked up so they could deposit boisterous kisses on his cheeks before going to their mother. Michel obliged smilingly, hugging them both just as exuberantly.

Casey hadn't seen Michel with children before. The picture he made with the little girls hugging his neck added another dimension to his character and brought a melting sensation to Casey's heart.

Taking her hand, he gave her his special lopsided smile. *"Courage, mon amie,"* he told her. Then he led her into the throng, introducing her to several children and one person after another—Claude and Jean and Anne-Marie, Pierre and André and Jacques and Charles, Madeleine, Guillaume, Jules, another Jacques. Remembering that she'd heard somewhere that the French hated to hear their language spoken badly, Casey didn't even attempt to use the few words she knew. Fortunately, everyone spoke at least some English, though none of them seemed to have mastered the *h* sound, dropping it off words like *hello* and *how* and *here*. Nobody seemed terribly thrilled to meet her.

Somewhere along the line she met a perfectly turned-out slender young woman who had the looks and style of an haute-couture model and boyishly cut silver-blond hair that contrasted marvelously with her body-hugging black gown. Her name was Angèle and she looked Casey over very carefully and unsmilingly before proffering a slender hand to be shaken. One of the cousin's

wives? Casey wondered as the introductions continued. No. Her last name was Peverell. And Michel had
seemed surprised to see her. "Jeanne invited me," the
glamorous young woman had said lightly, offering her
cheek for Michel to kiss.

Jeanne herself was a very beautiful woman, dressed
all in white, who looked far too young to be Michel's
mother. She had Michel's dark eyes and hair, but her
smile was forced. "Mademoiselle Templeton," she acknowledged in a brittle way that made Casey shrivel inside.

"*Maman,*" Michel said in a scolding voice. He was
looking at his mother with narrowed eyes.

She shrugged, obviously unfazed by his disapproval.
"Michel has shown you Paris?" she asked in what was
apparently meant to be an effort to show friendliness.

Casey nodded, trying to think of a comment that
would be tactful. Truth to tell, the flying glimpse of
Paris had left her with only a blurred impression of
massive gray stone, a host of Belle Époque houses,
sidewalk cafés, and the cloudy green water of the River
Seine—the only truly clear spot the gendarme on a corner of the rue de Rivoli who had made eyes at her in true
Gallic fashion while Michel waited for pedestrians to
cross.

"I'm hoping to have time to see it properly," she said
diplomatically.

"You will be staying long enough for sightseeing?"
the young woman named Angèle asked, materializing
at Michel's side.

"Casey is here for a few days only," Michel replied
shortly. He was still holding her hand. The rate of his
pulse told her he was nervous, too. But his hand—large
and square and capable—felt comforting all the same.

"I wanted her to stay longer," he added. "But she has a business to run."

"What kind of business?" Angèle asked, taking a glass of wine from a passing servant.

Casey decided to speak for herself. "I have a small shop. I sell antique jewelry and vintage and second-hand designer clothing."

"How interesting," Angèle said, looking bored. "It is difficult to believe that women of any distinction would wear used clothing, is it not, Jeanne?"

"Well, we're a clean nation—we take a lot of showers," Casey remarked, making Michel laugh delightedly.

"I don't know why I was worried. You take care of yourself very well," he murmured as he moved her on toward another group of people.

"Angèle isn't related to you, is she?" Casey asked.

He shook his head, then smiled his whimsical smile. "She would like to be, I think. She is one of the reasons—" He broke off. "Ah, here is Grandmère." He put one arm around Casey and another around an elegant woman who effortlessly projected Parisian chic from the top of her bobbed white hair to the pale blue shoes that matched both her deceptively simple evening gown and her eyes.

"Here are two of my favorite women," Michel said. "Grandmère, the family has been quite cool to Casey. Very Parisian. I am trusting you to make her feel welcome."

Hélène Rapide shook her head. "Pay no attention, Casey," she said in barely accented English. "The French often manifest coolness toward strangers. And I must tell you, there are times when certain members of this family are very cool toward me. I am not an original Rapide, you see—only by marriage. To this tribe, that makes a difference."

She took Casey's right hand between both of her own and looked closely at her. "You were right," she said to Michel. "She is truly lovely. Such luminous skin. Such vivid coloring. How my father would have loved to paint her." She smiled warmly at Casey. "My father was not a great artist, but he was a competent portraitist and he liked especially to paint beautiful women. Nude young women. My mother, *naturellement,* was not overly fond of his little hobby." She laughed merrily, infectiously, with Casey and Michel joining her.

"I am to be ignored because I am not on my feet?" a petulant male voice asked.

Michel apologized at once, stepping back to make room for his grandfather's wheelchair.

Jean-Paul was a big man, with the bold dark eyes of someone half his age, a sweep of white hair and a strong face—a jawline that meant business. Casey had expected to be totally intimidated by the patriarch of the family, but to her amazement she felt a strong and immediate liking for him. Michel would look like him when he grew old, she thought—the eyes, the unruly nature of the hair, the determined chin, had all been passed on.

Jean-Paul held her hand a full minute longer than necessary, while he studied Casey thoroughly. "So you are my competition," he said at last.

Casey met his gaze. "I don't think so, Monsieur Rapide. It is the gardening that competes with your wishes."

"What am I to do, my dear?" he asked softly.

Casey laughed nervously after a quick glance at Michel, who was watching his grandfather with an amazed expression in his dark eyes. It was obvious he hadn't expected his grandfather to take to Casey quite so easily. "Would it do any good for me to suggest you give in gracefully?" she asked.

Jean-Paul's explosion of laughter drew everyone's attention which they then focused on Casey, the obvious cause of Grandpère's good humor. One of the cousins—Sebastien?—murmured something in French that Casey roughly translated to mean it looked as if Grandpère liked Michel's little friend.

After that, everyone seemed even stiffer toward her. From one or two remarks made during the cocktail hour, Casey realized Angèle had spread the word about her occupation. Probably, she thought, they all looked upon her as some little gold-digger out to get her hands on the family fortune. Why hadn't it occurred to her before she came that the family might see her in that light? Because the thought hadn't crossed her mind, of course. How ironic that they should think that, when it was Michel's wealthy background that was most likely to come between them.

It was almost funny, the way they took turns interrogating her. While the family scattered themselves among the various tables, talking easily in French about the business or the Tour de France bicycle race that would be starting soon and would end in late July at the Champs-Élysées, or about Longchamps, which Casey seemed to remember was a famous racetrack, one by one, various family members came to sit beside her to "get acquainted."

By the time the children were sent off with their various nannies and the adults all went indoors for dinner, she was devoutly wishing she had never left Seattle. She was a misfit, here, just as she had been a misfit in school. All the old insecurities had come back to haunt her as one by one the cousins and uncles and various wives threw questions at her about her family and her education—questions that seemed designed to reveal her background, past and present. She had found herself sitting with braced shoulders, almost expecting someone to point at her and jeer, "That's the girl from the east side, the one whose father runs a mission for street people."

"This is one of your secondhand outfits?" Angèle asked in a not-quite-low-enough voice as they seated themselves in the intimidating dining room.

"One of my favorites," Casey said, lifting her chin.

Grandmère smiled at her—approvingly, she thought.

The array of silverware laid out on the enormous table was intimidating, but Casey kept an eye on Michel's mother and picked up the correct utensil a second after she did.

After the soup course, the entrée was served, each plate topped with a silver cover. Casey had taken off her cover before she realized there was nowhere to set it down. Luckily a sharp-eyed maid noticed her dilemma and rescued the cover. And then Casey saw that the maids and the butler—she supposed he was a butler—were lifting the covers off everyone else's plate. And Jeanne had noticed her gaffe. So had Angèle. Embarrassed, Casey glanced down the table to Michel, who winked at her.

It is a public service to provide people with free entertainment. She muttered Michel's words under her breath, and was comforted.

"Excuse me?" asked one of Michel's cousins, Charles, who had been seated beside her.

She smiled at him and shrugged. The French really knew what they were doing when they invented that shrug, she thought—it covered up nicely when you had no idea what to say.

Charles talked to her about the gilt-framed paintings on the walls of the dining room, which made her feel more at ease, until she noticed she had automatically shifted her fork into her right hand in order to eat her meal. She hadn't even realized what she'd done until she caught Jeanne looking down her aristocratic nose at the offending fork. She tried switching it over, which was fine for handling the lamb, but murder when it came to the green baby peas. After a minute's struggle, she gave up and decided you didn't necessarily have to do as the French did, just because you were in France.

"How did you meet Michel?" Angèle asked as they all drank bitterly strong coffee after dinner.

Casey glanced quickly at Michel. He had evidently overhead the question and was looking quite horrified. Did he really expect her to blurt out that she'd met him under very peculiar circumstances involving the theft of two vehicles amid some questions about a con artist who was cheating senior citizens out of their hard-earned savings?

What would they all say if she said instead that she had used some magic perfume given to her by an elderly lady of uncertain origin and Michel had popped up in her life like a genie out of a bottle?

"I'm sorry," she said to Angèle, realizing too much time had passed since the question had been asked. "I was distracted—jet lag is catching up with me, I'm afraid—I didn't hear what you said."

"I asked how you met Michel," the beautiful young woman repeated.

"He came into my shop to ask for...directions," Casey said promptly.

Michel's face showed relief.

Angèle appeared bored, which seemed to be her standard expression unless she happened to be gazing at Michel, in which case she looked attentive and charmed, adoring and adorable.

All in all, Casey felt she'd acquitted herself fairly well for her first day, but she was exhausted by the effort and excused herself as soon as she could, pleading jet lag once again.

The next few days passed quickly once the weekend was over and the cousins and uncles and aunts departed for their own homes. The château was relatively quiet, with only Michel's grandparents and mother and Casey and Michel and an assortment of servants. Only Angèle wandered in and out—apparently completely at home in the château.

Michel took Casey driving—back into Paris for a slower and more thorough tour, which gave her a better appreciation of the beauty of the city, out to the magnificent palace of Versailles with its terraced gardens and parks, and to Chartres to see its world-famous thirteenth-century cathedral.

He did not suggest taking her to see his grandfather's factories and when she asked why, he said, "I've been afraid to go anywhere near them. First thing you know, someone would ask me a question and I'd get involved in it and take my coat off and Grandpère would hear about it and have someone lock all the doors so I couldn't get out." He smiled at her. "I will visit just before I leave, to say hello and goodbye to everyone."

You *will* leave, then? she wanted to ask. But she restrained herself. Michel was under enough pressure; she didn't need to add to it.

On the evening before she was due to leave France, he drove her into the local village for some of the best pastries Casey had ever eaten.

"Does Angèle always spend so much time at the château?" she asked carefully as they sipped their espresso.

Michel shook his head and pushed his cup away. "Maman keeps inviting her," he said. "I began to tell you I think that Angèle was one of the reasons I needed you here with me. Maman has been pushing her at me ever since I came home. I was beginning to get nervous."

"You thought you might succumb?"

His look of horror was totally believable. "Never. Angèle, I must tell you, is a totally hedonistic young woman. She has never worked at anything. She plays bridge. And rides occasionally. Mostly I think she socializes—her mother is dead and she acts as her father's hostess. As far as I know, she does nothing else but sit around and look pretty." He glanced sideways at Casey. "I must admit she does that very well. However, I was afraid she might 'jump my bones,' as my young friend Sidney Arundel would say, and I would have to embarrass her by turning her down. As I recall, Angèle has never taken embarrassment lightly."

"You've known her a long time?"

"All my life. We were great friends when we were children." His mouth tightened and then he sighed again and reached for her hand. "We were lovers for a very short time, Casey. It was many years ago and quickly over. When it began I knew it would be nothing more than a short affair. I thought Angèle recognized that also. When it was over, she seemed perfectly happy to see it end, and we went back to being friends again. But now it seems I was mistaken. Angèle had not wanted it to be over.''

Casey could certainly identify with that. Was she supposed to recognize that *their* relationship was nothing more than a short affair? she wondered.

She sighed. ''The only reason Angèle married Gilles Peverell was because you had dropped her. She wanted to make you jealous. She is still madly in love with you.''

Astonished, he stared at her. ''Where did you hear that?''

''From your mother.''

He squeezed her hand. ''I am sorry, *ma chérie*. Maman has this idea that if I marry the girl next door then I will stay home. And she and Angèle play cards and go shopping together. They like each other.'' He sighed. ''They are both the products of a strong father who does not believe in women being anything but ornamental. They cannot really be blamed, I suppose.''

After a minute of silence, he went on, ''I think it is not that my mother does not like you, but that she cannot let herself like you, because you belong to my other life, the one that threatens her so. This is perhaps the main reason I needed you to come, because you are symbolic of that other life and I needed to be reminded of it.''

''Will you be coming back to that life soon?'' Casey finally dared ask, wondering as she did so how much security there was in being a symbol.

''I hope so,'' he said ambiguously. ''As soon as I am sure Grandpère is going to recover fully. Now that he is able to get up and walk around a little, I think he will soon be back to his old self."

The problem was, of course, that Grandpère's "old self" was very strong, and also very persuasive.

Michel was looking at her closely. "You did not believe, surely, that I was interested in Angèle?"

She shook her head. "There was a time that first day when I was ready to accidentally push her in the pond at the back of the château, but I remembered in time that I was brought up to be a lady."

He laughed, then leaned across the table to kiss her gently.

The proprietor of the small café beamed at them and discreetly bustled off to bring more espresso, giving them a few minutes alone. They'd had little private time, except when driving. At night, Michel had come to join her in the four-poster, and their lovemaking had been as wonderful as before. But whenever they were at the château during the day, it seemed to Casey that either Jeanne or Angèle was always watching them.

"Grandpère adores you," Michel said.

Casey nodded complacently. "I know. I adore him, too. I've enjoyed our daily visit with him. Some of your cousins seem terrified of him, and I guess I can see why. He's a very *determined* man. But he's really just a pussycat."

Michel laughed. "Don't tell him so. He thinks of himself as a tiger." He looked at her curiously. "What did you talk about yesterday when he invited you to have lunch in his study?"

She shook her head. "It was confidential."

"I need Michel here," Jean-Paul had told her bluntly. "If you were to marry him and move into the château, he would be content to stay."

"I don't think so," she'd said just as bluntly.

"Which?" he asked.

"One: he hasn't asked me to marry him. Two: I'd never consider moving into the château, and three: Michel wants to spend his life working in gardens, not factories or boardrooms."

"Why would you not move into the château?" he demanded. "Is it not beautiful?"

Casey sighed, looking around her at the extraordinary French Empire furniture, the series of equestrian paintings on the silk-covered walls, the Venetian fireplace. "I guess I prefer something smaller," she said as tactfully as possible.

Jean-Paul frowned mightily, following her gaze. "It *is* rather like living in a museum," he conceded. "I am used to it, I suppose. But you would not have to live here. We maintain residences in both Le Mans and Tours, and we could always build you a country home."

He raised his bristly eyebrows. "Would you marry Michel if he asked you?"

"I don't know," she answered honestly.

"He loves you. You love him. This I have seen for myself."

"Yes, but I'm not sure it's the kind of love that lasts forever."

"You think love *can* last forever?"

"Hasn't yours for Hélène?"

He'd smiled and began peeling a peach with a tiny silver knife. "You have been watching, Mademoiselle Casey."

"Yes, I have."

"Well, I can tell you this, Casey. No one can know in advance if love will last forever. One can only hope for the best."

"Then let me say that I will need to have a little more confidence before I can answer your question," she replied.

He had leaned back in his wing chair and smiled at her. Oh, he could smile just as charmingly, just as lopsidedly as Michel when he put his mind to it. "What is holding you back?" he asked.

"I don't fit in with all this," she said, waving a hand.

"So if I persuade Michel to stay here, you will not marry him?"

She swallowed. "I'm an American through and through, Monsieur Rapide. I couldn't just walk away from everything that means anything to me." She could hardly add the thought that this was in her mind—that if Michel were to allow himself to be talked into giving up his hopes for an independent future, he wouldn't be the kind of man she'd want to marry. She looked at Jean-Paul directly. "Why do I get the idea we are sparring here?"

"Because we are, *mademoiselle*. We are fighting for the possession of my grandson."

"But I don't want to possess him," she said at once.

He studied her face for a minute, then shrugged. "I was speaking symbolically, Casey."

"Were you?" she asked.

He raised his bristly white eyebrows again, his eyes narrowing. "You are accusing me of wanting to literally possess my grandson?"

She nodded. "I think you try to hold on too tightly. But if you love someone, you should hold them very loosely, with open hands, always prepared to let go."

He frowned and been silent for a few minutes, obviously thinking over what she had said. Finally he nodded. "That is a very wise statement, Casey. Where did you learn such wisdom?"

She had laughed. "I think I got it off a greeting card, actually."

His own laughter had joined hers.

"Shall I offer you a centime for your thoughts, Casey?" Michel asked. "Or are they worth a franc?"

She smiled at him. "I was thinking about your grandfather. Having met the rest of his grandchildren, I can understand why he wants you to stay. You're probably the only one who loves him."

Michel shook his head. "No, that isn't so. Charles, my oldest cousin, has modeled himself completely on Grandpère. He wishes to be as like him as it is possible to be. He is a good businessman also, and willing to devote his life and all his energies to the company. Grandpère knows this as well as I do, but he's advancing the idea that Charles is too boring and too earnest, and he has conceived a dislike of Charles's wife."

"The plump one."

"He is just being stubborn, trying to make me change my mind. Every time I argue with him he presses his hand to his heart as if he's about to have another attack."

"I've noticed that," Casey said with a smile. "It worried me at first, but I noticed he didn't do that all the time I was alone with him."

"Well, now that he's so much stronger, I'm going to try to sell him on the idea of Charles as CEO and Sebastien as his assistant. Sebastien is under thirty, but he has a good head, and he is also a company man."

Casey made a face. "Sebastien called me your little friend."

Michel grinned and leaned across the small table to kiss her again. "And aren't you my little friend?"

"Somehow it sounds better when you say it," she murmured, kissing him back.

MICHEL'S MOTHER greeted them in the foyer of the château on their return. She was still wearing the black silk two-piece she had worn to dinner and Casey felt a little uncomfortable in the slacks and shirt she'd changed into to go into the village. But Jeanne was charming to her. She had thawed considerably over the past few days, possibly following her father's lead. "Your last evening, Casey," she said with a rueful smile as Casey and Michel headed toward the stairs.

Casey hesitated, remembering that Jeanne rarely rose before noon. "Yes. I'll be leaving early in the morning. Perhaps I won't see you again." She came down a step and offered her right hand. "In case I don't see you..."

"But I have an idea," Jeanne said, smiling as she took Casey's hand between both of hers. "Why do you not join me in the little salon for a cup of hot chocolate? We can say our farewells there."

About to protest that she'd already indulged in enough empty calories for one evening, Casey was struck by the intensity of Jeanne's gaze. Evidently she really was anxious to spend some time with Casey. "Okay," she replied. "Sounds good to me. Michel?"

"Oui, certainement," he agreed.

His mother shook her head. "This invitation does not include you, Michel. It is for Casey alone."

Her tone was playful, but it seemed to Casey that there was a determined note in it, as well.

Once they were alone in the little salon, Jeanne seemed to forget about the cup of chocolate she'd promised Casey. Taking up a position in front of the empty fireplace, she gave Casey a long look, then said, "I have come to admire you very much in the last few days."

"I'm glad," Casey said simply.

"I think you are an honest young woman and I think you love my son. I can see also that he is enchanted by you." She paused as though to select her next words carefully, and it seemed to Casey there was something ominous about the silence that followed.

She wished Jeanne had used any other word than *enchanted*—it smacked too much of magic, and she'd just as soon forget that there was any possibility of magic being involved.

"Even though I find myself liking you," Jeanne continued finally, "I must admit to myself, as I'm sure you will admit, that you are not quite suitable...."

The kids at school were hovering somewhere behind Casey's left shoulder, jeering, pointing her out. She certainly couldn't come up with any immediate argument, and while she was still quivering from the word blows Jeanne had just delivered, the older woman went on confidently. "I think my son is wavering, Casey. I think there is a good chance I can persuade him to stay."

Casey shook her head. "I'm not so sure. He's pretty well set—"

"With that end in view," Jeanne went on as if Casey hadn't spoken, "I have decided to try to remove one temptation from my son's path."

Casey gazed at her for a full minute, her stomach tying itself into a knot that might never come undone. "You're talking about me, aren't you?"

Jeanne nodded briskly. So much for her apparent friendliness, Casey thought.

"We French are a practical race," Jeanne continued. "And I think you are practical, too. My son has told me about your business, and about your kindness to others—the young pregnant woman you have given a home to, for example."

Had Michel been trying to impress his mother with her meager accomplishments? Casey wondered. Probably.

"I have gathered for myself that you do not have a large income," Jeanne went on. "And I am sure it would help you to have an account to draw on to help with your various philanthropies. I am prepared to offer you twenty-five thousand American dollars to give up any idea of anything...permanent involving my son."

Casey had remained standing, but now she sat down hard on the nearest chair. "You're not serious."

"It is not enough? All I ask is that you return to the United States without putting any pressure on my son to join you."

She meant it. She really meant it. She thought she could buy Casey off.

Casey's first impulse was to say something very blunt and rude and to the point; but this was Michel's mother, and she was fighting to keep her son from going back to live thousands of miles away from her, and Casey could certainly sympathize with that.

She realized that she was staring at Jeanne and hadn't yet given her an answer to her offer. But what could she possibly say?

Standing, she shook her head and started across the room.

"Casey!" Jeanne exclaimed. "You cannot leave without answering me."

Casey found her voice then. "I have no answer for you, *madame,*" she said slowly. "You have misjudged me so much, I cannot find words."

"You will not take the money?"

Casey took a deep breath and looked at the woman steadily. "No, *madame,* I will not take the money. However, I think you are overestimating my power. I have no intention of interfering with Michel's plans, whatever they happen to be."

Jeanne was pale, but there was an expression of reluctant admiration in her dark eyes. "You will not use undue influence on my son?"

Would magic perfume come under the heading Undue Influence even if you'd only used it once, and that, more than two months ago? Casey wondered. Probably.

Unable to think of anything further to say, she turned on her heel and left the room.

CASEY WAS FIERCELY determined to put the conversation with Jeanne out of her mind. She would not tell Michel that his mother had tried to bribe her. She refused to cast herself in the role of adversary. If Michel wanted her, he would come back to Seattle. The next move was up to him. For now... this was her last night in France, possibly her last night with Michel, if Jeanne and Jean-Paul got their way.

When he came to her, she was already in bed, the room lighted only by a slash of light from the adjoining bathroom. He didn't ask what she and Jeanne had talked about; he didn't seem to want to talk at all, and Casey was content with that.

For a while he simply held her, then he began kissing the side of her neck, always a vulnerable spot where Casey was concerned. He sniffed at her skin once or twice, and Casey was afraid he was going to refer again to the perfume, which was certainly in the air, even though it was still safely tucked way in its golden bottle in Casey's medicine cabinet in Seattle.

No. She wasn't going to think about the perfume, either.

His hands moved over her, gently tracing the shape of her breasts, her waist, her hips, lifting her to him so that she could feel the power of his wanting, his mouth hungrily kissing her the while.

She wanted it to be perfect for him. Perhaps she wasn't above using undue influence, after all, she thought wryly, as she set off on a loving tour of his body.

His body was so hard. There was no softness anywhere—not even at the sides of his waist where even the most physically fit person often bulged a little bit. Not an ounce of fat on him. Only bone and muscles and sinew and smooth flesh to delight her hands and her lips as she moved slowly over him.

How dark his eyes were, shadowed in the dim light. And how firm his mouth as he brushed it against hers. She could feel the impatient pressure building and building inside her. For a while she tried to ignore it, but it kept rising inside her, forcing her to stop her teasing play and position herself so that Michel could enter her.

He came into her slowly, obviously not wanting to hurt her. Oh, but he was so thoughtful always and so loving in his loving. "I love you, Michel," she murmured as the pressure inside her built unbearably, and heard him say "I love you," just before the tightness in her groin gave way to a hot rushing that would surely never stop.

IN THE MORNING, Grandmère came down in a white quilted satin robe to say goodbye. Michel had gone to bring the car around to the front door while Casey waited in the foyer.

"I am glad I caught you, *ma petite,*" Grandmère said. "Last night, my daughter told me what she had said to you and I did not wish you to leave my house with—what do you call it?—a sour taste in your mouth."

"I know she loves Michel," Casey said.

"As you do."

"Yes."

Hélène took her hand and kissed her cheek. "*Bien.* Then you must not worry. I have seen that Michel loves you, also. And I have begun a campaign to make my husband see that our grandson Charles will make an excellent chief executive officer." She frowned. "Jean-Paul, unfortunately, does not approve of Charles's wife, but I think I can change his mind there, also. I shall certainly try."

Surprised, Casey looked at her questioningly. "You want Michel to return to the States?" she asked.

"I do not want to lose him, naturally. But I want what is best for him. His gardens have always been best for him. I intend reminding my husband that he himself rebelled when he was much younger than Michel.

When he became interested in the manufacture of automobiles he was only twenty-two. His family disapproved greatly. They had always been landowners. They had never worked for a living, other than the management of their estates. But Jean-Paul was fascinated by the automobile—sure that eventually, everyone in the whole world would wish to possess one. Everyone except his grandfather. *His* grandfather wanted nothing to do with the noisy, smelly things. I will remind Jean-Paul of all these things, Casey, you may be sure.''

Casey smiled gratefully, feeling much more confident of the future, now that this sensible and charming woman was on Michel's side. "Thank you, *madame*,'' she said softly. "And thank you also for trying to make me feel comfortable here.''

Hélène looked at her shrewdly. "But you are not comfortable, *ma petite*.''

Casey shook her head. "I've told you a little about my background. You must surely see—''

"But this is an *absurdité*, this bother with background. You will remember that my own father painted naked ladies. Family does not matter, wealth does not matter, race, religion, education—none of these things matter. What matters is the individual, the person. What matters is love.''

Hélène squeezed her hand. "I think you will be a very worthy addition to this family, Casey,'' she told her.

Casey shook her head. "There's been nothing said about marriage,'' she remarked.

Hélène's blue eyes twinkled. "My grandson is like many other men—he has never been eager for commitment, but he is a family man in spite of his rebellion.

And I have seen how he looks at you. I will expect an invitation to the wedding before the year is out.''

Casey returned Hélène's goodbye hug with affection before going down to the car. What would Hélène say, Casey wondered, if she were to tell her she hadn't dared think seriously about the possibility of marriage, because if her thoughts became reality once more, she would spend the rest of her life worrying that she *had* exercised undue influence?

CHAPTER THIRTEEN

SKIP GRANGER WAS standing outside the apartment door, wearing sweats, loaded down with a couple of grocery bags and an oddly shaped red-enameled pan with an electric cord dangling from it. He smiled at Sarah when she opened the door.

How could such a big, tough-looking man have such a gentle smile, Sarah wondered. And how could that same gentle smile have such a tumultuous effect on her nervous system? "What are you up to now?" she asked.

Skip grinned. "Came for lunch, kid. Not too much going on at The Grange today. You like Chinese food?"

Another cooking lesson, obviously. Since Casey went to France almost a week ago, Skip had taught her how to fix meat loaf, two ways to cook fish, and French onion soup. "I like chop suey," Sarah said warily.

"Chop suey isn't Chinese, chop suey's American." Without so much as a by-your-leave, he walked past her into the apartment and put his packages down on the kitchen counter. "It's just as I thought. You need some lessons in stir-frying. I'm going to start you off with Szechuan chicken. Be able to surprise Casey when she gets home later."

"Maybe I don't want to learn stir-frying," Sarah said flatly as she closed the door.

Skip ignored her, busily unloading the bags he'd brought. "Here you have your chicken breasts, your snow peas and your mushrooms," he went on cheerfully. "Brown rice—more nutritious than white—bean sprouts, a bottle of peanut oil for cooking, red pepper flakes for spice, green onions, garlic, soya sauce, a little ginger root, a little vinegar and cornstarch. And this—" he added, indicating the red pan "—is an electric wok, my gift to you."

He pulled out a saucepan from one of Casey's cabinets and measured water into it. "Got to get the rice started—takes longer for brown than white."

"Looks like a lot of work from where I stand," Sarah said, looking over the pile of ingredients.

"It is a lot of work. Takes almost an hour to prepare, six minutes to cook. You got anything better to do?"

Why did he keep coming over like this? Sarah wondered. Just when she'd get herself convinced he was never going to look at her as anything but a charity case and it would be better for her peace of mind if he'd stop turning up, there he'd be again, smiling, making her feel happy. She didn't trust feeling happy. Never had. Happiness never lasted very long and when it was over, the unhappiness was worse than before.

"I was going to clean house before Casey gets here," she told him.

He glanced around the large room. "Looks spotless already, you ask me."

Sarah sighed. "Okay—you win. What do I have to do?"

"Sit down at the table, shell half a cup of peanuts, and watch closely."

She couldn't help but admire the delicacy of his big hands as he peeled the outer skin from a bundle of green onions, the easy skill with which he cleaned and chopped the various items. He told her stories as he worked, entertaining her with the things that could go wrong in his restaurant, the strange people who sometimes came into his bar, making her laugh, making her feel good all over, making her feel happy.

"What about your ex-wife?" she asked as he deftly cut the chicken breasts into cubes. "Does she ever come into your restaurant?"

He glanced up. "Casey told you about Brenda?"

"Enough."

A shadow passed over his face, but was quickly gone. "Brenda doesn't come around anymore," he said with no expression in his voice.

"That bother you?" she asked.

"That relieves me," he stated firmly.

Could she possibly allow herself to hope? No, she was being foolish again. Skip Granger was *somebody*—a well-known figure in town, owner of a popular restaurant and bar, a well-to-do, good-looking mature man who could have his pick of women. What could he possibly see in a down-on-her-luck teenager twenty years younger than him, with a belly out to here and nothing to offer but the love that kept sparking inside her every time she saw him. It was pretty obvious he thought of her as only a kid. He'd even told Casey he'd considered adopting her. Probably a joke, but that had been a bad moment, when Casey told her that. Until then, she'd allowed herself to daydream. Stupid. With all that had happened to her, you'd think she'd have learned by now it didn't pay to daydream.

"You daydreaming?" Skip asked, making her almost jump off her chair. He took the heavy gold watch off his wrist and handed it to her. It still held the warmth of his body, and her fingers closed greedily around it. "I'm ready to start cooking this epicurean delight," he informed her. "Want you to time the operation. Give you practice timing contractions."

She used Amanda as an excuse for her lack of attention. "Baby's kicking," she said. "Guess she doesn't like the smell of those pepper flakes you're tossing around there." Feeling suddenly mischievous, she got up awkwardly from her chair and walked over to Skip. "You want to feel Amanda?" she asked.

He stared at her for a moment, then grinned. "Sure would. Can't say I ever did that."

She took his big hand and placed it carefully on her abdomen, watching his face. "This kid's going to be a gymnast," she announced softly, adding as Amanda landed a series of pretty hefty blows, "There goes one of her backward somersaults now."

A look of shock had appeared on Skip's face, but as she watched him, the look became one of awe, and then his expression softened altogether and she felt warmth and tenderness flow into her stretched flesh as he lightly caressed her abdomen. "Would you believe that?" he murmured. "Always thought it would be like a tickle— little tiny feet and hands moving like that. But that's a wallop if ever I felt one." Still cupping Sarah's abdomen, he spoke very softly, tilting his head down as if he were speaking to the baby. "Going to sign you up, little guy. Get you started out in football soon as possible."

"It's a girl," Sarah reminded him.

Straightening, he lifted his eyebrows. "You sure about that?"

"I know it."

He gave her another of those gentle smiles that set her blood zinging through her veins, making her heart beat like she'd run up four flights of stairs in one-hundred-degree heat. "Boy or girl, you've got one healthy little infant there, Sarah, my girl," he murmured.

Sarah, my girl. Sarah's love-starved heart seemed to swell inside her at the affection in his voice. Then her common sense took over. Skip had been moved by feeling the life inside her. Nothing more.

"Let's get on with this cooking demonstration," she said sharply.

Skip didn't move away from her right away. He was still looking down at her, one hand still resting lightly on her belly. There was a strange look on his face, but Sarah wasn't about to try to interpret it. She was through building castles in the sky, she decided.

CASEY ARRIVED a couple of hours later, in time to sample some of the Szechuan chicken heated up in the microwave. Skip had left a few minutes earlier after insisting on washing the dishes and cleaning up the kitchen. He had still seemed a little distracted, Sarah thought. Probably he was in a hurry to get back to his restaurant—back to his own life. He'd done his good deed for the day.

"This is wonderful," Casey said. "I skipped dinner on the airplane. My inner time clock's all out of whack again."

"How was your trip?" Sarah asked, seating herself at the other side of the gateleg table. She was worried about Casey. She looked unusually...somber.

Casey plied her chopsticks for a couple of minutes without answering, using the slim pieces of wood far more efficiently than Sarah had done. Sarah's face warmed as she remembered the suffocated feeling that had come over her when Skip took hold of her hand to show her exactly where to put her fingers so the chopsticks would work. Hadn't she sworn hatred toward all men all those months ago when her uncle had attacked her? What was she doing mooning over a man who was old enough to be her father?

It wasn't mooning, a solemn little voice said in her mind. This feeling she had for Skip was love. No doubt about that.

"Paris is a fascinating city," Casey said.

"Wasn't asking about Paris," Sarah replied.

Casey grinned ruefully. "I know that." She shook her head. "I don't know what to tell you, Sarah. It was such a mixture of things. Michel's family—well, some of them, his grandparents at least, were great. His mother—well, let's just say she didn't exactly take a shine to me. The rest—they were too busy worrying about their own positions in the family hierarchy to want to get to know me."

"And Michel?"

Again Casey shook her head. Then she put down her chopsticks and sighed. "I don't know, Sarah. Maybe he'll come back, maybe he won't. He wants to, but there's a lot of pressure on him to stay."

"He'll come back," Sarah said confidently. "I know it in my bones. Very psychic, my bones."

"Your bones were psychic, you wouldn't be in this fix," Casey reminded, gesturing at Sarah's abdomen.

"Truth in that," Sarah admitted judiciously.

Casey laughed, then seemed to throw off her somber mood, grinning suddenly at Sarah and picking up her chopsticks again. "I had this great idea on the airplane," she said after sampling a slice of mushroom. "I'm going to give a baby shower for you."

"Shower's supposed to be for a woman's friends," Sarah pointed out. "I've only got Jolene and her boyfriend. Not too sure I want to see them for a while."

"*I* have friends," Casey told her. "I owe them all a party. They've entertained me more than I've entertained them. I'll invite everyone I can think of. Marilyn, Barbara, Fumiko, Leslie, Dorrie. We'll make it a mixed shower, couples." She frowned, "Well, no, Barbara might feel bad, not having a husband anymore. Unless she wanted to invite someone else as an escort." She nodded, getting all her plans straight in her head. "No games," she added. "Just good food and lots of presents for Amanda."

"Nobody's going to want to come," Sarah protested.

Casey put her chopsticks down again and looked steadily into Sarah's eyes. "Everyone likes a party," she said. "What's truly bothering you?"

Sarah squirmed uncomfortably on the hard dining chair. "People going to look on me as a charity case."

"People are going to look at you as a nice young woman who's about to have a baby," Casey told her. "Everybody likes babies as much as they like parties."

"I've got nothing to wear," Sarah protested, looking down at her stretched-out T-shirt and worn jeans.

Casey grinned. "Spoken like a true member of the female sex. I'll see if there's anything in the store we can alter to fit. I remember this one smocked dress, kind of Empire style, cut pretty full. I meant to have you come into the shop to try it on, but then Michel called and it went out of my mind." She reached a hand across the table and laid it warmly over Sarah's hand. "Let me do this for you, Sarah. After all, if Michel doesn't come back I'm going to be a basket case—so then you can take care of me, and we'll be even."

Maybe Casey needed the planning of this party to make her feel better, Sarah thought. And the more she thought about it, the more excited she felt. Nobody had ever given a party for her before. "It's a deal," she said.

Casey squeezed her hand and released it, then raised her eyebrows. "There's a young man lives in the same apartment complex as Michel—Sidney Arundel?"

"The one delivered your flowers to the shop?"

Casey nodded. "He seems awfully nice. Should I invite him to the shower as your date?"

Sarah shuddered. "Lord, no, Casey. You lost your mind? What kind of guy wants to have a blind date with a pregnant woman?"

"You may have a point there." She shrugged. "Okay, I won't have a date, either, so we'll go it alone."

"Could always ask Skip," Sarah suggested, making her voice as casual as possible. "He's going to have a financial interest in this baby—temporarily, anyway." She concentrated on pouring Casey some green tea to go along with the last of her chicken. She hadn't wanted to try the green tea herself until Skip told her it was full of vitamin C. To her surprise she'd quite liked it. She poured another cup for herself, wondering if Casey was ever going to answer.

Finally she looked up, to find Casey frowning. "You don't want to ask Skip?"

Casey started. "Sure I do. Of course. I was just remembering something."

What she'd remembered was that now that Skip had agreed to lend her the money to pay Sarah's hospital bill, she had to figure out a way to pay him back. But she wasn't about to tell Sarah that.

THE PARTY WAS HELD a little over a week later. Casey had hoped that by some miracle Michel might return in time to attend, but when he called her a couple of days before, he still didn't seem sure how much longer he'd need to remain in France. Grandpère was much better, he told Casey, but still working on Michel to get him to stay.

And Angèle? Casey wanted to ask. Is she still working on you?

Actually, Casey had very solemnly and determinedly wished that Michel would return in time for the party, hoping that fairy godmother Inga might possibly be listening in. But obviously the powers that be had decided not to grant Casey's every wish. They had their own very selective interpretation of her heart's desire, she thought as she made a last-minute check of her appearance before her guests arrived. She had brought a lovely aqua silk blouse home from the shop and paired it with a pleated black silk skirt that almost reached her ankles, the two items pulled together by a wide aqua and black beaded belt she'd found at a flea market some time ago. For a second, she panicked, wondering if the top had been brought into the shop by any of the women who were attending the party, but then she remembered it was part of a consignment sent over by a woman in Bellevue.

Everyone had accepted her invitation, including Barbara. To Casey's dismay, when she opened the door to Barbara, the first arrival, she discovered she'd brought along Justin, of all people. He seemed a little embarrassed when he first greeted Casey, but relaxed when the rest of the guests arrived and he could mingle. Barbara kept glancing at him in a rather pleased and proprietary way whenever he spoke, Casey noticed. Could Barbara possibly have . . . designs on him? She'd always liked him. And of course she'd known him for years, ever since she and Marilyn were in school together. Well, well, well! she thought as she walked around the room offering stuffed mushrooms and crudités to her guests—it just might be that Justin was going to get his rich wife, after all.

Marilyn Kendrick looked like a ripened fruit about to burst, Casey thought. She was precariously balanced on a straight chair, having refused the sofa in case she wasn't able to get up again. Her face was shinier than usual, her eyes as blue as cornflowers. Her skin had never looked lovelier. Her husband, Ted, was keeping a wary eye on her; he hadn't left her side since they arrived. How wonderful to have someone so completely devoted to you, Casey reflected. How wonderful to be expecting the child that particular someone had fathered. How she wished— Hastily she cut off her thoughts and went into the kitchen to refill her serving tray.

"You okay?" she asked Sarah, who was measuring coffee beans into the grinder.

"Doing just fine," the girl replied, her brown eyes sparkling. "You got great friends, Casey. They've all been so nice to me."

"Brought lots of gifts, too," Casey said with a grin. "I knew they'd turn up trumps."

Actually, she was very proud of her friends. They had all responded with great tact and generosity when she'd described Sarah's situation to them.

"Skip didn't get here yet," Sarah commented.

Casey shrugged. "Said he'd be a little late, had to get through the restaurant's rush hour first. He'll make it, Sarah. He's very reliable."

"Oh, I wasn't worried," Sarah said airily. But she did seem nervous. Hardly surprising, considering all the strangers she'd had to meet this evening. Of all the people here, she'd only met Fumiko before. Fumiko had brought her husband, Goro, who didn't seem to be having a good time—he was sitting in one of Casey's hard-bottomed dining chairs, looking genial enough, but not joining in the conversation.

Perhaps he was nervous, too, like Sarah. Sarah must be hoping Skip would come soon. At least his was a familiar face.

"You look lovely," Casey told Sarah, hoping to make her feel more at ease. Not that the compliment was unfounded—Sarah did look very pretty in the gold-colored Empire-style dress Casey had brought home for her.

Sarah tossed her head, obviously pleased, making her dozens of braids swing in unison. "How do I smell?" she asked.

Casey sniffed in her general vicinity. "Nice," she said, though in truth she couldn't smell anything in particular.

Sarah gave her a sheepish smile. "You don't recognize it?"

Casey frowned. Surely Sarah couldn't possibly mean...

"I used a little of that perfume in your medicine cabinet," Sarah said hesitantly, obviously aware of Casey's frown. "Hope you don't mind. I just happened to see it when I was cleaning the bathroom earlier. Took it out and smelled it." She rolled her eyes. "Prettiest smell ever. Couldn't resist trying it." She looked anxiously at Casey. "You mad at me, Casey?"

Casey managed to shake her head, but speech was beyond her. Why had it never occurred to her that Sarah might come across the magic perfume? What if it worked for her as it had worked for Casey? It would be Casey's responsibility.

She became aware that Sarah was waiting for an answer, looking worried. "It's okay," she managed to croak, and then the doorbell rang.

Somehow she knew who it would be before Sarah opened the door. And there he was, all dressed up in a shirt and tie and a beautifully cut beige blazer and brown slacks, standing there grinning foolishly down at Sarah, a huge brightly wrapped package in his arms. Apparently he couldn't take his eyes off the girl. He looked positively smitten.

"Skip," Casey called out in a voice that was a little too loud. All conversation ceased. All eyes looked at her, than at the new arrival.

Skip, never one to embarrass easily, grinned a general greeting to the crowd, then made his way through them to Casey. "Something wrong, Case?" he asked.

She shook her head. "I just need your advice about the chicken casserole," she improvised. Her voice was still pitched a little too high. "The recipe calls for three sprigs of fresh rosemary and I haven't got any. How much dried rosemary should I use?"

"Half a teaspoon ought to do it," Skip said, then frowned. "Anything wrong, Case? You look kind of pale."

"I'm hot, that's all."

"Cool day today. Usual August. Guess we aren't going to get any more summer until September."

"I've been cooking, that's why I'm hot."

"Uh-huh." He looked at her, narrow-eyed. "Person gets flushed from heat."

"I'm okay, Skip," she assured him.

He nodded. "Good," he said, then went off to join the others, heading straight to where Sarah was standing swapping pregnancy stories with Marilyn.

Within minutes he was smiling broadly, keeping his gaze fixed on Sarah's face, his brown eyes gleaming. No doubt about it, Casey decided. She hadn't seen Skip look so bemused around a woman since Brenda had decamped. Not only bemused, but *enchanted*.

As for Sarah, she was quite obviously eating up Skip's attention, darting flirtatious glances at him when she thought no one else was watching her, letting him help her get settled in her favorite rocking chair when everyone decided it was time to open the presents. Working on the last of the dinner arrangements, Casey wished profoundly that she'd never suggested this shower. Somebody was going to get hurt here, and she didn't want that happening to either Skip or Sarah.

Everyone but Casey seemed to have a good time at the shower. Ted Kendrick and Skip swapped football stories, Justin held forth on a couple of his favorite classic movies, with Barbara nodding and smiling alongside him. Leslie turned out to have a talent for palm reading, which Casey had never suspected, telling Sarah her baby was going to do something in politics. Sarah simply nodded. "Planned right along for Amanda to be president," she said amid general good-natured laughter.

After dinner, no one seemed inclined to leave. Sign of a successful party, Casey told herself, wishing they'd all get up and go so she could worry in private about Sarah and the magic perfume.

And then about nine o'clock she noticed that Marilyn Kendrick was sitting forward on the edge of her chair, holding on to its wooden arms with hands that trembled. Her body was braced, her eyes closed tightly, her mouth clamped firmly shut.

"Marilyn!" Casey exclaimed just as Ted caught sight of his wife's discomfort and knelt in front of her chair.

"Breathe through your mouth, honey," he said urgently and Marilyn obediently puffed audibly. A moment later she relaxed and everyone in the room breathed a sigh of relief. Ted had glanced at his watch and now he was gazing at Marilyn's face, waiting. When the next pain struck, Marilyn's back arched as if someone had struck her. The knuckles of both hands turned white as she gripped the chair arms. Her mouth shaped into a surprised O and her eyes grew wide as her body grew rigid.

"Relax, honey. Breathe the way you learned," Ted said calmly.

When the contraction ended, he hauled his wife out of the chair and eased her toward the door. "Sorry to break up the party," he said cheerfully. "Looks like all this baby talk stirred things up."

"Call me when the baby's born?" Casey asked as the couple went through the door.

"You bet," Ted said.

Marilyn smiled weakly. "It's not so bad, Sarah," she called to the younger girl, then grimaced as another contraction hit and she had to hang on to the doorjamb for a few seconds.

"Nothing to it," Sarah remarked. "I can see that for a fact."

Everyone laughed, then started making preparations to leave, wishing Sarah well as she thanked them for all the wonderful gifts they had brought.

"That was a terrific party," Sarah said when only she and Skip and Casey were left.

Skip grinned at her. "Lots of loot."

"That infant seat you brought is the best thing," she told him. "Never did see one as comfortable looking as that."

"Even a little guy needs comfort," he replied, looking embarrassed.

"Little girl," Sarah corrected him.

They exchanged a smile that turned each of their faces luminous. What the hell was she going to do? Casey wondered. This whole situation was her fault, her responsibility.

Skip was frowning now. "Seemed like Marilyn was in a lot of pain."

"That's the way it is with childbirth," Sarah explained matter-of-factly. "Marilyn will be okay. She's got Ted with her."

Skip nodded. "Sure seem to love each other a whole lot, those two." He frowned again. "Don't like to think of you going through all that alone," he added.

They exchanged a glance that seemed to Casey to be loaded with meaning.

"I'm going to be right there with Sarah," Casey said flatly. "She won't be alone for a minute if I can help it."

Casey might have been invisible for all the attention Skip and Sarah paid her. They were still staring at each other, looking now as if they'd never seen each other before. Looking moonstruck.

What on earth was she going to do?

Excusing herself, as if anybody was going to notice she was leaving, she went into the bathroom, took the golden bottle out of the medicine cabinet and stared at it as if she hoped to find some kind of instructions written on it. First, she had to get Skip out of here, she decided. Then she had to hide this bottle somewhere safe so Sarah wouldn't use it again—God only knew what would happen if she tried a second dose. Then she had to find a way to keep Sarah and Skip separated until the perfume had a chance to wear off—if it ever did.

Holding the bottle, she had unthinkingly removed the stopper. Once again the smell of it wafted around her, bringing thoughts of Michel and the wonderful fourposter bed they'd made love in while she was in France. She could almost hear his voice murmuring in her ear, feel his sensitive fingers touching her, his arms pulling her close.

Were these the kinds of thoughts Sarah and Skip were having about each other? If so, then the power of the perfume was confirmed. She had trapped Michel into a relationship, using undue influence.

The doorbell rang.

Hastily replacing the stopper, she stuffed the bottle in the pocket of her pleated skirt. Had one of the guests forgotten something? she wondered, hurrying out of the bathroom. Skip and Sarah were sorting through the packages together, folding the wrapping paper, so engrossed in their own low-voiced conversation they apparently hadn't heard the doorbell. Her concern rapidly increasing, Casey passed them by and flung open the door.

Michel.

He was wearing the dark knit shirt and white chinos he'd evidently traveled in, his dark hair tousled over his forehead. He was clutching a bouquet of Shasta daisies, evidently newly picked. He was smiling his whimsical smile, obviously pleased that he'd managed to surprise her.

For at least half a minute, Casey stared up at him in shock. Where had he suddenly appeared from? He hadn't intended coming back to Seattle today. The bottle in her pocket seemed heavy, pulling her down. Had opening it precipitated another genie effect?

She wasn't ready to see Michel. She had to think about this new problem with Sarah and Skip and the whole moral implication of her own use of the perfume. Maybe Michel was just an illusion, a dream. Maybe if she closed her eyes, he'd disappear in a puff of smoke. She tried it, just in case, closing her eyes tightly, then opening them again.

He was still standing there, gazing lovingly at her—gazing at her as though she were the most enchanting woman in the world, gazing at her intently, as though he could absorb all of her with his eyes. There was a smile playing around his lips, making her want to smile back, making her want to kiss him, touch him. But she must hold herself away from him, even if it hurt him. She had to tell him, confess to him, warn him....

"Chérie?" he said questioningly. Then he stepped inside the apartment and set the flowers down on a little Victorian table, took her in his arms and pulled her close to his hard body. A second later, he was kissing her with the ardent thirst of a man who had been traveling in the desert and had just found water. As the heady aroma of roses drifted all around her, she couldn't seem to remember what it was she was supposed to warn him about.

CHAPTER FOURTEEN

WHEN SHE WOKE UP, she wasn't sure at first where she was. She was only sure she shouldn't be there.

Michel's bedroom. What was she doing in Michel's bedroom?

Casey almost groaned aloud as she remembered Michel looking over her shoulder after his passionate greeting and discovering Skip and Sarah kneeling over the pile of presents, watching Michel and Casey, both of them smiling. While Casey was still in shock Michel had greeted Skip, introduced himself to Sarah, admired the infant seat she was caressing proudly, then propelled Casey out of the apartment and downstairs into his car.

All the way over here she had rehearsed how she would tell Michel about the perfume. But then when they arrived, he had taken her into his arms immediately, his lips claiming hers, the sweet warmth of his breath mingling with her own. Before she knew it she was naked and so was he and they were in bed together making wild and passionate love, heedless of the apartment's thin walls, heedless of anything but their need for each other.

They had made love half the night. And now it was almost sunup and she still hadn't told him about the perfume. She sat up, clasping her knees. In the cold light of day it seemed an impossible story to tell. She needed time to think about it, time to work it all out in her own mind, time to reach some kind of definite conclusion about her relationship with Michel. When she did tell him, she thought with a sinking heart, she might not *have* a relationship with Michel.

She became aware that Michel was awake, looking up at her. "Good morning, *chérie,*" he murmured, his voice husky with sleep. Then one strong arm came up to her shoulder, easing her down under the warm blankets.

"I have to go," she said urgently.

He shook his head, pulling her against him. "It is barely light outside. Another hour, *chérie*. I need at least another hour with you in my arms before I face the day." He was stroking her bottom gently, his hand warm and tender against her flesh.

"But you must have a lot to do. You haven't even unpacked."

"It is a Sunday," he pointed out. "I do not need to report to the office until tomorrow. My drawings and calculations are complete. And the unpacking can wait. I do not foresee a need for any clothing today."

He kissed her, wondering why her body was feeling so suddenly stiff. Come to think of it, when he first arrived at her apartment, she had not reacted as he had hoped, had expected, to his homecoming. She had seemed almost sorry to see him.

Once they were in bed, she had been her usual loving self, moving with him as though their lovemaking had been choreographed in advance, seeming to know instinctively what would please him most, opening her body to him without hesitation when he touched her in a certain way.

Now she seemed stiff again, reluctant. Smiling reassuringly at her, he released her and excused himself to use the bathroom. When he returned, she'd gathered up all her clothing, and she scooted into the bathroom without more than a shy smile that didn't quite reach her eyes.

He had coffee ready when she emerged fully dressed. For a moment he thought she was going to refuse even that, but after a few seconds of obvious wavering she sat down and picked up the cup he'd poured for her. "You cannot possibly stay?" he asked.

She shook her head. "I'm worried about Sarah. I should never have gone off and left her alone with Skip like that."

"You surely do not think he would...what, take advantage of her? In her condition?"

"No, of course not." She didn't look as sure of that as she sounded. "I think Skip likes her," she said worriedly.

"She seems likable."

"I mean, he *really* likes her." She frowned. "I feel responsible. It's all my fault."

"Because you gave her a home when she needed one? You've done only good things for Sarah, *chérie*. I fail to see any problem in Skip liking her. Even if he *really* likes her."

She showed no amusement at his imitation of her. "He's almost old enough to be her father," she said.

"But he is not her father. Some women like older men," he pointed out.

She shook her head and set her coffee cup down. "I have to go," she insisted. "I have to make sure she's okay."

She wasn't making eye contact with him at all, he realized. Something was wrong—not just her worry about Sarah, but something else. Something to do with him. He felt as though someone had struck him in the chest with a sharp rock and he couldn't get his breath. If he lost Casey now... "Are you angry with me, Casey?" he asked.

She had stood and turned away as though she were going to walk out without even a goodbye kiss. Now she glanced at him as if startled and shook her head, then hesitated. She looked so pretty in her blue-green blouse. The luminous silk brought out the intense color of her eyes and contrasted flatteringly with her red hair. She had left her hair down, the way he preferred it.

All at once she was looking at him with an apologetic expression. "I haven't even asked about your grandfather," she said.

"He is much better," he assured her. "Before I left he was walking every day in the garden. I placed a bench near the rose garden so that he could rest when necessary."

Mention of the rose garden seemed to make her agitated again, but she listened intently as he told her about watching his grandmother walking with Grandpère, holding his arm as though it were she who might need the support. "It was something very nice to see, the two of them walking together in my garden," he said.

Taking advantage of the softening he saw in her face, he stood up and went to her, slipping his arms around her and kissing her lightly. "Grandmère said to give you her love. And Maman also asked me to pass on her regards."

She looked at him directly then, as if she expected him to say something more about his mother, but then she shook her head a little and asked, "How does Grandpère—your grandfather—feel about you coming back to Seattle?"

He laughed shortly. "About as you would expect. He did not give me his blessing, but he did allow that he understood. Grandmère has been working hard, praising Charles and Sebastien. I did my part, reminding him that Charles is the most knowledgeable of us all about the regulations governing installation of antipollution equipment. Europe has always trailed behind the United States in reducing automobile emissions. Rapide is environmentally aware, but has not kept up with all the new standards. Charles's favorite small talk deals with catalytic converters and fuel-injection systems and platinum- and rhodium-coated cylinders. Grandpère knows how brilliant Charles is, but he was so stubbornly set on having me take over, he would not admit Charles is perfect for the job. But now he has finally reconciled himself to my departure, it seems. He at least let me go without making me feel guilty this time."

He laughed shortly. "As soon as he seemed reconciled, I left before he could change his mind. That is why I did not take time to telephone you to announce my homecoming. I hope my arrival was not too much of a shock."

Tell me it was a wonderfully pleasant shock, he wanted to urge her. Tell me it was the best thing that ever happened to you. Tell me you have longed for me to come.

"That's okay," she replied vaguely. Then her gaze shifted and he felt a resistance in her body again. "I really do have to go," she said.

"I will see you later?"

She hesitated, then fumbled with the shoulder strap of her purse as though it had developed a knot only she could see. "I've got so much to do, Michel. I'd like to go by the hospital this afternoon and check on Marilyn Kendrick—she went into labor at the party last night."

"It appears you had an interesting party. I wish I could have arrived in time to take part."

She nodded, still not looking at him. "I made a wish that you would, but . . ." She was becoming agitated again, heat rising into her face, coloring her cheekbones. Jamming her hands into the pockets of her skirt, she blushed even more, and pulled out a small golden bottle with her right hand. "I completely forgot it was here," she muttered. "What if it had broken and spattered all over me?" She shuddered, then carefully placed the object in her purse. "I'll call you," she said after another awkward pause.

Why did he feel he might never see her again? Why was she behaving so strangely? "You are experiencing the flight response again for some reason?" he asked her. "You are 'going to your room' again?"

She shook her head a little too quickly.

"Casey?"

"I have to go." She glanced at his face, then away. "I will call, honestly."

"I do not believe this is only to do with Sarah. In some way I have offended you. Please tell me what I have done, Casey."

"You've done nothing. It's just that I . . . have to do some thinking."

"About you and me?"

She looked miserable—so miserable he didn't have the heart to question her any further, even though he desperately needed to know for his own peace of mind what had gone wrong between them.

His family? Was she upset over the way some members of his family had treated her? He'd had a few heated words to say to them himself.

She was heading for the door again. "Casey," he said softly. She stopped but didn't turn around, her shoulders hunching as though she expected him to question her again. "I drove you over here," he reminded her.

"I'll take a cab. I don't want to bother you."

As though anything concerning her could be a bother to him. "I will call a taxi for you," he told her, not wanting to distress her further.

"Thank you," she said. "I'll wait for it outside." Her voice was so polite, he felt it might turn his blood to ice.

SARAH WAS VACUUMING when Casey arrived home. She was alone. Casey's relief took the form of a gushing sigh that seemed to let the stuffing out of her body so that she almost folded down to the floor. "Hi," she managed to say.

Sarah grinned cheerfully and carried on without a pause, humming as she worked.

"What time did Skip leave?" Casey asked after she'd changed into jeans and a shirt.

Sarah was wrapping the vacuum-cleaner cord around the back of the machine. "Eleven, maybe," she said and smiled again, her whole face lighting up this time.

"Is everything okay?" Casey asked.

Sarah looked at her sharply, probably surprised at the tense note that had come into Casey's voice. "Why shouldn't it be?" she asked.

"I don't know. I got the feeling something had changed between you and Skip at the party. I sort of worried about you last night."

Sarah laughed. "Way you looked when Michel took you out of here, I shouldn't have thought you were going to worry about anything. Looked stunned, you ask me. Like a woman in love, if I ever saw one." Her eyes narrowed again. "What you think, Skip was going to rape me?"

"Of course not."

"But you got the idea he was maybe interested in me—that way?"

Casey took a deep breath and sat down at the gateleg table. "Something like that, yes."

Sarah beamed, then tugged her T-shirt down over her belly and patted her bulging abdomen complacently. "Got that idea myself."

"You don't mind?"

"Why should I mind? Skip's a wonderful man."

"I thought you didn't like him all that much."

"Meant you to think that," she said, sitting down in the opposite chair, her eyes gleaming. "Didn't want you knowing I had the hots for him myself. Seemed pretty stupid, someone with a baby just about to pop into the world getting romantic ideas. And it looked like Skip saw me as some little kid got herself in trouble. So I was protecting my pride. Learned how to do that over the years."

Casey looked at her closely. There was a glow about her that hadn't been there before. In her eyes, in her skin. "Did he...*say* anything?"

Sarah grinned. "Like what?"

"Well, I mean, anything romantic—like how you looked, how you smelled."

"Said I looked pretty. Didn't notice the perfume, I guess." She frowned. "That what this is about, Casey. You mind that I used your perfume?"

"No, it's not that I mind. I just..." Why on earth had she said anything at all, she wondered. There was no way she was going to tell Sarah the truth about the perfume. "I guess I just wondered what got into Skip all of a sudden," she finished lamely.

"Maybe it was my new dress," Sarah suggested.

Fat chance, Casey thought, suddenly seeing Inga's conspiratorial smile again.

She had to do something here; that much was obvious. But short of trying to inveigle Brenda back into Skip's life—which would be a disaster—she didn't have a thought in her head. Except that she suddenly didn't want to borrow money for Sarah's baby from Skip anymore. Which meant she had to find another source.

Barbara? she wondered. Then shook her head. Barbara had enough on her plate with her divorce going through and Justin in the picture.

Marilyn? Probably not a good idea to borrow from friends, anyway.

"You going to see Skip again?" she asked.

Sarah shrugged. "I don't know. He didn't say." She looked gloomy at the thought. But then she brightened. "He knows where I am," she said confidently. Then she grinned at Casey. "My turn," she announced. "How are things with Michel?"

"His grandfather's getting better," Casey said.

"Wasn't asking about his grandfather."

"Michel's fine," Casey stated flatly.

"But?"

Casey shook her head. "I don't want to talk about Michel. I have to think about things a while, make up my mind..." She let her voice trail off, aware of Sarah's sympathetic expression. "I think I'll go down to the store," she announced abruptly.

"You and Michel will work everything out, Casey," Sarah said softly.

Casey nodded, not at all sure she agreed.

After doing a few things at the shop that could easily have been postponed until Monday, she drove to the hospital and looked in on Marilyn, then admired Scott Boyd Kendrick through the nursery windows. The baby had arrived very soon after his parents got to the hospital. "I didn't even have time to get nervous," Marilyn had told her.

He was a beautiful baby; as blond as his mother, round-faced and contented-looking like his father. Casey allowed herself a couple of minutes of wishing—generally, not specifically—that she might have a baby someday, then she returned to the shop and went on a blitz of dusting. There was something about dusting, she thought, that precluded thinking; and she'd found, after all, that she didn't want to think, even though she now had all the time she needed.

When she got through dusting, she checked every dress and skirt and jacket in the shop for creases, then rearranged all the jewelry in the display case. She could get another job, she thought suddenly. Not instead of this one, of course, but as well as. If she had another job she could earn the money for Sarah's baby, if she could get the hospital to let her pay the bill off on a monthly basis. And if she had another job she would be too busy to see much of Michel. And maybe she could decide what to do.

At about three o'clock, the telephone rang. Thinking it might be Michel, redirected by Sarah, she almost didn't answer it, but the ringing persisted and at last she picked up the receiver and said hello.

To her surprise, the caller was a woman who owned an antique shop up close to the Canadian border. A customer who regularly dropped in on her way from Bellingham to British Columbia had mentioned that she and her husband had been victimized by a con man, she said. Seemed the man had sold the couple some stuff supposed to get rid of termites or something like that.

"Carpenter ants?" Casey queried.

"That's it," the woman replied. "I remembered you asking for information if I came across any. I don't know too many details. Just that it was Bellingham, and the man drove a red Porsche just like you'd said. And he had a foreign accent. My friend thought he might be from Puerto Rico."

"Do you know when it happened?" Casey asked.

"Last week," the woman told her.

When Michel was in France. Carefully, Casey took down the customer's name and address and phone number, thanked the dealer and hung up, then considered what to do. She certainly wasn't ready to talk to Michel yet, but she had to get this information to him right away.

At last, she checked with directory service under Sidney Arundel, dialed his number and found to her relief that the young man was at home. Directing him to write everything down, she gave him all the information and asked him to deliver it to Michel as soon as possible, which he agreed to do. Then she left the shop and walked down to the waterfront. Obviously, she had to think things through now, whether she wanted to or not.

ON MONDAY MORNING, Michel walked the Cartwright Tower rooftop again with Cartwright and Roger Prestergard. After lunch, the two men joined him in his new office. As they leaned over his massive desk, poring over the detailed renderings he had prepared while in France, Michel decided he was pleased with the way the meeting was going. He was also amused that the two men did not fit stereotyped images. Prestergard, the developer, was slight and elegant, hair combed just so, dapper in white shirt and striped tie and knife-creased slacks. He was fussy about details but quick to grasp overall perspective.

Cartwright, whose wealth and philanthropy were legendary, was a giant of a man with curly gray hair, wearing his usual uniform—blue jeans and running shoes and a T-shirt, this one with a race-car logo emblazoned across the back. He was most concerned with good design. In the beginning, some of Cartwright's preconceptions had threatened to conflict with Michel's ideas, but Cartwright was a reasonable man and had shown a willingness to listen.

"What have you got under this small lawn area?" Prestergard asked, straightening up and smoothing his already smooth hair.

"One hundred and fifty millimeters of soil laid over glass-fiber matting," Michel answered.

"And these plants, what are they?"

"I plan to use mostly evergreens so we won't have a cleanup problem. Rhododendrons, azaleas, japonica, juniper."

Prestergard nodded. "Plenty of sitting room, logical traffic patterns. Timed irrigation. Looks good to me."

Cartwright was still hunched over the desk. "Those screens are ingenious," he commented and Michel let out a breath he hadn't realized he was holding. It was going to be okay.

"Took some tips from the Japanese," he confessed. "Kept everything in miniature to suggest a parklike landscape."

Cartwright smiled. "Some buildings in Tokyo have a whole kiddie playground on the roof. Do anything they put their minds to, the Japanese."

"I can have working drawings and materials lists ready by the end of the week," Michel said.

Cartwright and Prestergard exchanged a glance, then Cartwright nodded. "We'd like you to oversee the project to completion," he said.

"No problem," Michel assured him.

The two men turned back to look at the drawings again just as the phone buzzed. Michel walked around the desk to answer it, hoping it might be Casey. He'd tried to reach her yesterday after receiving her message from Sidney, but without success. Sarah had said she had no idea where she'd gone if she wasn't at the shop. He had no idea why Casey had chosen to send the message by such a circuitous route instead of calling him herself.

"Sergeant Bennett," the voice on the other end announced.

Michel flashed a quick glance at the others but they were talking between themselves, pointing out something on the plans, paying no attention to him for the moment.

"What can I do for you?" he asked carefully.

WHEN THE DOORBELL RANG, Sarah was sure it must be Skip. It was just about the right time of the day for him to be coming over to help her figure out what to cook for dinner. She had wished all day that he would come. She'd really thought he might call the previous day, but he hadn't. She was disappointed but not yet willing to relinquish hope.

The tall thin man outside the door was a stranger—at least she didn't know who he was, though he looked vaguely familiar, as if she might have glimpsed him somewhere.

She didn't like the way he looked at her, his eyelids hooded over eyes that were set too close together. She held onto the heavy door ready to slam it in his face if he took one step forward.

"Name's Vern Gilbert," the man said in a gravelly voice, passing a hand over his thinning sandy hair.

She relaxed. A rapist or burglar probably wouldn't introduce himself. "You selling something?" she asked.

His laughter had no mirth in it. "I own this building," he said.

Vern Gilbert. The landlord. Of course. Casey didn't like him. Sarah could see why—something not nice about that smirk on his face.

"This is a studio apartment," he said.

"No kidding," Sarah answered before she realized she shouldn't antagonize Casey's landlord. He was heavily into rules, Casey had said. "What can I do for you?" she asked more politely.

"Studio apartment's meant for one-person occupancy," he said. "One person only. It's in the rental agreement."

"Just passing through, myself," Sarah answered hastily.

His eyes narrowed. "You've been here five weeks come tomorrow."

She *had* seen him around, skulking in the halls and the building's foyer. Casey had told her about the cat incident and they'd both laughed. This wasn't so funny. "I'm a slow traveler," she explained.

"You figuring on moving on soon?" he asked with heavy emphasis on the last word. "Sure as shootin', one of you has to."

"Day before yesterday," Sarah said, then remembered she was supposed to be mollifying this man. "Planning on going today, as it happens," she added airily.

His face showed suspicion. "Sure enough? Now, isn't that a coincidence. Sure was a long visit."

"Casey's a good hostess. And a good tenant for you, Mr. Gilbert."

"Still got to mind the rules," he said. Then he smoothed his thin hair again and smiled slyly. "Bon voyage," he told her, adding "I'll be watching," before he turned away.

Sarah carefully closed and locked the door, then rushed for the phone to call Casey.

Fumiko answered. "Casey had to go out," she said.

"Where did she go?" Sarah asked.

"Some kind of interview. Didn't know when she'd be back."

After she'd hung up the telephone, Sarah glanced at Casey's chiming clock. Three o'clock. Damn. Where *was* Casey? With Michel, maybe? What the hell was she going to do? There was no way she could go back to Jolene's place. And after five weeks of comfort, it would be harder than ever to go back to the streets.

She shook her head, picking up the telephone receiver again. She had known even while she was talking to Vern Gilbert that there was only one person could get her out of this difficult situation.

"Skip," she said when he answered. "I need help."

He came over right away, his tough face getting tougher as she described Vern Gilbert's visit. When she was done, he pulled one of Casey's dining chairs close to her rocker and took her hands in his. "First thing, you have to stop worrying," he began. "Nobody's going to let you go back to the street." He looked at her directly. "We could possibly fight this—but if we make difficulties for Casey with her landlord he might make things uncomfortable for her and we don't want that, do we?"

She shook her head, liking the sound of that "we"— she'd never had anyone talk about "we" where she was concerned. It gave her a good, warm safe feeling when Skip did it.

"So what we have to decide is where you are going to live. Which as I see it comes down to two choices. One, we could find you an apartment by yourself, which isn't too good an idea."

"Don't have the money," Sarah said flatly.

"Wasn't talking about money," Skip replied. "Don't like the thought of you being alone for your last month of pregnancy. Now, it's also possible that Casey might consider moving with you to another apartment, but I'm not sure she can afford a move right now."

"She can't," Sarah said.

"So that leaves us with one alternative, which happens to be something I was thinking about all day yesterday."

"Which is?"

"That I own an extra-large condominium that has plenty of room for one very pregnant lady."

Lady. She liked the sound of that, too. "You mean you'd let me rent some space?" she asked, wanting to be sure.

"I mean I want you to move in with me as my lady. If you want to—if you don't think that's taking advantage of you when you've got problems. And if you'd say yes for some reason other than that you need a place to stay."

"Oh, Skip," she said, feeling herself filling with sunshine, feeling happiness bursting inside her until her whole face must be one big smile. "You sure?"

He stood up, looking stern, then held out a hand to help her to her feet, too. "Think it might be possible for me to put my arms around you?" he asked.

She nodded, still smiling fit to burst. "You got long arms," she pointed out.

He held her gently, then kissed her very delicately on her forehead, then on her mouth. "No strings," he said. "Seems to me we ought to wait for the little guy to be born before we make any lasting arrangements."

"Little girl," she corrected happily.

He was still looking serious. "I'm a lot of years down the road ahead of you, Sarah. You've got to take that into consideration."

"One thing *you* should take into consideration," she added solemnly.

He frowned. "What's that?"

She took a deep breath. "I love you, Skip."

His face went through a whole transformation she'd never seen before, glowing like a light had switched on inside him. But then he looked stern again and she held her breath.

"This is ridiculous, you know. Old man like me."

She tipped her head back. "How old are you?"

"Thirty-nine."

She laughed. "Ancient is right. Guess I'll be ancient myself, someday. Happens to everybody sooner or later."

"Don't know what's got into me."

"Don't you?"

He looked thoughtful. "Seem to have felt something coming on ever since I met you," he said. "Kept telling myself it was just affection for this little unfortunate child who got herself pregnant, but knew all along it was more than that. Seemed to crystallize at that party Saturday night."

"Crystallize into what?"

He grinned. "Going to get the words out of me, aren't you?" He took a deep breath. "I love you, Sarah Bailey," he said tenderly. Then he hesitated. "I still think you should wait awhile before committing yourself. See how you feel."

"I know how I feel," Sarah insisted. "I know you are the kindest, dearest man ever, and if I can be with you I'm going to be the happiest woman in the world."

He grinned down at her. "You sure *look* happy."

She grinned, feeling some action inside her belly. "Amanda's kicking up her heels, too."

"Is that so?" Keeping one arm around Sarah's shoulders, he spread one of his big hands on her swollen abdomen. Amanda poked his hand with a delicate foot. "Maybe it is a girl, at that," he admitted.

"That going to be a problem with you?"

He shook his head. "I've developed this terrible fondness for little girls all of a sudden," he said. Then he dipped his head and kissed her with all the powerful emotion that had been building inside him since the first time he saw her—and thrilled to the fact that she was kissing him back with matching passion.

He'd finally done something right, he decided. Maybe reading Brenda's romance novels had done him some good, after all. It sure looked as if this particular story was going to have a happy ending.

CHAPTER FIFTEEN

"HOW WAS THE interview?" Fumiko asked.

It was only natural that she'd be curious. Casey hadn't given her any reason for her sudden call asking her to take over Second Time Around for an undetermined time. Usually Casey was very open with her friends, but right now she wasn't up to revealing anything. She made a "so-so" motion with her right hand. "Was it busy around here?" she asked.

Fumiko grinned and repeated Casey's gesture. "Sold that pink-and-black cocktail suit. Looked terrible on the lady that bought it—she had *blue* hair—but she insisted it was what she wanted. Barbara Harriman called to say she'd be bringing something in."

Casey nodded.

"Anything wrong?" Fumiko asked.

Casey shook her head.

"Guess I'd better get going. Kids will be getting hungry. You sure you're okay?"

"I'm sure," Casey said, and managed a smile.

"Sure enjoyed the shower the other night," Fumiko told her as she checked through her huge handbag for her car keys, pulling out a pacifier, a toy racing car and a folded diaper during the search. "Goro, too. He was impressed, the way Ted Kendrick fussed around Marilyn," she said. "Brought me breakfast in bed the next morning. Major breakthrough. Now all I have to do is keep reminding him about all the flowers Michel sends you and maybe he'll mend his ways." She hesitated on her way to the door. "Michel get back from France yet?"

Casey nodded. "Right after the party."

Fumiko studied her face, her own expression thoughtful. "Things not so good, huh?"

"Everything's fine," Casey assured her, which was certainly far from the truth.

A half hour later Michel burst into the shop. "We have things to celebrate," he said, looking jubilant, evidently not realizing Casey was not alone.

He looked wonderful. Impeccably dressed in his navy blazer and gray slacks, he was carrying a bunch of red roses wrapped in cellophane. "No time to go home for flowers, *chérie*," he told her, presenting the bouquet with a flourish. "I had to go to a flower shop this time. But of course I had to bring flowers, there is good news all around."

Barbara Harriman moved away from the side wall where she had been examining some of Casey's more recent acquisitions, her thin face alight with interest. Not ten minutes ago she had brought in the beaded dress she'd worn to Sarah's shower, telling Casey she could put it on sale; she'd already worn it three times. Now she was smiling meaningfully at Casey, obviously expecting an introduction. "My friend Barbara Harriman, Michel Smith," Casey said.

"Ah, the landscape architect," Barbara replied.

Michel smiled sheepishly as they shook hands. "You must forgive me, *madame*. I do not usually enter buildings so impetuously." Then he laughed and glanced sideways at Casey. "Well, perhaps I do," he amended. He bowed slightly, to Barbara's obvious delight and said, "Excuse me, I will fade into the walls while you finish your business."

"I don't see how he could possibly fade into the walls," Barbara remarked too loudly as she followed Michel admiringly with her gaze. "Congratulations, Casey," she added more quietly. "I couldn't imagine why you'd ditch Justin, but I'm beginning to get a glimmer."

"I didn't exactly ditch Justin," Casey murmured. "I told him I was seeing Michel and he ditched me."

"Justin never did like sharing," Barbara commented.

Casey could hardly tell her that it wasn't jealousy that had caused Justin to dump her—not without explaining Justin's quest for a rich wife, which wouldn't be a very sporting thing to do.

"I'm getting the feeling you're pretty fond of Justin," she remarked as she wrote Barbara a receipt for the clothing she'd brought in.

"Amazing, isn't it?" Barbara said cheerfully. "There he was all those years and I thought of him only as Marilyn's brother. Now . . . well, he's suddenly looking like someone I could care for. And he does seem to be showing an interest."

"I hope it works out for you," Casey told her, meaning that sincerely, hoping at the same time that Justin wasn't really more attracted by Barbara's money than herself.

"You, too," Barbara said with an arch glance toward Michel.

Michel came over to the counter as soon as Barbara left. "You see, your friend approves of me," he remarked happily, obviously having overheard Barbara's remarks.

Casey looked at him helplessly. She had hoped for a little more time before another confrontation with Michel. She still had no idea how to explain....

"You look very smart, *chérie*." he said. "Very businesslike. No vintage clothing today."

She glanced down at her tan rayon suit. "I had an...appointment. I just got back a few minutes ago." She shook her head. "You said you had good news," she reminded him.

He beamed at her. "Three times good news. First, I have a—what do you call it?—a go-ahead on my rooftop garden."

"That *is* good news. Congratulations."

He waved his hand in a dismissive gesture. "There is more. The police have discovered my Porsche in Portland, Oregon. It is in good condition—only the tape deck removed and the speakers."

"Did you tell the police about the woman in Bellingham?"

"Of course, early this morning. That is the third and best part of my news. Sergeant Bennett has called the police there and confirmed that the young man and woman have been operating their...con game in that city. He has told me that when all the facts are in I will be—what is the expression he used?—I will be off the hook." He grinned. "This is a very good expression. I have felt that I was hanging on a hook since all of this began."

He reached across the counter and took hold of her hand. "Thank you, *chérie,* for finding out about the people in Bellingham. Though I do not understand why you could not telephone me with such fine information. You did not wish to speak with me?"

"I was still thinking."

"Ah, yes. Thinking." He raised an eyebrow, but when she didn't offer any further explanation he shrugged and went on. "Sidney said you spoke with an antique dealer?"

"A woman I know. Actually, I talked to all the dealers I could think of. I figured sooner or later one of them might hear something."

"You are very resourceful, *chérie*. And as always, very kind. You have given me back my dignity. I will think of a way to thank you properly when we are in more private circumstances." His dark eyes held promises that made her heart start beating fast against her rib cage. Then he kissed her hand lightly. "I must ask for a favor again, Casey. I need someone to drive me to Portland so that I can bring the automobile back. Is it possible that you could do so tomorrow evening?" He smiled at her—a slow, sensual smile that made her breasts ache and her breath catch in her throat. "I thought perhaps we could stay for the night in Portland, drive back to Seattle on Wednesday morning."

Casey's heart sank. She wanted to help him, of course, but she certainly couldn't spend another night with him without explaining about the perfume. Besides which, she would probably be busy on Tuesday evening, and every evening thereafter. "I have to open the shop at nine," she protested, withdrawing her hand from his.

"We can leave Portland very early Wednesday morning."

"But I have so much to do. I can't just go dashing around the countryside. I have responsibilities, Michel." She had spoken curtly, aware that she wanted nothing more than to go with him, to spend the night in his arms; but she couldn't do that again, she mustn't—it wasn't fair to him.

Her sharp tone had hurt him, obviously. Hating to see the bright anticipation fading from his face, she turned away to put the roses in a vase, aware even as she did so that their fragrance was reminding her of that other perfume.

"It is all right, Casey," he said after a moment. "I will ask Sidney to drive with me."

She nodded, then looked up to find him gazing at her in a bewildered way. "I do not understand what is happening here, Casey," he said softly. "I think there is something you are not telling me. You said you wanted time to think, but I cannot imagine what is necessary for you to think about. Is it that my family has hurt you? My mother said she had perhaps offended you but would not tell me why. Is this what is wrong?"

She shook her head. "This has nothing to do with your mother." She certainly wasn't ever going to tell him what his mother had done, and she was relieved Jeanne hadn't confessed about the offer of money she'd made. She'd hate to feel she had in any way caused trouble between Michel and his mother. "Your mother did not offend me," she added, just to make sure.

He came around the counter and put his hands on her shoulders. Immediately her knees felt weak and she wanted nothing more than to just forget about the damn perfume and melt into his arms and tell him yes, she'd go with him to Portland tomorrow; yes, she'd spend the night; yes, she'd do anything he wanted her to.

She drew herself up, looking at him directly. "I have to talk to you, Michel," she said. "There's something I have to explain to you."

"We could have dinner at Étienne's, perhaps?"

She considered. Neutral territory would probably be best. That way she wouldn't suddenly find herself in bed with Michel without having had a chance to explain anything. "Okay," she agreed. "But first I have to go by my apartment. I want to tell Sarah we don't have to rely on Skip, after all."

He looked bewildered again. "I do not understand."

She took a deep breath. "Skip was going to lend me the money to pay for Sarah's hospitalization. Then I got worried about how I was going to pay him back. And then he got interested in Sarah and I decided it would be best if I could get the money from another source. So I'm going to take a job."

"You are closing your shop? But I thought you loved it."

"I do. And I'm not closing it. I'm taking a second job, in the evenings, working with a personnel service that places people in temporary jobs. That's what my appointment was. I went looking for part-time work and the supervisor offered me employment with the company. It's pretty good pay. I'll close the shop at six and go over there and work until nine or ten. This way, I can take care of Sarah myself."

His hands tightened on her shoulders, his face softening. "You would do this, work such long hours, go without time off—all for Sarah?"

She shrugged. "It seems the best thing to do."

"You have accepted this job?"

"I said I'd call tomorrow. But I'm going to take it, Michel. I have to. It won't be forever, after all. Just until Sarah can get on her feet. Between us we can manage, I think."

"But this is unnecessary," he said. "I can help Sarah. I did not know there was this money problem. I should have done, I suppose, when you told me Sarah's circumstances, but I imagined there was some kind of welfare system that would provide."

"Sarah doesn't want to get involved with any more agencies. She had a bad experience with the last one." She looked at him gratefully. "I appreciate your offer, Michel, but this isn't your responsibility."

"It is as much mine as it is yours," he argued. "The point is that I have more than enough money. I have no objection to using Rapide money for a purpose such as this. I certainly cannot stand by and see you work yourself to a shadow when it is no problem at all for me to provide the money. No, Casey," he said when she opened her mouth to protest. "I do not think you can speak for Sarah. I think you must let her accept or reject my offer for herself."

There was truth in what he said. And it would be such a relief if she didn't have to take the second job. She hadn't liked the look of the office or the supervisor, and she certainly didn't relish the idea of working twelve-to-thirteen hours a day. Besides which she would have to walk to her car alone, late at night.

"We'll let Sarah decide, then," she said. Feeling relieved, she managed a smile. "You'll have to be prepared to have her clean your apartment from end to end every day. My place has never looked so good. I think she spends the whole day cleaning. I've tried to get her to stop, but she doesn't pay any attention to me. She'll probably be scrubbing the floor when we get there."

But Sarah wasn't scrubbing the floor. She wasn't even home. Casey wasn't too concerned until she realized that all of Sarah's clothing had been removed from her closet. Even the shower gifts had been taken away. It was as though Sarah had never been there, except that the floor and furniture glowed from her waxing.

Luckily, before Casey could start worrying in earnest, Sarah returned, beaming, looking very pretty in a yellow maternity top Marilyn Kendrick had brought over for her on Saturday. She hugged Casey, then Michel, in an exuberant show of good spirits. "Got news," she crowed. "Got news you aren't going to believe."

"You have gone to live with Skip Granger," Michel said.

She stared at him openmouthed, looking so comically astonished that Michel laughed.

Casey fumbled blindly behind herself and sank down onto the daybed.

"How did you know?" Sarah asked.

Michel grinned. "I saw the way Skip was looking at you on Saturday night. I would never have believed that tough-looking face of his could acquire such a loving expression. It *is* love, *n'est-ce pas?*"

"Nesser what?" Sarah queried.

"It is an expression to mean is it not so," Michel explained.

"Well, it sure is," she said, with warmth in her voice. "Going to get married, that's how much love there is."

"But Sarah," Casey protested weakly, trying to pull herself together.

"Guess I'd better start at the beginning," Sarah said to her. "Vern Gilbert came by earlier."

Casey rallied, sitting up straight. "What did *he* want?"

"Wanted to know what I was doing living here. Told him I was passing through and he told me to keep on passing. Studio apartments meant for single occupancy, he says.''

Casey pushed herself to her feet, feeling heat rush to her face. "I'll see about that," she burst out angrily.

Sarah put her hands on Casey's shoulders and pushed her back down on the daybed. "Far as I'm concerned, Vern Gilbert is my fairy godmother," she said. "Going to say prayers for his health the rest of my life. No knowing how long it would have taken for Skip Granger to get around to admitting he loved me if it wasn't for Vern Gilbert coming and me calling Skip to ask him what I should do.''

"But Sarah, why didn't you call *me?*" Casey asked.

Sarah grinned. "I called you. Guess you were out with your main man here.''

"She was out having a job interview," Michel told her.

"Michel," Casey exclaimed, shaking her head.

Michel ignored her, looking directly at Sarah. "She was going to take a second job so she could help you with your hospital bills," he told the girl.

Sarah lowered herself awkwardly beside Casey and put her arms around her. There were tears in her eyes. "You're the best friend anyone ever had," she declared.

Casey lightly tugged a handful of braids. "Not so bad yourself," she said affectionately, then glanced up at Michel. "Michel came over here to offer to pay for your hospitalization himself," she told the girl.

Sarah's face turned up to Michel. "That the truth?"

Michel looked embarrassed. "I've got plenty of money, Sarah. I can still do it if you need me to. Unless Skip..."

Sarah climbed carefully to her feet and hugged him, too. "Life looks pretty good when there are people like you and Casey in it," she told him. "But neither one of you needs to worry about me anymore. Skip and I are a team now. He's even going to hire someone to come take care of Amanda and me the first month or so." She grinned at Casey, her eyes still suspiciously bright. "I suggested Fumiko. You said she always needed money and I reckon she knows all about taking care of babies." She paused for breath, then added, "You ever see Skip's condo?"

Casey nodded.

"He's even got a white leather sofa," Sarah crowed. "All my life I wanted a white leather sofa." Her face became very solemn all of a sudden, the tears starting up again. "All my life I wanted someone to love. Now I've got you two and Skip and Amanda." She shook her head, making her braids swing. "Going to make myself cry all over my new clothes, I keep on this way." Wiping her eyes with the back of her hand, she headed for the door. "Got to get back to Skip. He's waiting downstairs. Going to take me to dinner at his restaurant. Wants everyone to meet me. Can you beat that? He loves me," she added with wonder in her voice, stopping to look at Casey, then at Michel, her face radiant. "Skip Granger loves me. And he's going to love Amanda. I know he is. Though she might have to play football whether she wants to or not." She giggled and turned back to the door. "Listen to me, I'm getting hysterical. I've got to go."

"But Sarah," Casey croaked, suddenly remembering that she had to stop this whole thing from happening. She stood again, but Sarah was already out the door.

"This is terrible," Casey said, sitting down again, feeling totally stunned.

Michel sat down on the daybed beside her, feeling more mystified than ever by Casey's odd behavior. "How can you say that, *chérie?* Sarah looks happier than anyone I ever saw. Skip's face, Saturday night, leads me to believe he is also happy. Why, then, are you so obviously unhappy?"

"He's twenty years older than she is."

"This is not important when there is love, Casey."

"They hardly know each other."

"Sometimes lightning strikes. As it struck with you and me, *n'est ce pas?*" He put his arms around her and kissed her gently. "It is not so bad to be struck by lightning, Casey."

She didn't even seem to notice he was kissing her; there was no response from her lips at all. And her face was very pale. It was as though she were in shock.

Michel persevered, brushing her mouth tenderly with his own, stroking her hair. And after a minute or so, she sighed and her mouth began moving under his. Probably he should question her some more, find out what was going on in her mind, but now that she was responding, it seemed much more enjoyable to go on kissing her.

Very slowly and cautiously, he began unbuttoning her blouse, then slipped it and her jacket off her in one smooth motion that she didn't even seem to notice. Lovingly he kissed her nose and her eyelids and her forehead. As usual, she smelled wonderful. Where was the source of that delightful fragrance? Behind her ear? Yes. Delicately, he traced the outline of her jaw with the tip of his tongue, moving downward until he found the hollow of her throat where her pulse was beating erratically. Here was more of that erotic, seductive perfume.

Her arms were around him now, but she was not yet fully relaxed. "You don't understand," she muttered, as he reached behind her and unfastened her bra.

"But of course I do, *chérie*," he murmured. Then his lips found the rounded tip of her breast, which was already erect and ready for his kiss. Cautiously he eased her back against the piled cushions and applied himself to the other breast, reining himself in, allowing only gentle, delicate caresses that would not startle her into awareness.

Yes. Here, too, was the scent of roses, tinged with something else that hinted exotically of spice. It must be a body oil she used, or a soap, something that permeated every part of her, something that tasted as ambrosial as it smelled.

"What are you doing?" Casey demanded, her suddenly alert voice startling him, her body stiffening away from him.

He smiled at her and stroked her breast tenderly, hoping to gentle her. But she pulled away and sat up and began putting on her clothing, her fingers agitated. "We were going to Étienne's," she reminded him.

He shook his head. "I have changed my mind, *chérie*. I am not moving from this place until you tell me what is the problem between us. I am going to stay here until you satisfy all my questions, whether it takes a week or a month or a year."

Her lovely green eyes were clouded by the anxiety that nibbled at her and drew her away from him.

"Tell me," he said.

She had finished buttoning her blouse. Now she stood and tucked it into her skirt, then picked up the jacket he'd taken off her and took it to hang in the armoire against the wall. "Would you like some coffee?" she asked.

"No," he said firmly, sitting up very straight and planting his feet on the floor. "I would not like coffee, I would not like wine, I would not like dinner. I am on a thirst and hunger strike until you talk to me."

He had hoped to make her smile, but her eyes still looked haunted. Sitting down opposite him in her small rocking chair, she gazed at him in a troubled way. Then she sighed and he saw that she had made a decision. He leaned forward, waiting.

"The day before I met you I went to an antique show at the Kingdome," she told him. "There was a woman named Inga, a strange sort of woman, and she insisted on giving me some perfume that she said was made especially for her family."

"It was in a small golden bottle?" he asked, remembering her agitation when she discovered such a bottle in her skirt pocket the previous morning.

She nodded. "A very beautiful bottle—Saracenic glass. Very old. Inga told me the perfume was very special. Magic. Anyone who used it would be given their heart's desire, she said."

Using sheer strength of will, he managed not to smile. "You used it?" he asked.

She nodded. "Not five minutes later you came barreling into my shop."

There was a silence and he finally realized she had finished her story. "I am not sure I understand," he said.

"Michel, it's as clear as daylight. I used the perfume and you came into my life and were attracted to me. Right away, you said."

He nodded. "That is so."

She spread her hands in front of her, palms upward. "Inga was right, don't you see? It really was a magic perfume. Which means it cast some sort of spell on you. At first I was afraid of what might happen if it wore off. But it didn't wear off. I don't think it's ever going to wear off. And that's not all. After I met Inga, it got so if I thought about you wearing certain clothing, that's what you wore. If I thought of roses, you sent me roses. Wallflowers, and you sent me wallflowers."

"You spoke of this before." He shook his head. "Coincidence, Casey."

"And the bluebells, and pansies? Gladioli? Each time, I thought about them before you sent them. I wished you would tell me you loved me...and you did."

"The supersensitivity that develops between lovers, perhaps."

She shook her head. "How about when you were five thousand miles away and I wished you would come back to Seattle in time for Sarah's shower and you arrived that same night."

"A little late, I am afraid." He allowed himself a small smile. "Perhaps you were confused by the time-zone difference?"

"Don't make fun of this, Michel," she said in a warning tone. "It's all true. And now I'm afraid..."

"Of what, *chérie?*" he asked gently when she hesitated.

"I'm afraid you only love me because of the perfume. Because you can't help yourself."

"I cannot help myself, that is true," he murmured. "But Casey, dear, lovely Casey, I do not comprehend what the problem is here. Women have used perfume to attract men since the beginning of time. There is a classic poem of India—"The Ritusanhara"—that speaks of women perfuming themselves with sandalwood to coax their lovers to burning desire."

"But that's not the same—"

"You must remember that I work with flowers always. I am used to perfume and I know its power. The essential oils secreted by flowers, those same oils used in perfume making, *call* to pollinators. That is what the fragrance is *for*. You see how natural it is for perfume to be effective? Many, many animals use scents to stimulate sexual responses. And you have surely heard of pheromones."

"I've heard of them, yes, but I don't think—"

"Pheromones are scent signals one insect sends to another. The word is made up of two Greek words, *pherein*—to bear along, and -*mone*—an excitement."

She was looking at him in a bewildered way. "You're making it sound almost normal to have a magic perfume."

He shook his head. "No, Casey, I am assuring you that your perfume, wonderfully fragrant as it is, is *not* magic."

Her face had closed again. "You don't believe me."

"It is not a case of believing you or not believing you," he protested. "I am merely—"

"I used the perfume only once, Michel," she said flatly.

He frowned.

"That first day. That was the only time I ever used the perfume. Inga told me I shouldn't use it more than once, and I was so shaken by the results I wouldn't have used it again, anyway. I was so shaken I didn't use *any* kind of perfume. Since that first day I haven't used scent or perfumed soap or cologne or bath powder or anything with any odor to it at all.''

She was leaning forward now, looking at him very intently.

''But you smell always so beautiful, like roses mixed with exotic spices,'' he murmured. ''A few minutes ago, I smelled it on you again—that same wonderful fragrance that I smelled the first time I met you.''

''Exactly,'' she said triumphantly. ''I smelled it, too. I smell it every time I'm with you. But I'm not wearing any perfume, I swear to you. And I never smell it at any other time.''

He realized he was staring at her. He felt dazed, stunned by what she was saying. And then another thought struck him and he laughed.

''Don't you dare laugh at me, Michel,'' she said through her teeth.

He shook his head. ''I am not laughing at you, *chérie*. I am laughing at the thought that perhaps your concern for Sarah stems from the same cause.''

Two spots of pink appeared on her cheekbones. ''She used the perfume, yes. I had put it away in my medicine cabinet and she came across it and used it the day of the baby shower. When Skip arrived I could see him...succumb. He looked...*enchanted*.'' She was sounding very agitated again.

''But, *chérie*,'' he continued soothingly, ''you said this woman at the antique show—this Inga—told you the perfume would bring a person's heart's desire, so it follows surely that Skip must have been Sarah's heart's desire. So where is the harm?''

He watched her consider that for several seconds, then a look of wonder crossed her face. ''I hadn't thought of that. Sarah did say she'd liked Skip all along,

but didn't think he could see her as a grown woman."
She shook her head. "That doesn't work, either, Michel. What about Skip's heart's desire?"

"He did not need someone to love?"

"Well, yes, he did. But—" She giggled suddenly, surprising him. "It's ironic in a way. I told Skip about the perfume—he was the only person I did tell. And he refused to believe any perfume could be magic. He was quite adamant about it. He as good as implied I should be locked up in a state institution. But the perfume got to him, anyway. Serves him right."

There was a silence, then Michel said teasingly, "I suppose with all of this, I must have been your heart's desire?"

"I didn't even know you."

"But your heart desired *something, someone?*"

The pink in her cheeks deepened to a vivid shade of rose as she remembered that she had originally wanted to galvanize Justin into action. She had wanted so desperately for someone to love her. "Well, maybe so," she said briskly. "I do remember thinking about a husband and children. I went through a whole thing there of envying women who had babies."

"You still wish to have babies?"

She nodded. "Very much."

"That is good. I adore babies. And children like me, too."

She remembered his cousin's children clinging to him. The memory brought a smile to her face. But then it faded. "The thing that worries me is that you didn't get any choice in the matter," she said slowly.

"Ah, but there I must disagree, *chérie*. I do not think any perfume on earth could have drawn me if I had not wished to be drawn. I was not drawn until I saw you, at which time you became *my* heart's desire." He smiled at her. "So you see it all worked out very well."

Taking advantage of the confusion that was showing on her face, he stood up, pulled her out of the rocker and sat her on the daybed with him, putting his arm around her shoulders and pulling her close to his side. "When I plant a garden, Casey," he told her, dropping a kiss on her hair, "I use several methods of planting, seeds and bulbs and tubers and small shrubs. It does not matter what I use. What matters is the beauty of the result. Whether your perfume is magic or not, the fact is that I love you and you love me. It is the same for Skip and Sarah. They have found one another. How it happened does not matter."

"Sarah did look very happy," Casey murmured, allowing her head to rest on his shoulder.

He kissed her forehead. "You brought her that happiness," he reminded her.

She sat up straight suddenly, looking astonished. "Well!" she exclaimed.

What now? he wondered. But she was smiling. Whatever had struck her had driven away the clouds from her eyes. They were shining so green they dazzled him. "Remember I told you I have never forgotten the aphorisms my father used to quote to me?"

"Yes, but I am not sure what an aphorism is, Casey. Do you know the French word for it?"

She shook her head. "It means a short, wise saying. I just remembered another one, very clearly, as though my father was saying it in my ear. *Train up a child in the way she should go, and when she is old she will not depart from it.*"

It was going to take him a lifetime to learn to follow the complex workings of her mind. An enjoyable lifetime. "It is from the Bible?" he asked.

She nodded, looking excited, her green eyes glowing with pleasure. "It must mean I did the right thing for Sarah, don't you think? He sounded pleased." She blushed. "I don't mean that I actually hear voices," she added hastily. "You'll be getting the idea I really am totally crazy. It's just that I remember the things my father taught me and I hear them the way he said them, as though he were speaking in my mind. The voice is coming from my own memory, of course, but if it sounded approving, then deep down I must approve of the things I did for Sarah—even including bringing the perfume home."

"That is a possible interpretation," he said, ready to agree with anything that would make her realize nothing she had done could possibly have hurt Sarah. Or Skip. Or Michel Gervais Smith.

He pulled her closer into his arms, leaning back with her against the pillows. "It is all right now, *chérie?*" he asked. "We are friends again? More than friends?"

She nodded, raising one hand to lightly touch his cheek, her thumb grazing his mouth. "I guess I made too much of Inga's perfume," she said. "It just seemed so impossible that someone like you should love me."

"Ah! This, then, is why you have projected so much effort into finding reasons for my love. You have convinced yourself you are not worthy of my love. Why? Because I am rich?"

She shook her head. "That doesn't seem to matter anymore."

"*Bien.* Nor should it. I do love you, Casey, and I wish very much to make love to you. May I please have your permission?"

She smiled at him and he thought that if he lived to be as old as his grandfather he would never tire of watching her smile. Taking the smile as permission, he began carefully unbuttoning her blouse again. A vein showed in her throat, pulsing slightly. Leaning over her he kissed it, then trailed kisses down to her breast.

Her hands held his head, urging him closer. He wanted to take off his clothing, but he didn't want to leave her, to take a chance on her changing her mind. Carefully he tried to ease his jacket off, while still kissing her. He heard her laugh softly—the most erotic sound—and then she was helping him, making a game out of stripping him, pulling the rest of her own clothes off, dropping them haphazardly on the floor. And then she lay back, smiling, her glorious hair tumbling against the pillows. A moment later he was inside her, loving her.

"I have yet more good news to pass on to you," he said after a long, lovely while.

She was wrapped closely around him, their legs and arms so entwined they might never free themselves, Michel thought, which would surely not be such a terrible state of affairs. "I have heard this afternoon from a real-estate agent I know," he informed her. "He tells me the house I have had my eye on for the past two years has come on the market and I am invited to make an offer. So first I must ask you, as I am now gainfully employed and about to become a houseowner, is it possible that you might consider becoming my wife?"

Her face shone with the answer before she gave it to him. "I would marry you if you were still a shuttle-bus driver," she said.

"But it is more important that you should want to marry me for who I am," he insisted.

"I do," she said, and kissed him very lovingly and thoroughly—so thoroughly that he almost forgot he had not yet finished this conversation. "The house is on Bainbridge Island, *chérie*. Does this please you? I know that you like it there."

Alarm filled her eyes. "Michel, it's happening again. You're fulfilling wishes. I've wanted to live on Bainbridge Island ever since the first time I went there."

"So, then, it will be accomplished," he said, ignoring the resurgence of her fear, touching his mouth to hers, teasing at her lips until they parted to his. Feeling her body relax again, he thought that it was all part of her enchantment, this superstitious nature of hers. He would never try to explain away every last part of it; it would remain part of their own personal mystique—the private mystery that every loving couple should share.

It occurred to him as Casey began to move under him again that he *wasn't able* to explain all of it. Even as this thought crossed his mind, he realized that the smell of her perfume was once more in the air, rising all around them like a cloud, redolent of rose petals and mysterious spices, intoxicating him. For a moment he felt a small tremor of superstition himself, but then Casey's hands touched him in sensitive places and he let the thought drift away from him, to be replaced by the joy of feeling her close. Gazing at her lovingly, he noticed that her face held the inward-listening expression he was coming to know and love. "Has your father another wise saying for us, *chérie?*" he asked.

She shook her head, smiling brilliantly. "Not my father—Virgil. *Love conquers all things.*"

THE ARTICLE IN the Sunday newspaper was quite long. Skip Granger, after all, had been a well-known figure in town for a long time, and all of his many accomplishments had to be included. Now it seemed his wife Sarah had given birth to a baby girl, to be named Amanda. There was some mystery about the wife, according to the reporter—a secret marriage performed without any of Skip's many fans knowing anything about it. He was the happiest man in the world, Skip was quoted as saying.

Inga wasn't quite sure why the article had drawn her attention. She knew where Skip's restaurant was, but had never eaten there. Nor had she ever met the man. But she found herself pleased, as she always was when someone proclaimed happiness. There was too little happiness in the world.

Turning to the *J* portion of the paper, she found the section she had been searching for originally, the section she had checked every Sunday for several months now. And there it was at last, among all the other happily smiling couples, the announcement she had been waiting for, together with a photograph of a darkly handsome man and a radiant young woman in a lovely vintage-lace bridal dress and veil.

"Cassandra Templeton and Michel Gervais Smith were married September 29th."

"A landscape architect," Inga murmured, reading the rest of the text. "A Frenchman, too. Very romantic. Well done, Cassandra."

Folding the newspaper carefully so that the picture was uppermost, Inga propped it against the lamp on the small drum table next to her wing chair and gazed at it for a long time.

She was smiling.